TERROR IN THE WOODS

There was no time to hesitate, no time to ask questions or even to think. I scarcely noticed Timmy's weight in my arms. I had never run so swiftly in my life. We splashed across the stream, taking no time for the stones, and raced on. As we reached the shore, my heart was pounding, and I could scarcely breathe. We stood for a moment in stunned disbelief.

She turned about, looking wildly in all directions, and I could have cried for her. She was so beautiful, even in this strange, tormented frenzy. Her dark hair flowed about her shoulders, standing out sharply against the bright white of her loose terrycloth beach dress which settled against the slim, graceful lines of her body.

We will send you a free catalog on request. Any titles not in your local book store can be purchased by mail. Send the price of the book plus 50¢ shipping charge to Tower Books, P.O. Box 270, Norwalk, Connecticut 06852.

Titles currently in print are available for industrial and sales promotion at reduced rates. Address inquiries to Tower Publications, Inc., Two Park Avenue, New York, New York 10016, Attention: Premium Sales Department.

THE
JAGGED
EDGE

Wendy Westervelt

TOWER BOOKS  NEW YORK CITY

A TOWER BOOK

Published by

Tower Publications, Inc.
Two Park Avenue
New York, N.Y. 10016

Copyright © 1979 by Wendy L. Westervelt

Chapter One

The setting sun flooded the evening sky with orange and rose and cast glitters across the water as I drove along the smooth curve of the lakeside road. The wind blew gently against my arm through an open window, a little cooler now that the shadows were longer. It had been a hot day for driving, but in Michigan's northern woods, even July nights were likely to be chilly. I welcomed the fresher air, breathing deeply of the sweet, strong pine scent.

It had been four years since I had made this drive, and the beauty of the rolling hills and shining waters struck me with full impact. I remembered how lovely the scenery had been before, but now, driving alone, I noticed even more. I could well understand how Lily would want to live here.

Four years ago, my older brother Gary, his wife Alice, her sister Lily, and I had driven up north to look at the house Lily had decided to buy. The four of us had stayed all summer long, moving in Lily's things, making repairs, redecorating, and enjoying the summer activities. I could hardly wait to see the place again, and to see Lily. We had been fast friends for as long as I could remember, but after high school our ways had separated. She had come to her north woods paradise to follow her dream—nature photography—and I had gone to the university, preparing to be an English teacher. We met every year at Christmastime back in our home town, but other than that we had little contact except through letters.

The road turned away from the lake, plunging deep into the woods. Pines, oaks, maples, and birches towered on both sides, their branches almost meeting overhead. A chipmunk skittered across the road, and I could hear blue jays and red squirrels calling and scolding in the distance. I rounded a last turn, and the big old fieldstone house came into view. Mrs. Norfolk stood by her mailbox on the other side of the road. I slowed down and waved to her, smiling.

"Hello, Kimberlee," she said, with an odd, forced smile.

How strange, I thought, but then I really didn't know her very well. It was hard to believe that four years had passed since the four of us had had such marvelous times with her children, Eric and Karen Norfolk.

As the car rolled on I caught glimpses of the big green Norfolk house. It was set well back from the road, almost hidden by the trees. I saw the brilliant red of the geranium bed that flourished in the front yard and re-membered with instant nostalgia a huge, fragrant bouquet that Eric had presented to Lily one hot August afternoon. I remembered, too, the bright sparkle that had lit her pretty green eyes as we arranged the flowers together afterward.

I pulled into the drive, fully expecting to see Lily burst exuberantly from the house. The place looked very quiet. The door was completely shut. I got out and slammed the car door and was at once greeted by wild barking from within the house. I ran up the stone steps, fishing in my purse for a key, and hastily opened the door. Freddy dashed past me, made a racing circle about the front lawn, and rejoined me hesitantly on the porch. I doubted he would remember me; four years ago he had only been a puppy. I knelt down, waiting for the magnificent creature to come and make friends.

I had never even heard of a Bernese Mountain dog

until one day Lily showed me a picture of one and said that was the type of dog she wanted. Freddy was certainly impressive, a large, sturdy, black dog with precise white-and-tan markings. He watched me carefully and finally walked over to sniff me and let me scratch his head. I knew that he would watch me constantly but would accept me.

I took my suitcase from the car and carried it into the house. Everything inside brought back memories of the summer when we had discovered and created the interior of the place, from the huge stone fireplace in the living room to the tiny copper bumblebee that sat on a stack of papers next to the telephone in the hallway.

I stood just inside the door for a few moments, savoring each reminder of that wonderful time. Studying the pattern of the carpet, I thought of the radiating happiness at Gary and Alice's wedding. They had been married in the beginning of May, but by mid-June there had still been a special glow in the air. As I noticed the fine grain of the wood paneling and the odor of staining fluid returned to me in memory, I also thought of graduating from high school, full of high hopes, afraid of nothing.

My dreams had seemed so simple and safe then. I had been so sure and confident about becoming a teacher. Everyone had encouraged me, assuring me there would always be a need and a place for teachers. The doubts had come later, from half-ignored employment prospect data and articles on population growth. By my senior year at the university I had not bothered to elect the education courses but had simply fulfilled my degree requirements in literature. Somewhere I had lost my sense of direction and purpose, but now, reliving choice moments of a simpler time, I could almost convince myself that it didn't matter, that I would find a new objective now and reach out for it.

Freddy jarred me from these reflections by chasing his dish across the kitchen floor, dashing up to me, and

7

throwing it down at my feet, but my mood remained untouchably high. I did begin to wonder just how long Lily had been gone that Freddy should be so desperately hungry, but it was not long before I located a can of dog food and satisfactorily handled one problem. While Freddy ate, I looked about casually for a note of some kind, reluctant to allow Lily's absence to disturb, annoy, or depress me.

As I had no idea when Lily would return and there would be another good hour of daylight, I decided to take Freddy and go for a walk behind the house. Just outside the back door was a small cultivated area planted with tomato vines, a few rather scrawny rose bushes, and an abundance of bright orange tiger lilies. In the center of the lily bed, three or four bulbs produced the sunny yellow variety that the missing Lily especially loved.

Thinking of this made me smile to myself, because it was so characteristic of Lily to love best what was unusual or hard to find. The whole idea of living alone in an isolated spot surrounded by nature was quite different from what most young women thought inviting, yet for Lily it was the ideal life. The Bernese Mountain dog trotting along the garden path beside me was just what Lily liked too; rare, practically unheard of, beautiful. I could easily see the charm of the things Lily loved so much, yet I had always liked the orange lilies just as much as the yellow ones.

Beyond the back yard with its small garden lay a huge stretch of forest. At the point where the garden path reached the trees, Lily had placed a bird feeder, and six large sunflowers grew up around it. The feeder was really for the squirrels too, and as Freddy ran ahead of me past the box a beautiful gray squirrel with a full, silvery tail jumped agilely to the closest tree and scurried up a few branches to watch me pass below.

The forest was lush, cool, and fragrant in the fading sunlight. The ferns that grew thickly to both sides of the path brushed softly against my legs and the warm, sweet scent of huckleberries and wild blueberries reached me subtly beneath the stronger, heady freshness of the pines. As I passed an arborvitae tree, I plucked a small network of tender, flat needles from one of the lower branches and savored their pleasant, tangy taste.

The path was carpeted with a thin layer of rust-brown pine needles and ashy birch and poplar leaves. In places where thick roots protruded, a fine green moss grew, and an old stump to one side of my walkway boasted the bright red nubbins called British soldier. Beneath the ferns I noticed different varieties of mushrooms growing: little white ones, some that were bright yellow-orange, and a few large brown ones. The biggest brown one was notched all around the edge with tiny tooth marks, so I judged it to be edible.

In the distance I could hear the clear gurgle of water running over rocks, and knew I was approaching the stream. Freddy danced along ahead, obviously enjoying the outing immensely. He surprised a chipmunk crossing the path, and the little fellow darted up a tree, chipping at us disapprovingly. I wished I had remembered to bring some peanuts.

Freddy had dropped back beside me for a moment, but as we rounded a turn in the path and came in view of the stream, he bounded ahead to splash playfully in the water. I followed the stepping stones across the little brook, noticing the mossy emerald-green covering on the rocks and watching the dragonflies darting and circling above the surface of the water. I remembered how amazed Lily and I had been one afternoon while picnicking beside the stream to see a funny little nymph crawl from the water, shed its outer covering, and fly away perhaps an hour later to play with the others in the afternoon sun. The casing had remained stuck tight on the log for two or three weeks, then a heavy rain had washed it away.

On the far side of the stream, the path branched in

two directions. The more worn side followed the stream and led to a lake. The other was slightly overgrown and meandered through another stretch of forest before it finally opened out into a vast expanse of open, rolling countryside. I decided to go quickly along the stream for a glimpse of the lake before turning back.

The walk from the house to the shore of the lake was about half a mile and could be made easily in about fifteen minutes. I had taken a little longer because I savored so many half-forgotten details.

I reached the lake and felt at once its breathtaking beauty. As the sky darkened overhead, the water reflected soft gray-violet and mirrored the earliest stars and an almost circular waxing moon. The thin margin of beach, golden in the sunlight, now rimmed the quiet water in a pale, muted beige. The tall trees of the far shore stood out clearly, black against the deepening violet.

I would want to see all this again in the golden warmth of afternoon. But for now I called to Freddy and we retraced our steps, heading back to the house. Early fireflies dotted sharp sparks of light in the tall grasses that edged the stream, and after I carefully made my way across the stone steps, I hurried along the path, thinking Lily must surely be home by now.

Freddy walked beside me now, and as we emerged from the woods together, I thought I caught a glimpse of movement in the shadows near the back porch steps. I ran across the garden calling Lily's name joyfully, Freddy barking as he bounded along, racing me. I stopped at the foot of the wooden stairs, hearing no answer and seeing no sign of anyone. I took a circle around the house, as I was quite sure the motion had been outside and that the door had not since opened, but no one was to be found. Perhaps I had not seen anyone after all.

Freddy was still sniffing around the corner of the house, so I went in alone. Something thudded against the plastic wastebasket, then flopped across the floor. I flipped on the light switch and saw a large perch gasping helplessly on the floor. I reached into one of the lower cupboards to find a pan, filled it with water, and rather squeamishly picked up the poor creature by the tail. While the fish calmed down, I filled the sink with water, then poured it from the pan to the sink.

It had been foolish not to lock the door but there were only three houses set out here in the woods and an expanse of isolating forest surrounding them. There seemed little need for many precautions, and I had been gone for less than an hour. I checked as quickly as I could to see if anything was missing. My purse was there, with the wallet still in it, and my suitcase was untouched. None of Lily's thing appeared to be missing. Why would anyone come into Lily's house and put a fish on the kitchen floor?

I went back to the kitchen and, as I passed the note-board, a new slip of paper caught my eye. Someone had scrawled across a sheet of orange paper, "That's what you are!" and tacked it up for me to find. It took little puzzling to see what was meant. I was, in a sense, a fish out of water. I did not know the people who lived here, Lily was gone, and I was not exactly in my element. But why should someone bother to point this out so cruelly? Someone intended to frighten me, perhaps to make me leave. It could only be one of the inhabitants of the other two houses, for Lily would simply not have invited me if I was not supposed to come. It made me wonder if Lily was in some sort of trouble. But I never gave leaving a serious thought. I would have to stay and see what was going on.

Putting all this aside, I decided to take care of the poor fish. I found a flashlight, scooped the fish up in the pan, locked the doors this time, and called to a puzzled Freddy to make another quick trip to the lake. When I had let the fish go I ran back to the house, hurried inside, and locked the door behind me. Freddy lay down in the corner and went to sleep, leaving me feeling terribly alone.

I sat restlessly on the couch for a while, then, thinking back over what had happened, I could almost laugh. It was really a ridiculous trick to have pulled, yet somehow it was not just a funny practical joke. If I had not come right away the fish would have been dead. Was that what someone intended for me? No, of course not. That was silly. I decided that I had better occupy myself to keep away such ghastly thoughts.

I remembered that Lily's darkroom was set up in the basement, and I was sure there would be something there to keep me busy. It was a real workshop, and could always use straightening, if nothing else. Lily always said so in her letters, complaining that she had no time to spend on simple cleaning. Well, I had all night, if I wanted, and nothing better to do. I could think of no sensible action to take to help solve the problem I suspected. I knew too little.

I wandered back through the kitchen, glancing thankfully at Freddy, who opened one eye at the sound of my footsteps, then made my way down the stairs that led to the basement. Half of the basement was devoted to the furnace, hot-water heater, and other necessary utilities. The rest was Lily's darkroom, which, as a professional photographer, she used a great deal and had planned very elaborately.

I started my work by gathering the half-dozen coffee cans scattered about the room and dumping their contents of scrap film and bent mounts into the main wastebasket. By the time I had done that the wastebasket was overflowing, so I took it out into the other half of the basement and dumped it into the incinerator. Next, I matched numbers on shelves to numbers on cans and bottles, and cleared the counter completely. This system of Lily's allowed me to pick up properly without knowing much about what I was doing. The floor was dusty, so I got the vacuum cleaner out of the closet. Then I scrubbed the salmon-colored counters with soapy water and polished them dry with a cloth. I looked at the central work table to see what might need to be done there.

Lily had been in the process of mounting slides. There were about three rolls of film still unmounted. This was something I knew how to do, so I set about cutting the frames of film apart, preparing the cardboard mounts, and putting the film carefully and securely between the protective edges. It was routine work, but fascinating to me, because I had not seen many of Lily's pictures for a long time. I held each frame up to the light, enjoying the lovely flowers, insects, birds, and squirrels that Lily loved to photograph. She had some very good shots of a raccoon and two frames of a porcupine as well.

As I began the third roll, I was a little surprised by the subject. Lily had taken nearly a whole roll of pictures of a darling little blond boy between two and three years old. He had green eyes, much like hers, and the same fair hair. In some of the pictures he was feeding peanuts to a chipmunk, in a few he played with Freddy, and in others he simply smiled charmingly at the camera. The roll had been taken in the garden with the lily bed as background. I wondered who the little fellow could be. He certainly was an attractive child, and he looked very happy. The thought crossed my mind that he looked enough like Lily to be her own, but this was a strange conclusion to jump to, and at the time I really gave the matter no more than idle consideration.

As I completed the roll, I glanced at my watch and found that midnight was already fifteen minutes past. I had been up before six o'clock that morning, as I had had some last-minute preparations to make before starting the trip after lunch. It had been a long day, and I suddenly felt very tired and a little disappointed about the way my vacation had started. I climbed the stairs, passed a sleeping Freddy in the kitchen, and crossed the living room to the couch, switching off lights as I went.

13

I sat down with a sigh and stared for a moment at the shadow of my suitcase, which was cast by a small light that I had left on in the hall. Then I kicked my shoes off and lay down, drifting quickly into a light, uneasy sleep.

Some time later I awoke feeling vaguely chilly and saw Freddy padding softly across the floor to join me. I had probably been roused by the slight sound of his toe-nails clicking on the kitchen linoleum. I got up to get a sweater from my suitcase, and stroked Freddy's head as I settled back down on the couch. I decided that in the morning I would move into the room that had been mine before. Perhaps that way I would feel more at home. Deep down, thought, I knew the problem was more difficult to solve. Until I knew where Lily was and why she had been in such a hurry to leave that she had not told me what was going on, I would be on edge.

Feeling totally unable to sleep, I looked at my watch in the light from the hall, and found it to be three o'clock. I knew that, in order to get any real rest at all, I would have to make some plans for the following day. Lily had mentioned the Norfolks to me in several letters. Perhaps they might know what had become of her. I would go to see them in the morning, right after I un-packed. I might even find some clue concerning the intent of the flopping fish and the note, though this bothered me far less than Lily's absence. Yes, that was the sensible thing to do. It must have been about half-past three when I finally fell soundly asleep.

The midsummer morning sun woke me early and, though I had slept soundly, the hours between three-thirty and six were painfully inadequate. For a moment I felt inclined to lie still and drift off to sleep again, but the unanswered question of Lily's disappearance cleared my mind before that could happen. There was no point in wasting time, so I took my suitcase upstairs and began to reacquaint myself with the room I was sure Lily would want me to use.

The beautiful oak floor, too lovely to be completely

hidden by carpeting, was as I remembered it, covered only in places by soft moss-green throw rugs. The walls were also natural wood, and I remembered what a job Eric and Gary had had to strip away the old layers of paint and restore the lovely grained surface. The bed-spread was a vivid daffodil yellow and a chair had been upholstered in the same lively shade. The rest of the furniture—a dressing table, two straight chairs, a dresser, and a night stand—were of rich, warm cherry wood. The room had one large window which looked out upon Lily's garden and part of the forest. In the distance, the clear blue sky was reflected intensely in the lake's deep water.

The dressing table was placed almost directly opposite the window, and the large mirror above it was like a picture on the wall, repeating the outdoor scene. I glanced at myself in its clear, undeceiving surface, but was not pleased by what I saw. My hair had been treated roughly the day before and my white blouse was water-spotted from the fish incident. There was a dark gray streak across its right shoulder that I could not identify, and the inevitable little wrinkles showing that the blouse had been slept in. I had a lot to do before calling on the Norfolks.

I pulled open the dresser drawer, ready to begin un-packing, and found a photograph of Lily and myself, taken four years ago. On the back we had scrawled our names—Kim Harris and Lily Pentwood. It was not a serious picture, but rather a vacation snapshot. I wore orange shorts and a pale yellow blouse; Lily a solid sky-blue short set. We were about the same height, Lily perhaps an inch shorter, and we both wore our hair straight and parted in the center, though hers was blonde and mine dark. In the picture, Lily laughed vivaciously at the camera while I smiled guardedly. Eric Norfolk had taken the picture, and Lily had been greatly impressed with him from the first. I, being transient, had felt the need to be unobtrusive.

I set the photograph on top of the dresser and turned to begin my unpacking, wondering what had ever come of this relationship. Lily's letters during the first few months had been full of Eric, but after that he was mentioned only occasionally, and always in connection with his mother or his sister, never alone.

When I had filled two drawers of the dresser and hung a few things in the large, walk-in closet, I stepped into the adjoining bathroom to begin freshening my appearance. I noticed right away that Lily had put out a set of towels for me. She clearly had been anticipating my visit, glad that I was coming, as she had said in the last letter. Something unexpected must have come up, something so important that it had made her forget even to leave me a note. I hoped the Norfolks would know what had happened.

When I had showered, combed my hair, put on short navy blue culottes and a coral-colored blouse, I felt much better. I finished with a little light makeup, and this time the large mirror was far more complimentary. The big brown eyes that looked at me from the glass were bright and eager, perhaps a little too excited, and the morning sun caught auburn tints in my long, straight hair.

I ran downstairs, glimpsing a clock that taunted my impatience by reading only ten past seven, and decided to find something to eat for breakfast. Freddy came with me to the kitchen, and I guessed he was hungry again. I unlocked the back door and let him out into the garden. While he loped around the house I got two eggs out of the refrigerator—one for Freddy, one for myself—and fried them. I also made myself a cup of instant coffee with hot tap water. When Freddy came in, I put his egg in his dish, ate mine quickly out of the pan, and drank the cup of coffee. I had only a pan, fork, and cup to wash, and I was ready to call on the Norfolks by a quarter to eight.

It was early, but I didn't feel like waiting any longer.

There was a chance that the Norfolks would see me, though it was certainly an unusual hour for visitors. My questions were not usual, either, and they gave me an excuse.

I locked the front door behind me, slipping the key into my pocket. Freddy was more than willing to stay on the porch, so I didn't encourage him to accompany me. He would serve well as a hindrance to any more practical jokes or hazy threats—whichever the fish and the note had actually been.

The sky was cloudless and intensely blue and the sun was already warm. The grass glistened with quickly drying dewdrops, and the trilling of the unseen songbirds was light and delicate, almost elusive when the wind caught the leaves and set them rustling. I could imagine their little brown bodies perched high in the thick greenery, lone piccolo players piping joyfully amidst the surrounding orchestra, nearly drowned out by violins and cellos. Then the wind would still, and the songs would pour forth, clear and tranquil, blending occasionally, at other times one single melody surpassing all the others.

A cloud passed over the sun, and at the same time a strong gust of wind blew, chilling and penetrating. The bird songs were lost to me, and I hurried on toward the Norfolks', shivering from the fresh morning air and a curiously keyed-up feeling I could not suppress.

There is no telling what I would have done if Mrs. Norfolk had not been up and out watering her geraniums. It is quite likely that I would have gone straight up to the door and pressed the doorbell until someone came. Fortunately, it was not necessary to display my concern so dramatically. It even seemed almost natural that I should walk up her drive and begin chatting nervously to Mrs. Norfolks' rigid, unwelcoming back.

I had not expected much of a welcome, but when Mrs. Norfolk remained kneeling over the flowers, not even looking up, while I greeted her hesitantly and made comments about the weather, I knew this was more than mere lack of friendliness. She had no wish at all to talk to me. I grew uneasy, just looking at her back, and my talk trailed off into nothing. I saw no way to retrieve my lost fragments of small talk, so I regathered my thoughts and approached her more directly with the subject that most needed attention.

"It's strange that Lily isn't here to meet me. She knew I was coming. In fact, I was invited," I began, still a little timidly.

She turned to face me then, her hazel eyes completely expressionless, a faint tension about her mouth. I remained silent, hoping she would say something, but when she did not, I pressed her further.

"I wondered if you knew where she is. She mentions you so often in her letters that I thought she might have told you."

Realizing that at this point the conversation demanded some comment from her, Mrs. Norfolk looked away and said reluctantly, "Lily left yesterday— early in the afternoon."

"Did she say where she was going? When she'd be back?"

Mrs. Norfolk refused to meet my eyes and rubbed her hands together while she considered what reply to make. Just when her silence was becoming awkward, Karen came to the door carrying a large bundle that I could not see clearly because of the distance and the screen door.

"Mother—" she began, then stopped short at the sight of me and turned abruptly back into the house.

"Well, I'd better go see what Karen wants," Mrs. Norfolk said quickly, with relief.

I persistently kept pace with her, saying, "May I come in?"

"I guess so," she snapped, hurrying past me and letting the screen door slam shut in my face.

Determined by now to be just as ill-mannered a guest

as she was a hostess, I snatched open the door and found my way to the now deserted living room. There I sat down to wait for someone to show up and talk to me.

It was a long time before anyone came to see what I was doing. While I waited I studied the pretty room. The walls were warm beige, the carpet soft fawn, and the furniture shades of brown accented by pale orange. A large potted plant stood in one corner and on one of the end tables there was a lamp with a driftwood sculpture base. A lovely sunset painting stood out warmly on one wall, glowing rose, peach and yellow, and a large vase of geraniums splashed color into a quiet corner of the room.

In another corner, I noticed a set of shelves filled with interesting little objects. I got up to examine these more closely. One shelf was devoted to natural treasures: shells, pine cones, birch bark, a few colorful stones. Another held exquisite little wood carvings: a seagull, a squirrel, a woodpecker, a chickadee, and a raccoon, all painted carefully by hand. A third level held a music box with two little wooden children, a boy and a girl, sitting side by side on a bench. At their feet, tiny sparrows pecked at scattered grain, and a squirrel sat up on its hinds legs, asking for a nut.

As I turned from this delightful collection, I noticed a small gold picture frame sitting on one of the tables. I crossed to look at it, and stopped short in surprise. The picture it held was of the same blond child Lily had photographed. In this picture he was a little younger, but I was sure that I was not mistaken about his identity. There was no doubt he was the child who had played in Lily's garden.

Not wishing to be caught staring at the photograph until I had a chance to think it over, I began pacing about the room idly. This did not last long, however, for Karen finally came to greet me. She looked a little pale, and her smile quivered nervously, though she was trying to be friendly.

"Kim! How good it is to see you, really! It's been a long time."

"Yes, it has, though I hadn't realized that it had been this long."

"What do you mean? Because of Mother? Please—there's so much to talk over. Don't insist on going too fast."

"I only asked your mother where Lily was and when she'd be back."

"Please, Kim, don't ask any questions. Mother has been very w—ah—working very hard lately. She can't be bothered with Lily right now. I'll try to help you when I can."

I was sure she had been about to say that her mother was very worried. With every minute I became more apprehensive, more sure that Lily needed help. Even her friends were unwilling or unable to communicate with me.

"Do you know where she is, Karen? Surely she must have said something."

"I'm not exactly sure where she was going. But it's nothing to worry about, believe me. She'll be back within a week, I should think. A pity she didn't tell you."

"Well, it can't be helped now," I said, sensing that I would get no further. "How is Eric? I've been looking forward to seeing all of you again."

I had expected this to put Karen at ease, to let her think that I was satisfied that Lily would soon return. To my surprise, she became more flustered than ever, starting up from her chair and crossing the room to study the wood carvings I had so recently admired.

At last, she laughed giddily. "Oh, Eric's fine. He isn't here now either, though. This trip must be terribly disappointing."

I could think of nothing more to say, and suddenly I felt as if I could not leave that tense, agonized house soon enough. How could I ask about the fish or the child? I understood these things far less than I understood Lily's absence, and I was on shaky enough ground trying to discuss that. Karen and her mother were not even inventing excuses for Lily's absence or trying to devise a consistent story. I could only assume that they were paralyzed by fear, and try to fight my own increasing tension.

When I made a move to go, Karen began to relax a little. She came with me to the door and out into the front yard, smiling the same vaguely insincere smile she had worn since she had come to talk to me. Yet I could find nothing malicious in her attempts at natural conversation as she asked how things had been going for me lately, and her failure to meet my eyes directly might have been nothing more than reservation, for I was, after all, practically a stranger. When we reached the road, she left me abruptly, hurrying back toward the house.

As I watched Karen's retreating figure, I would have given much more than a penny to know the thoughts that went on inside her dark honey blonde head. I was undecided about the Norfolks, totally unprepared to trust them, but not sure if I needed to watch them with suspicion. My presence disturbed them greatly—but why should it? Why could they not be honest with me if some serious problem existed? Were they trying to conceal something that would damage them if I should find out about it?

I was deep in thought as I strode along the road, and I didn't notice Denise and Kent Robinson until Denise hailed me with a light and cheery, "Hello, stranger." This jesting use of the word implied a familiarity I was not sure we shared, but she was very friendly and all smiles, a welcome relief from the thundershower atmosphere at the Norfolks'. During the summer four years ago we had seen very little of the Robinsons. While Karen, Eric, and their mother had gone out of their way

21

to welcome us, the Robinsons had waved from a distance or called to us from the road as they went past. Lily had mentioned Denise and Kent in a few of the early letters, and it seemed to me that there had been a cousin, Paul, as well, but I could not remember the details clearly. I knew very little about the occupants of the third house, and was glad of this chance to learn more.

The brother and sister pair walked along beside me, having turned around, as if they had planned to meet me and accompany me. They were both dark and slim, taller than average, athletic and graceful. Denise was four years older than I, just the same age as my older brother Gary and his wife Alice, a year younger than Kent, who was twenty-seven. This kind of information Lily had gathered masterfully and passed on to me, but I knew nothing else about them—nothing at all that could help me now.

"We were going to the lake when we met you, Kim. Come with us, why don't you? Bring Freddy, if you like. We've got a boat, and Kent would love to show off for you," Denise encouraged me.

"Yes, do come. Denise, why not make a picnic of it? Let's show Kim a good time," Kent added charmingly.

"If only I knew what Lily's up to, I'd love it. But what if she comes home while we're gone? I should be here."

"Nonsense. There's no telling when she'll be back. Leave a note and come with us," Denise said firmly.

Deciding that I should not risk missing my only chance to get to know the Robinsons, I said, "You've convinced me. I'll be ready in a few minutes. Thanks—it will be marvelous."

They hurried back to their house, and I to Lily's. I was very glad I had made up my mind to go. Even if I could discover nothing about Lily's absence, I would have a good time. It was better to have some relaxation than to sit and worry in the big empty house.

Chapter Two

Freddy lay peacefully on the porch, straightening to alertness as I approached, then trotting easily down the steps to meet me, his tail swaying gently from side to side. As I touched his silky head, the knowledge that I had, at least in the dog, a true friend swept through me warmly, then ebbed into loneliness as I realized that of all my acquaintances of the past few hours, Freddy was the only one I could completely trust.

This was perhaps being a little paranoid, though, for the house had not been touched in my absence, nor had Freddy been disturbed in any way. The whole mystery might be nothing more than a misunderstanding and a practical joke, so I forced myself to stave off this persisting gloom by at least acting carefree.

I ran up the stairs to get my swim suit and a pair of sunglasses, though I was not sure I would have occasion to use either. It was better to be prepared than left out, in any case. At the last minute, I snatched up a terry cloth beach jacket, thinking that this could double as a towel after our swim was finished. Then I went back downstairs to the kitchen, where I found a small scrap of paper and jotted a quick note for Lily, in case she came home before we returned. This I tacked up on the same board that had held the disconcerting message only hours before, then left the house on the heels of an excited Freddy, stopping only to lock the door before heading down the road to the Robinsons' residence.

The sun was higher now, and the grasses in the drive that had been moist with dew earlier now felt warm and vaguely dusty as they brushed my sandaled feet. Queen Anne's lace grew abundantly along the edge of the hard-packed dirt road, each rich, creamy circle breathing forth a sweet, fresh fragrance that invited small amber honeybees into its frothy depths. Further back from the road's shoulder, a plant of butterfly weed caught my eye with a brilliant blaze of orange. I noticed too that a taller, sturdier relative milkweed flowered richly pink along the roadside. On one stalk crawled a yellow, black, and white striped caterpillar, the infant stage of the monarch butterfly. Overhead I heard the twitter and rustle of birds, and looked to see a robin feeding a few of the last berries from a Juneberry bush to her nearly full-grown yet still speckled young.

It was a perfect day for the sort of outing Denise and Kent had planned, and as I neared their house, I was truly feeling more relaxed. Just as I turned into the drive, they came out the front door, laughing and chattering, in a real party mood. I stood waiting for them, and as Kent approached, he reached out to pat Freddy, who stood beside me. His gesture had caused me no concern, for I knew the dog was normally friendly, but at the sight of Kent's hand, Freddy tensed, uttering a soft, low growl, and moved back a step. I put a hand down lightly to quiet him, and looked up quickly, catching a flash of anger in Kent's eyes before his face cleared and he laughed.

"Come on, boy—don't you remember me?" he coaxed, then added, turning to me, "I guess he doesn't know me very well."

Seeing no reason to make any apology, I changed the subject as we headed off toward the lake. "It was really nice of you to include me in this party. With Lily gone I would never have been so ambitious on my own, but it's a perfect day. It would have been a shame to waste it."

"Yes, we did so want you to come along and enjoy it

with us," Denise agreed, smiling at me, and also at her still slightly ruffled brother. From my position between them, I saw her deliberate attempt to catch his eyes above my head, but Kent glanced away quickly, still watching Freddy, who ran along some distance ahead of us. Some message had passed between them nonetheless, for his color rose slightly, then faded, and he began joking lightly with his sister, whose careful face showed no trace of any emotion other than the cordiality she had openly expressed to me.

I listened appreciatively to their easy, witty banter, laughing softly when it was appropriate, but mostly just smiling silently. Much of what they were saying did not include me, and they made few efforts to draw me into their conversation. After a time, I stopped paying attention to them and withdrew to my own thoughts.

I watched the road beneath my feet, hard, tawny sand and bits of shattered rock. A fossil fern caught my eye, and a dusty blue-jay feather blew across in front of us. If I had been alone, I might have reached over to pick up the etched rock, but as it was, I walked on without hesitating. Presently, I no longer saw the little stones, just a vague sandy blur.

I knew that when we got back from the lake I would have to call my parents to tell them I had arrived. Normally, I would have called the night before, but with Lily gone, I hadn't known what to say. I didn't want to alarm them, but I could hardly say she was here and we were having a fine time. Until I decided what to tell them, I couldn't call them, but if they got no call soon, they would begin to worry, or at least to think me rather thoughtless. There could be no more putting it off.

I began too to wonder if there was something I should do to try to locate Lily. I certainly didn't want to call in the authorities and make a great issue of her absence if there was any reasonable chance that she was simply off on some private affair. She would never let me hear the end of it if my concern went so far unnecessarily. I would not really blame her if she was even annoyed with me. But how great a chance was there that Lily would have left home on the day of my planned arrival and not even bother to tell me, unless she was in some sort of difficulty?

If only I could uncover some more information on my own it would be so much easier. How these people, Lily's neighbors in an isolated location like this, could be so ignorant, or why they should be so unwilling to tell me what they knew, was more than I could figure out. Since I hardly knew Denise and Kent at all, it was much harder to ask them straightforward questions than it had been to ask Karen, but it was clear that this was essential, for they volunteered nothing.

"Where have you been, Kim?" Denise asked edgily.

"What do you mean?" I countered, smiling uncertainly and a little defensively because I had entirely lost track of their conversation.

"Well, I asked you twice how long you would be staying in Lily's house."

"Oh, I'm sorry. I was planning to stay about a month. Now I guess I'll wait for her return, then play it by ear. I really couldn't tell you for sure. I wish I knew where she is."

"You're really worried, aren't you?" she said, smiling almost mockingly.

"Why shouldn't I be? It's not at all like her, and no one here seems to have any notion what's become of her. Or at least no one has been willing to tell me. I have a feeling Karen knows something. What do you think?"

If only she would talk, now that the subject had been brought up. It would be no use to mention it again unless I got some response now.

"Oh, undoubtedly she does," Kent spoke quickly, a little sharply. Then he added more smoothly, "Your friend Lily and the Norfolks have not always been good friends, but their affairs are somehow inevitably tied together."

"As far as we're concerned, Lily is a bit of a loner, really. At least, she doesn't seek out our company often. She seems quite a strange, eccentric little thing," Denise commented, with a tinge of scorn in her voice. Then, remembering that I was, after all, a good friend of Lily's, she added hastily, "Oh, do pardon my saying so. I suppose that's often the way with people of unusual talent. As far as her disappearance goes, I wouldn't give it a thought, if I were you. She'll be back soon, no doubt. It would have been much out of character for her to tell us anything about her plans. But please don't brood about it. It makes me uneasy."

She and Kent laughed uncontrollably, and I wondered if anything in the world could truly make those two uneasy. In fact, they seemed so exuberant and high-spirited that I did not for a minute challenge their complete innocence and ignorance. Their position was much more clear than the Norfolks' was. I felt no compulsion to rely on that brother-and-sister pair, for they seemed completely detached, absorbed in their own lives. Yet, this same uninvolved quality made me feel that, with the Robinsons, I was on safe, neutral ground.

"I'm sure you're right, Denise," I said, smiling. "Lily could show up any time, and until she does, there's no point in worrying. We'll know what's up soon enough."

We turned off the road to follow a narrow path through the woods, single file, Kent holding back branches for me, I for Denise, Denise leaving them to swish back into place. At this point, it was only a few yards from the road to the lake. There the path continued along the shoreline, eventually merging into the one that led from Lily's back yard.

I had actually been a little unsure of exactly where we were going, for I had never gone with Denise and Kent to the lake. All during that summer four years before, Lily and I had watched them walking past on the road, obviously going to the lake, but I had never investigated the path they used. Now I could see that this access was perfectly satisfactory, but also I was intrigued by the circular walkway I could easily envision. I was glad to become more acquainted with the countryside surrounding Lily's house. Before, almost all of our attention had been focused on the house itself and the land that came along with it.

The Robinsons had a dock and two boats located at the end of the lake where the three of us now stood. I realized when I saw the boats that I had never even seen the lake properly, for Lily had no boat. I hoped that Denise or Kent would remember to offer me a tour, and I determined to suggest it before the afternoon was over if the opportunity presented itself.

A fresh wind blew over the sparkling water, almost chill, though the day was warm and clear. Back at the house, surrounded by thick woods except for the drive, which was filled with sunlight, I had relished little snatches of this breeze, for they prevented the heat from becoming noticeably uncomfortable. Here, though, the wind was strong and unbroken, and I found myself rubbing crossed arms to keep my skin from prickling with the unexpected cold.

Denise ran lightly out onto the dock, then stood gazing into the water. Kent set the picnic basket he had been carrying in the shade of a large hemlock tree, and slid down beside it, leaning back against the broad, sturdy trunk. I thought perhaps I would join him there and try to start a friendly conversation in which Lily had no part, but Denise saw me hesitate and motioned me to her side.

"Well, how do you like it?" she asked, gesturing to include the entire lake.

"Why, it's beautiful. I love it," I said candidly, and we laughed together.

"I'm glad you feel that way. It means a lot to all of us too. Everyone who lives near it can't help but feel its influence."

Denise seemed lost in a strange, intense passion, caught in a spell of her own creation. She stared silently into the depths of the clear water, smiling faintly, almost as if she had forgotten my presence.

"You must all be very fortunate, then," I remarked quietly. "It's certainly a beautiful influence."

Denise said nothing, but glanced at me almost expressionlessly, as if what I had said surprised her, though I could not see why. In any case, her pensive mood completely evaporated.

"So—how have things been going for you and your brother and his wife? It's been a while since we heard from you," Denise said pleasantly.

"Oh, just fine. What about you two—and your cousin—Paul, is it?"

"Yes, Paul."

"Well, what is it, Denise? You didn't answer my question."

"Oh, no, I didn't. Kent and I are fine, of course," she said, laughing. Then, growing more serious, she glanced at me mysteriously and lowered her voice slightly. "I'm not sure what to say about Paul. I wouldn't want to mislead you."

"In what way?" I asked cautiously.

"It's hard to explain. It's just that Paul is very troubled—very upset. These past few years have been really rough for him. Just a few months before you were here last time, if you remember, his father was killed in a plane crash." She paused, as if to collect her thoughts and perhaps to see what effect her words were having on me.

"No, I didn't know about it. I don't think anyone ever mentioned it before."

"Maybe not. Anyway, he was staying with us for the summer, because his mother—well—needed time to get over it. She was my father's sister, and naturally we didn't want Paul left at loose ends."

"I don't understand. I would have thought his

29

mother would have welcomed her son's support.''

"Yes, I guess that's usually true. But in this case the problem was more serious. Poor Aunt Helen was completely overcome by her husband's death. She needed total rest and the best of care. She was institutionalized for nearly a year.''

By this time, I felt that I was hearing more than I ought to about someone I did not even know from a very casual acquaintance. Yet I had asked about her cousin, and if Denise wanted to talk about it, it did not seem my place to stop her.

"Well," she continued, "Paul put off starting college for one semester, because we were told by the doctor that Aunt Helen was making good progress and should be able to return home some time that fall. Paul didn't want to be involved with school when she first came home, and, all things considered, everyone agreed with his decision. Toward the end of November, Paul and Aunt Helen moved back into their own house. Things appeared to be going smoothly enough, and Paul arranged to start classes during the winter quarter, which began in January. They lived close enough to the college for Paul to attend classes during the day and still live at home. As far as we knew, everything was settling down to normal. Then one day toward the end of March, we got a phone call from Paul, saying that his mother was dead and asking us to come down as soon as possible, which we did. When we got there, he told us what had happened.

"It seems that Paul had met a girl in school, and they were beginning to spend quite a bit of time together. Oh, nothing unusual, but it meant evenings out. Aunt Helen really did approve of it and was pleased for Paul, but the long hours alone were hard on her. She would start thinking about the future, when Paul would marry and leave home, and it would make her extremely depressed. Paul tried every way to reassure her, and he limited the time he spent with Sara, out of consideration for Aunt Helen. But the idea was strong in her mind and a constant worry. Anyway, that evening Paul had taken Sara out to dinner, and then they went to a poetry reading on campus. Sara was an English major and liked that kind of thing. Paul got home about ten-thirty and found that Aunt Helen had shot herself. You can imagine the shock of that! Well, he blamed himself for months, and cut Sara completely out of his life.

"Sara was an interesting girl, though. She really loved him, and she seemed to understand what he was going through. When he finally began to come out of it and realize that it was not really his fault and that he still had a life to live, she was waiting for him. About two years after Aunt Helen's death, they were married.

"I think Paul was really happy then. Four months after the marriage, they found they were going to have a child. It was as if time really had healed things for Paul. Then, that winter, Sara was driving from their house to the campus, and her car skidded on the ice and crashed into a tree. Both she and the baby were killed. That was just last winter."

For several minutes, neither of us said anything. The story seemed incredible. It was too much to happen to any one man. At last I felt I must respond in some way.

"I really don't know what to say, Denise. I'm glad you told me, so I can avoid opening old wounds if I should meet Paul some time. How is he now? That was an awful lot to go through."

"He's really been put through the wringer, all right. Naturally, there are some scars. He seems to get more withdrawn as time goes on. Sometimes he acts hostile to us, especially to Kent, though I know he doesn't mean anything by it. He reacts strongly even to small tensions. I guess he's a little bit paranoid—I don't know. All I'm really trying to do is to explain the situation, so you won't be surprised by anything Paul might say to you.

"The other thing that's been in my mind is Paul's protection. Now, I know you're concerned because Lily isn't here. We all wonder about it. But I did hope, if you knew all this, you would leave Paul out of it. I mean, I'm sure he doesn't know anything about it. The whole thing would just upset him. I probably shouldn't have said anything, but—"

"No, no, I think you're right. I'm glad you told me. Don't worry about it," I assured her quickly.

This story eclipsed my concern for Lily almost completely. It was like seeing a terribly sad movie on television, only there was no way to change channels, and when the allotted two hours were up, it just ran on and on. The conclusion had not been written.

Just as this point, Kent came out to join us, laughing at our gloom but not asking about its cause. His main concern was to erase it and get the party under way. Denise brightened spontaneously, as if she had completely forgotten all that she had said to me. I pushed it to the back of my mind and began again to enjoy the remarkable beauty of the lake and the lovely day.

Ken proposed a tour of the lake, and Denise and I responded enthusiastically. When Freddy saw that we were getting into the larger fiberglass boat, he dashed over to join us. Kent said nothing, but Denise, with a good-natured grin, invited him to jump in. I was a little embarrassed, because Freddy had been swimming in the lake and rolling around in the sand, making himself a completely unpresentable mess. His disheveled state was accepted with remarkable hospitality.

The Robinsons seemed to enjoy telling me about the lake and pointing out special landmarks. They told me to watch carefully for the wildlife, and often pointed things out to me that I would have missed, if not for their keen, experienced eyes.

The lake did not have a simple, circular shoreline, but many coves and inlets protruding from the expanse of open water. The quieter, more secluded places were havens for the shyest creatures. We saw a great blue heron posing as a stick of driftwood and a green heron running swiftly along a log. Six or seven turtles basked on an old log in the sunlight, and kingfishers perched on the dead branches that stretched over the water. Several muskrats were swimming in different places on the lake, each with its mouth full of lush, aquatic vegetation. Peering down into the water in the shallower places, I saw an occasional young perch, bluegill, or bass. The most breathtaking sight of all was in a little inlet with so shallow a channel that Kent had to shut off the motor while Denise rowed us through. A lovely doe and her small fawn stood at the water's edge, drinking. They looked up at us, startled, watched for a few seconds, then melted into the shadows.

The part of the lake that was deeper and more open had a different kind of joy all its own. There, Kent thrust the speed control to its fastest setting, and I felt the sensations of wind and spray, surrounded by the glorious privacy of the motor's roar. Denise showed me the rainbows in the spray at the side of the boat, and we laughed as the wind caught drops of water and showered them on us. There were two good-sized islands in this part of the lake, and Kent drove us around them in sweeping circles.

When we reached the far end of the lake, Kent slowed down to show me where the highway passed near the shore. There was a place to park the boat there, and Kent explained that there was a little store perhaps a quarter of a mile's walk down another road that branched off from the main one at this point. This made it possible to pick up a few groceries by boat rather than by car if one felt so inclined.

After we returned to the dock, Kent and Denise began to unpack the picnic lunch they had brought: cold fried chicken, potato chips, pickles, carrot sticks, beer, and soft drinks. Kent had brought a radio, which we listened to as we ate and talked. Freddy was a terrible tease, and drove Denise and me to hysterical laughter by knocking over and lapping up as much as possible of Kent's half-finished can of beer. I cannot recall exactly what Kent's reaction was, but by this time he had surely come to accept the dog, for any scowl or disgruntled behavior would have been strikingly out of place.

After lunch we took turns changing into our swimsuits in the little shanty that had been erected for that purpose, then lay in the sun lazily listening to the radio. The sun was hot by this time, and when we had all begun to feel the heat, Kent jumped up, ran out a few feet into the water, and began splashing Denise and then me. It was not long before we were all out in the lake, swimming with sure strokes away from the shore.

It had been a long time since I had experienced the sheer exhilaration of that cool, sparkling water, but I was a fairly competent swimmer. Denise and Kent were both very strong and quite tireless swimmers. We swam a long distance out from shore before I gave a thought to the fatigue that would eventually overcome my unaccustomed muscles. I was not so inexperienced that I failed to notice the first signs of overexertion, however, and shortly afterward I told Denise and Kent that I was going to head back in toward shore. Somewhat to my surprise, they agreed amiably to turn back also rather than continuing without me. We reached the beach in the same high spirits in which we had left it.

A short time later, we collected the items we had brought with us and started back to the road. It was not yet late in the afternoon, but Kent was planning to drive to one of the larger neighboring towns, about twenty miles away, and he had to be there before five-thirty. He asked me if I wanted to go along, but I declined, thinking I should wait for Lily, half expecting she would show up that evening.

For a few hours I had not thought about Lily's absence or the tragedy of Paul's life, but as I walked alone up Lily's driveway, having left the Robinsons in easy, high spirits, my mood slipped gradually downward. I entered the house with Freddy, fed him another can of dog food, and sat doing nothing for perhaps a half-hour. At last I decided to force myself to cheer up enough to call my parents and give them an unalarming account of the situation.

This was harder to do than I had imagined, because I really was worried about Lily. Though I tried to sound as if I accepted her spur-of-the-moment absence as a natural thing, there must have been a betraying note of doubt in my voice, for I received a good deal of consolation and some advice that no one really expected I would follow. They suggested that I call the police and place a missing-persons report. I answered hedgingly that perhaps I would do it later. I also said I would call again to let them know what happened, and told them about the Robinsons' picnic party. I did not mention the fish and the note, the young blond child, or Paul, and after I hung up, I felt the full depression that I had been staving off since leaving Kent and Denise an hour earlier.

Restlessly, I glanced again at all the more obvious places where Lily might have left a message for me. In desperation, I searched them all once more with fruitless thoroughness. Toward the end of this futile effort, I began to think that perhaps I should try to remember places where Lily might have thought I would look but which would mean nothing to anyone else. Since I had been unable to find any answers while talking with the neighbors, I could only hope that some clue concerning Lily's whereabouts might still be found in the house itself.

After a moment's reflection, I did remember a set of hiding places only Lily and I knew about. The old house had built-in secret compartments and a passageway that the two of us had discovered and had mentioned to no one else. We had no way of knowing if we had found them all, but I remembered that we had found several. It was a more difficult task to remember where these were located four years later.

The first one I was able to recall was behind a loose stone in the wall beside the fireplace. I ran my hands lightly over the stonework, feeling for the free section of wall. At last I felt one of the rocks slip beneath my fingers, reached for it anxiously, and pulled it out. The space behind it was small, perhaps one cubic foot. I could run my hand over the entire interior surface in a matter of seconds, and that was all the time it took to deflate one possible hope.

The passageway, I remembered, had an entrance behind a section of bookcase in Lily's room upstairs, so I hurried up the steps to investigate that possibility. After moving some light furniture and working for several minutes on opening the disguised door, I managed to open up the concealed walkway. There was nothing near the entrance, and beyond the first few feet it was too dark to see anything. I went back to my room to get a flashlight before walking through the secret hallway. On my way back I remembered another little compartment behind a mirror in one of the spare rooms, and I stopped to check it, with no success. Later, when I had searched every inch of passageway and still found nothing, the idea of secret hiding places had lost its charm. I persisted only because I had no other plan, and I realized that until all of the places I could recall had been checked, I would still have some doubt that they were all empty.

It took several hours and many trips up and down the stairs to complete this meaningless task. I didn't remember the places I was looking for in any logical, room-by-room order. When at last I was quite finished with this procedure, I climbed the stairs one final time to take a good look at Lily's room.

I was convinced that Lily had left me no explicit information about her plans, but perhaps some subtle indications might be found by a critical study of her wardrobe and her luggage. I swiftly encountered a problem in this line of investigation, because I didn't know anything about Lily's current clothes. I could see what was left, but I had no way of knowing what was gone. In the end, I could only conclude that most of her things were still in her room, so she was not planning any long absence. It was hard to tell whether any departure had been planned at all, but the absence of a comb and brush from the dressing table and the lack of a toothbrush in the adjoining bath suggested comfortingly that at least hasty last-minute preparations had been made. With this scant note of optimism I concluded my career as supersleuth and descended the stairs to watch some television.

I had not quite reached the set to turn it on before I had thought of another possible source of information. I decided to call Gary, as it was still only nine o'clock, and find out if Lily had left any word with Alice. This would have to be done in a casual way that would not be unduly upsetting, in case Alice knew nothing, either.

I placed the call, began the conversation in a sparkling tone of voice, then slipped in my inquiry as inconspicuously as possible. Alice was not at home, and Gary knew nothing about Lily's plans, but then, he hadn't known I was going to visit her, either. He said he would ask Alice about it when she got back, and that Alice would call me if she wanted to talk. I cautioned him not to make the story sound more important or mysterious than was actually the case, and we hung up.

As I turned from the telephone, I saw Denise walking up to the front door, and I went outside to meet her.

"Come on over and see some late fireworks!" she called as she approached. "We have some sparklers and things left over from the Fourth, and if you'll come, we'll use them to celebrate in your honor."

"Sure, just a minute. I want to get a jacket. Come on in, if you want to."

I ran upstairs to get my jacket, checked to see that Freddy was sleeping calmly in the kitchen, then locked the door after Denise and myself.

"Heard anything from Lily?" she asked.

"No, not yet. She won't be gone for long, though, because most of her clothes are still here."

"Oh, well, that's a good sign," she remarked absently, then changed the subject. "Paul's home now. He's anxious to meet you, but a little shy—you know. Do be nice, okay?"

I told her that of course I would be nice, but I could not help feeling a certain tension about meeting Paul. Making an effort to be especially agreeable would only make me cautious, self-conscious, and uncomfortable. I really dreaded the encounter. I knew nothing at all about Paul except what Denise had told me.

As we came in sight of the house, I noticed a young man sitting on the front porch, and I supposed that he was Paul. Denise confirmed this as we drew closer. When we reached comfortable speaking distance, Denise introduced us, and Paul got up and walked down the steps to meet me, extending his right hand. As he smiled and greeted me I noticed that he was slightly shorter than Kent, his hair somewhat lighter, and that he was probably a little bit younger than his cousins—closer to my age.

Denise immediately began talking, I supposed to cover up any unpleasant silence that might have occurred. After giving a brief, rather chattery account of our afternoon, she suddenly brightened and turned to Paul.

"I know what, Paul—be a dear and set up some of the sparklers so that they spell out Kim's name. Out on the hill in back would be nice, don't you think? I think it's a great idea. Don't you?"

Paul had been looking at her with a mild and, I thought, rather unkind amazement. At last he said that it would be nice, and left to do as she had suggested.

"He does so need to be involved. If I didn't ask him to do things for me, he'd just sit somewhere and brood. Half the time he doesn't even hear what anyone says to him. But he does try. He's really a great guy," Denise said.

"Well, come on in and meet Shag. She's our cat. Paul never used to like her much because she was always catching something—a bird or a chipmunk. He always said we ought to have her declawed. About a month ago, he just quietly picked her up, took her in to the vet, and had it done. I was a little upset at first, but it does save the birds. She's been a perfect angel ever since. I guess it was a good idea."

"She's very pretty. I've always liked cats, except for the way they catch things. That's a good solution," I said as I stroked the little calico cat. Shag purred and rubbed against my legs lovingly, then ran past me into the living room.

Denise did not invite me past the foyer, but I had the impression that the Robinsons' home was very beautiful with its high cathedral ceiling and gracefully curving staircase. Something told me that everything about the place, both its architecture and interior decoration, would be tastefully done and the best that money could buy. Perhaps, in the fashion of more modern houses, it did not have as many rooms as Lily's house, but it was large enough to represent a small fortune, I was sure. I would have liked to see just a glimpse of the living room, but Denise was anxious for me to join Paul.

"Well, you'd better go out and see how Paul is doing. You can help light the sparklers. I'll be along in a minute," she directed cheerfully.

I followed her in the direction that Paul had gone. As I rounded the corner of the house, I could see him on a hill about a hundred yards in the distance. When he saw me, he waved and struck a match to light the single sparkler he would use to light all the others. I hurried toward him and, as the separation narrowed, I saw Kent coming up over the other side of the hill.

"Hey, that looks great, Paul," he said enthusiastically.

What happened next I did not see clearly, because I was too far away. Kent came up close behind Paul and seemed to stumble. It was then that I noticed he was carrying a small red gasoline container. As he tripped, some of the gasoline must have spilled onto Paul's clothing, and the unexpected impact of Kent's hand on Paul's arm as he tried to regain his balance caused some of the sparks from the sparkler to ignite the gasoline-drenched cloth. Paul dropped the sparkler and stepped on it to put it out as he clapped a hand to the first flicker of flame on his shirt, hoping to smother it. He was fortunately successful in this, but he did burn his hand in the process.

As I hurried up, Kent was apologizing and explaining how this freakish accident must have happened, but Paul turned to him angrily.

"It will take a lot more than this kind of thing to get rid of me, Kent," he snapped, with carefully controlled fury.

"Wait a minute—wait a minute!" Kent protested, shaken. "I wasn't trying to hurt you. Believe me. Let's go to the house and fix that hand."

"Never mind it," Paul said tersely. "Come on, Kim, let's light these sparklers. I'll take care of it later."

Kent nodded to me unsmilingly, and left with a slight shrug of his shoulders. This I took as an apology to me, a statement that he had not meant to upset anything.

Paul was lighting two sparklers, slowly and reflectively. At last he handed me one wordlessly and began lighting some of the others that would eventually form my name. When we had finished, we stood back to watch while my name sizzled brightly against the hillside. After a short time, the tiny fireworks sputtered and went out.

"That was wonderful, Paul. Thank you," I said, with a warm smile.

"I'm glad you liked it," he answered pleasantly.

This exterior calm puzzled me, because I knew from

40

the scene I had witnessed earlier that inside he was seething with emotion. I wanted to find some topic of conversation that would put us both at ease, but before I could think of anything to say, Kent and Denise joined us.

As soon as his cousins arrived, Paul excused himself, saying that he had better go treat his hand. His bitterness was gone, but I could tell that the ill-feeling ran deep between Paul and his cousins, at least on Paul's part. I wondered why he should feel this way about them. Nothing Denise had told me could explain this animosity between Paul and his cousins. I felt it was a shame that whatever was bothering Paul couldn't be straightened out in some way.

After he was gone, Denise and Kent were quietly apologetic. I had half expected them to recapture the party spirit, but this time they did not even pretend lightheartedness. Instead, they explained that they really ought to be with Paul—that he would need them. I quickly offered to call it a night, thanked them for including me, and returned to Lily's house.

When I had entered the house and locked the door behind me, I called to Freddy to come upstairs with me. Though I had felt tired earlier in the evening, now that it was the appropriate time to get some sleep, I felt a false stimulation. Even when I lay resting in the warm softness of the bed, sleep did not come to me. My mind was too full of all the things that had happened that day.

My acquaintance with Paul had confirmed a lot of what Denise had told me earlier. I had seen for myself the complexities of the younger cousin, his reticence, his hostility, the paranoia that had surfaced under the tension of the accident with the fire. Yet, now that I knew Paul, I no longer felt inclined to avoid him. I wanted to understand him better. Denise's explanation did not seem completely satisfactory, because there was a calm, thoughtful side to his nature that it ignored. He had greeted me with kind reserve, with no trace of hostility or resentment. I wondered if we might not become friends.

As I drifted off to sleep, I began to think about Lily—where she might be and how I could find out. In my sleep, these thoughts mingled into a nightmare frenzy. I was standing in an enormous room filled with small boxes, opening them one after another, always to find them empty. The light was fading and I knew I had to hurry, but the boxes began sticking shut. I tried to open one last box but, for some reason, it would not come open. I kept trying, but with no success, and the longer this went on, the more sure I became that *this* box contained what I was searching for. At last, when I was on the verge of tears, the box sprang open. At first I thought it was empty like all the others, but suddenly I saw a flame starting inside it which grew and spread. The next thing I knew, all of the boxes were flaming, and I was caught in the middle, suffocating. I woke suddenly and found myself drenched with perspiration, my mouth dry with fear.

I rose from the bed to open the window and stood before it until I shivered from the chill. I slipped back under the covers and tried once more to sleep, but the best I could manage was light, short snatches. Finally, as the first signs of morning were already apparent in the east, I fell soundly asleep.

Chapter Three

It was not until several hours later that I reawakened to find the mid-morning sun streaming through the window. I felt much better after having slept, but when I discovered that it was already nearly ten o'clock, I was filled with impatient annoyance that sent me into a flurry of activity.

It did not take me long to dress and comb my hair, though I was delayed by a dresser knob that pulled off under the pressure of a hasty tug. I managed to edge the drawer open and decided to leave it that way, with the knob inside. I did not stop to make the bed, but pulled the door shut to hide the disarray.

I found Freddy waiting for me down in the kitchen, and I realized that the dog had probably been awake for quite a while, though I had not heard him leave my room. I opened the back door on another beautiful morning, warmer than the day before, and tinged with a pleasant haziness that fell short of oppressive humidity. Freddy brushed past me as I held the screen door open and loped across the yard and into the woods.

While I drank a warm cup of instant coffee, I checked Lily's supply of groceries. There was not much food on hand—just a few slices of bread, some margarine, a slightly rubbery carrot, a few cans of fruit, some partially used bottles of sauces and relishes, and a few teaspoons of instant coffee. I decided to go into town that afternoon to do some shopping.

I had just finished my search of the kitchen when the phone rang. Alice was calling, in a somewhat agitated frame of mind.

"Kim, where on earth have you been? I've been going half out of my mind wondering what's going on up there! I called twice last night after you called Gary, but we figured when there was no answer that you were tired and had gone to bed early, or else were out for some reason. Then this morning I called again, once around eight, then about nine, and still no answer! I didn't know what to think!"

"I'm really sorry, Alice. I should have called you back last night when I got in. It wasn't really too late. This morning I just overslept. I didn't hear the phone ring from upstairs."

"Oh, it doesn't matter. What I really want to ask about is Lily."

"Well, there's no news here. I was hoping you'd know where she was. I guess we'll find out when she wants us to know," I answered carefully, trying to keep my concern out of my voice.

"I suppose so. But it's not like Lily to do this. That's what makes me worry."

"There's probably a good explanation, Alice," I reassured her. "But, still, if you want me to actively investigate this—I mean call the police, or whatever you think best—I'll do it."

"I think—no. Not yet. If we wait a little while she'll show up. Let's keep in touch, though. I may change my mind if we don't get word soon."

"All right, Alice. Thanks for calling. I'll let you know if I hear anything—and you do the same, okay?"

"Fine, Kim. 'Bye."

As I set down the phone, I felt more worried and uneasy than before. I knew these were feelings that both Alice and I shared, though we both were making an effort to conceal this useless emotion. I did begin to wonder just how long we would be able to restrain the impulse to call for official help. If it had not been for Alice's decision to wait, I might have phoned the police today. As it was, I felt miserably torn between two opposing courses. Waiting was difficult, but I had not yet settled upon any productive action. Until I had made a firm decision about what I should do, I knew I had no other real choice but to wait.

I walked back to the kitchen and looked out the back door for Freddy. He was nowhere in sight, so I left the house to find him. Since I had seen him enter the woods, I started my search in that direction.

I was surprised by the warmth of the sun as I walked across the yard. A few roses lent their sweet fragrance to the air, and I bent over a particularly lovely pink bud to savor its faint aroma more closely. A big, furry bumble-bee buzed near my ear, and I backed away slowly to watch it enter the flower. Smaller, amber honeybees were collecting pollen from the little white clover blossoms sprinkled throughout the grass. As I made my way toward the woods, I watched where I put my feet, carefully avoiding the tiny creatures.

I had scarcely reached the edge of the woods, however, when I heard a shrill yelp of pain. The sound came from the direction of the road, so I quickly retraced my steps, leaving it up to the bees to clear the way this time. I ran around the house and up the drive to the road, where I called for Freddy. He did not appear right away, but I heard raised voices at the Robinsons', so I proceeded in that direction.

As I reached their drive, Freddy pulled away from Denise and slunk toward me, then broke into a run. I reached out a hand to him, and he stopped to receive my gentle caresses. He seemed reluctant to go back toward Denise with me, but I wanted to find out what had happened. I left him sitting in the drive as I continued forward to meet Denise.

"What happened?" I asked breathlessly.

Denise had appeared quite flushed at first, but now,

as she answered me, her face was a mask of composure.

"Freddy was chasing Shag. I've told Lily many times that I don't like him coming over here. Dogs need to be taught when their actions are wrong. He cried when I struck him, but he's not really hurt."

"It would have been better if you had left the discipline to me. I am responsible for him since Lily isn't here. I'm sorry he chased your cat, and I'll keep him under tighter control from now on. But still, I would rather you hadn't hit him."

I hoped my tone of voice conveyed the anger I felt, though I had to soften my words with apology. I was not yet ready to shift my mood to the light banter in which Denise tried to engage me, and my face must have shown it because she dropped her chatter for a more serious truly conciliatory line.

"Oh, Kim—please don't let this upset you! If I'd known Freddy was going to cry out I never would have done it. I didn't hit him all that hard. I don't know what to say. . .Please, don't let this spoil everything," she coaxed.

"Oh, never mind. It's not that serious a problem. It's all right. Think no more of it," I relented self-consciously.

As Denise glowed with the pleasure of success, I noticed Paul standing on the porch of the Robinson house. His expression was hard to read, but I knew instantly that he had overheard our conversation and that it had not pleased him. When he caught my eyes on him, he turned without any look of recognition and disappeared into the house.

It seemed so unlike Denise to have hit Freddy, especially to have struck him hard enough to cause him to cry out in pain. A possible explanation suddenly presented itself to me, and I turned to Denise to see if I was right.

"Denise, did you hit Freddy, or did Paul?"

"Why do you ask?" she countered with slight surprise.

"Oh, I don't know. Just a hunch. I saw Paul standing back there listening to us, and when he realized that I'd seen him he left. I thought maybe you didn't want to let me think he'd done it, so you said you had yourself. If I'm wrong, just forget it."

"No, you're not wrong," she said, after rather a long pause. "I hope you can understand why I tried to cover up for him. I didn't want you to feel angry with Paul so I took the blame for it. I figured there was some reserve of friendship between us which would soften your feelings. Though I think you're quite soft-hearted, anyway."

She flashed her quick, charming smile, but I was not sure whether she meant that as a compliment or an insult, so I ignored the remark entirely.

"Actually, I understand what happened better this way," I explained to her. "Thank you for telling me the truth."

"I guess that's always the better way. Now it's all clear between us, and no more need be said about it."

"Right. Well, I've got to be going now. And Freddy won't bother you again."

I left feeling that Denise had allowed me to share a secret part of her life. I felt trusted, and this gave me new confidence. I thought I could rely on Kent and Denise to be honest with me, and Paul's problems need concern neither me nor Lily in any important way. If I wanted help with finding Lily, at a later time, I would turn first to Denise and her brother.

I watched Freddy closely as we walked back to the house, assuring myself that he really was unhurt. As I threw an old ball a few times for him, I remembered that I had again left the door unlocked. Whoever it was who had wanted to frighten me before had now had another opportunity. It was with curiosity and apprehension that I reentered the house.

Nothing seemed to be out of place, and I felt amused by my feeling of relief. I called to Freddy to come in, and after he had reluctantly joined me, I filled his dish with water and prepared to go to town. I ran upstairs to get my purse and a sweater that I probably would not use, and on my way back to the kitchen, decided to check the front door.

As I stepped into the hall I noticed some grains of sand beneath my feet and wondered when I had been so careless about tracking dirt into Lily's house. I found that the door was locked, as I had known it would be, and turned back quickly, only to stop in amazement, staring at the floor.

A vase of straw flowers had stood on the hall table, and apparently the arrangement had been supported in a sand base. The vase now lay shattered into many pieces, with the sand and flowers spreading across the floor. Someone had written a message in the sand, tracing the letters with a hasty finger. I smoothed it out with a rough sweep of my foot, but not before the words had done their job. I felt shaken and perhaps a little hysterical, but I stood very still until the image of the erased message had reduced itself from a shouted slogan to quiet words in my mind.

I was (am?) here, it had said. It was senseless to be upset by what was no more than a practical joke. Yet no longer could I see it as a trivial, unthreatening occurrence.

The note had implied that its author might still be in the house. I really had no desire at all to find out if that was the case, and I felt almost sure that it was not, but neither did I want to lock Lily's valuable dog into the house with a possibly malicious stranger. I forced myself to check through every room in the house, even the basement, before saying goodbye to Freddy and locking the back door behind me.

As I stood beside my car fumbling through my purse

with a slightly unsteady hand, Kent came up the drive behind me. I did not hear him until he spoke, and when he did, I dropped the entire frustrating collection of clutter.

"Is anything the matter?" he asked as I knelt down to scoop up the contents of my purse.

"No, of course not. What could be the matter?" I answered with unnecessary vehemence and a nervous giggle. I had found the keys while replacing the rest of my things in the purse, so I was now ready to go.

"I thought you seemed a little nervous, that's all," he explained.

"Too much coffee, I guess," I suggested casually.

He seemed to accept this explanation and dismissed the topic. I unlocked the car door and tossed my purse onto the front seat before turning back to Kent.

"I'm going to town. Lily's supplies are really low."

"I'd offer you a boat ride across the lake, but the little store over there has a rather limited selection of basics. Great for everyday things like milk or bread, but to really stock up you need to go to the larger grocery."

"That's what I thought. Besides, I'd like to see Dipper Point. I haven't been in yet on this trip, and I remember what a charming place it is."

"I'd offer to drive you, but I suppose we'd be better off with separate transportation. I can't be gone too long today. Tell you what—you go ahead, and I'll drive in and meet you at the restaurant by the train station. We can have lunch and I'll show you around a little, then I can head back, and you'll have your own car to stay and do your shopping afterwards."

"That sounds great. I'd love it," I told him, with a sincere smile of appreciation.

I watched as he walked back down the drive, a little smile still lingering on my lips. He turned as he reached the road and waved to me, and I reciprocated, laughing.

I realized as I started up the car engine that my tense, frightened feeling had melted away entirely. After a few moments with Kent I felt incredibly relaxed and happy. As I turned the car around and headed out of the drive, I reflected serenely on the marvelous effect he had on me. At that time, I had not yet thought that this feeling Kent produced in me was a vulnerable and unguarded state as well as a pleasant one.

The drive into Dipper Point took about twenty minutes. The road wound through otherwise untouched wilderness. Occasionally a mailbox at the side of the road signaled a residence, but all that was visible from my car were the narrow, nearly overgrown driveways. As I neared the town, the area showed increasing signs of habitation. The natural forest trees thinned, though they always remained present in scatterings, and the scenery changed to the more orderly pattern of orchards. Some of the land was rolling hillside, and horses or small herds of cattle grazed leisurely in the pastures of small farms.

Dipper Point itself is a small, quiet collection of homes, mostly two-story buildings, with the character lent by age. Some of the houses are year-round residences, others are summer homes, but in July it's hard to tell them apart. As I drove past, I noticed that the lawns were for the most part well kept, thick, and dark green with summer growth. The colorful splash of gardens added a special attractiveness to many of the yards, and I saw a happy group of young children playing tag in the shade of a huge old oak tree. I could hear their laugher and the delighted yapping of their little dog even after I had driven well past them.

The streets which I had chosen to take to get to the depot were the residential ones, though I knew the town also had a small business distict. I decided to leave that for later, when I went to do my shopping.

The train station was situated charmingly on a small hill overlooking the bay and the town's marina. I parked my car in the gravel parking lot and got out to sit at one of the outdoor tables. The tables and chairs were painted in cheerful yellow and green shades, and some of the tables had matching canopies. I decided to sit at one of the unshaded tables, at least until the sun became too hot for me.

As I waited, I watched the seagulls dipping down to the water, then soaring up out of sight into the blue sky. I looked at the fifteen or twenty boats that were docked in the marina. These were considerably larger than the boats Kent and Denise had for use on the inland lake. Though the bay had quieter waters than the main body of Lake Michigan, its waves were larger than those of an inland lake, even in calm weather. High winds often caused the water to be very rough. From Dipper Point's marina, the opening of the bay onto the big lake was only a short distance.

A young girl walked briskly from the restaurant door to my table, menu in hand. She smiled a welcome and asked, a she handed me the menu, if I wanted to order right away or later. I told her I was waiting for someone and that we would order together when he came.

I glanced idly at the menu for a few seconds, then turned in my chair to watch for Kent's arrival. After a few minutes, I moved to one of the shaded tables, and just after I had done so, Kent pulled into the parking lot in his red Cougar.

He glanced at the menu on the table in front of me and asked if I had decided what I wanted. We both ordered bacon-and-tomato sandwiches and iced tea.

As we ate, Kent told me a little about himself and his family. My intuition about the Robinsons' affluence had been accurate. Kent's parents were spending the summer in Europe. They owned a house in the south of France. Mr. Robinson had made enormous sums of money in oil, and Kent had a small fortune of his own. He planned to become a partner in the management of his father's oil wells which would one day belong to him.

Kent had produced this information in response to a

couple of general questions about his family and his plans for the future. I could not help but notice, however, that he spoke with indifference, answering me with polite brevity. I turned to the surroundings to provide a more congenial topic of conversation.

"The marina is so lovely, especially on a day like this," I observed, gazing at the docked boats.

"Yes, it is," he agreed. "One of the boats down there belonged to my grandfather. He used to run a boat service for the tourists in the summer after he retired from his position at the University. It wasn't a very lucrative business, but he enjoyed it, and he used to let me take some of the tours when I had some spare time. That must have been ten years ago, but sometimes I still dream of starting up the business again, this time with more funds. If we had ten boats instead of one, charged higher fares, ran more tours. . . But Dad says it can only lose money because there's fuel to pay for, and maintenance, and the wages of all the tour guides. The funny thing is I know he's right, but the idea still fascinates me. At the very least we could get the one boat in shape, and I could take the tours myself."

I could tell by Kent's expression that this project meant a great deal to him. I wanted to give him my wholehearted encouragement, as the idea appealed to me too. I could imagine joyful hours of planning in the weeks to come if Kent would allow me to help in the early stages of the venture. Still, another little voice told me not to get involved, not to be too encouraging, when this plan would most likely lead to financial disaster. In the end, I only said with a smile that I thought it was an interesting idea.

This did not seem to satisfy him, and for a few minutes, he was quiet and looked to be thinking unpleasant thoughts. I did not want our lunch to end with Kent brooding on the failure of his plans and unhappy with my lack of enthusiasm about them. Suddenly I thought of a plan of my own that would help in the immediate situation.

"Kent, is the boat in working order now?" I asked speculatively.

"Why, yes. Dad wanted to sell it, but since Denise and I like it, he said it didn't make too much difference one way or the other. It needs varnish and paint, maybe some new seat cushions, but otherwise it's fine."

"I'd love to see it. Maybe we could even go out in it if you have time."

He glanced at his watch, his mood brightening with anticipation. He paid the check and we walked quickly down to the boats. Kent said he did not have much time but he didn't want to pass up this chance to show off the *Betsy Ann*.

"Let me show you how to drive it," he said as we pulled away from the marina.

Kent was a good teacher, and instructed me with enthusiasm and patience. For my part, I was more than willing to learn, and soon I was doing quite well on my own. It wasn't really that different from driving a car.

After we had made a big circle around the bay, Kent told me to pull in to the dock. I assumed that would be the end of the boating excursion, and thanked him for taking me and showing me how to handle the boat.

"You don't have to come in if you want to have a better ride," he said, as we pulled up to the dock. "There's an island out there, beyond the horizon. You could head out to see that. Don't worry about the key—you can give it to me later. I'll have Paul come down later this afternoon to tie up the boat for the night, and you can give it to him then."

"Why, that would be fun, Kent, but are you sure? I mean, maybe I should wait till a time when you can come along."

"Don't be silly. We can do it together another time. Go ahead."

"What about the fuel?"

"It should be nearly full. I asked Paul to fill it up this morning, since he was in town."

"Okay, fine. Thanks a lot."

I turned to look back as I headed out from shore in the direction Kent had pointed, and saw that he had stopped to wave. I sounded the horn lightly as he turned to climb the hill to his car.

I was captured by the sound of the water, the sparkle of the sunlight, and the graceful flight of the gulls. I had even managed to force my worries about Lily from my mind for the time being. The boat sped along toward the horizon, steadily opening up the distance between itself and the shore. The direction Kent had indicated seemed to lead to open water, but I accepted his statement that there was an island out there somewhere, and continued. The boat was very stable and, though cumulus clouds billowed softly in the west, the weather, for now, was clear.

Suddenly the motor coughed twice and stopped. I was no expert where mechanical devices were concerned, but it sounded to me like I had run out of fuel. I looked around for a container that might hold extra gas for such emergencies, but I saw none. I was dubious about my ability to refill the tank, anyway, since I hadn't asked Kent anything about that. I walked to the stern of the boat and poked about looking for a gas gauge. I finally found it. Its needle rested on the empty mark. I also found what I was sure was the proper refueling place, if only someone would pass by within signalling distance.

I had no choice but to drift with the waves and wait. I told myself there was no real danger, only inconvenience. I remembered that I had asked Kent about the fuel, and that he had assured me that Paul had taken care of it. Obviously, he had not. I wondered if this oversight had been intentional, or just an accident.

The shoreline was little more than a blur, and I doubted that Paul would see me stranded so far from shore, even if he did finally come to take care of the *Betsy Ann*. I probably wouldn't get any help for quite some time. This thought depressed me a little, but I determined to enjoy the afternoon sun anyway, since making myself miserable would have no positive effect on the situation.

I had been watching for boats for about an hour when at last I saw one passing by close enough to hear a signal. I sounded the horn several times, but the only response I received was an answering horn blast. They probably thought I was fishing or else they didn't want to take the time to stop.

My arms were getting dreadfully sunburned, and I was uncomfortably hot. I had just about decided to put on my sweater to keep my arms from getting any worse, even though it was much too warm for it. Before I had done so, the sun mercifully vanished beneath the rising bank of clouds.

I had practically stopped looking for boats when I was aroused by the sound of an approaching engine. I looked up to see that, at last, someone had noticed my predicament. I had no doubt that whoever it was had decided to come over and inquire about my trouble.

The boat pulled up within a few yards, and the driver shut off the engine and stood up. It was Paul, and I shouted to him.

"Paul, am I ever glad to see you!"

"What's the problem?"

"Out of gas," I answered.

"All right. I've brought some along."

Before long, the two boats were tied together with ropes. Paul joined me easily and set about refueling the empty tank.

"That ought to be just enough to reach shore. I'll

watch, though. You really ought to check on things like that, Kim. It could be dangerous."

"Well, I asked Kent. I guess he made a mistake."

"You have to look out for *yourself*," he said, a little sternly.

He had put me on the defensive and, though I knew he was right, I thought his tone was uncalled for. I had not intended to place any blame on him, but the words came out before I could really think.

"I don't see why you should be so angry when it's your fault anyway," I snapped.

He stopped pouring the fuel for a moment and looked at me appraisingly. "What do you mean by that?" he asked coldly.

"Oh, nothing," I murmured, embarrassed. "I didn't mean to say that. It's just that Kent said he asked you to fill it this morning. You couldn't have known we would be using it. It wasn't planned."

His color rose slightly, but I could tell that his annoyance was no longer with me. He turned to finish pouring the fuel and I sat down, tired, puzzled, and a bit ashamed of my temper.

Paul turned back to me with a smile. "That's all taken care of. I'm certainly sorry this happened. I didn't get word from Kent to refuel the boat until about two-thirty. When I got to the dock and saw the boat gone, I figured there had been some mixup. Kent had said you were going to drive out a ways into the big lake later in the afternoon. I borrowed a boat from a friend and headed out this way. It was just lucky that I saw you."

"I should say it was. I don't understand—"

Paul shook his head and said gently, "I don't want to frighten you, Kim, but you really must be careful. I don't mean just about the boat. Be watchful of everything, as watchful as possible. I don't want to frighten you," he repeated, with a sudden laugh. "I certainly sound ominous, don't I? Forget it. It was just an accident. Misunderstandings like that happen all the time to everybody.''

"Yes, I guess they do," I said, but I was not so sure, and I knew Paul had his doubts too. Perhaps he knew that this one had been planned. I didn't know whom to believe.

Paul told me he would meet me at the dock and we headed for shore. I followed him because I was no longer confident of my sense of direction. I was glad to get back to Dipper Point, and I didn't wait while Paul tied up the boats. I gave him the key, turned down his offer of dinner, and hurried to my car.

I drove down to the main streets of Dipper Point and parked my car in a central location. I had about an hour before most of the little shops closed, an hour and a half before the grocery shut its doors for the night. I saw a gift shop at the end of the street that sold Indian crafts, and I walked down to look. It was a fascinating little store, and I purchased a small, brightly painted totem pole for Lily. On my way back to the grocery, I left the package in my car.

I decided not to spend a lot of time shopping but just to pick up a few items. I had started pushing my cart up the first aisle when I stopped short, unable to believe my eyes.

Lily was standing a few feet away, picking out a pack of cigarettes. She had her back to me, but I would have recognized her long blonde hair and casual stance anywhere.

"Lily!" I exclaimed. "When did you get back? I couldn't imagine—"

The girl turned toward me with a slightly hostile gaze, and I realized that I had made a mistake. She was like Lily in every respect when her face was not in view but when she turned to me, I knew instantly that I was wrong. Though beneath her heavy makeup the girl was pretty enough, she had a very different face from Lily's.

"I'm sorry. I thought you were someone else," I explained quickly.

She snatched up the cigarettes and rushed out the door without paying for them. The clerk shouted after her and bustled over to the door, threatening to call the police.

"Don't do that," I said impulsively. "I'll pay for them. It was my fault she took off like that."

The clerk sputtered with annoyance, but accepted my offer. I realized, as I paid for the cigarettes, that I should have known it was not Lily, since Lily didn't smoke.

After that, I went back to my own shopping, and finished quickly without further delays. I had some difficulty balancing the two heavy sacks of groceries while I unlocked the car door, but I managed, and was soon on my way back to Lily's house.

As I unlocked the back door and called to Freddy, I realized with a sudden shock that I hadn't even wondered if Lily might be there. I could scarcely believe that I had given up so easily. Perhaps to prove to myself that this was not true, that I had only forgotten because I was tired and confused, I walked through the first floor of the house looking for a sign of Lily's presence. I saw nothing, but before I had completely finished, there was a knock at the front door.

As I hurried to answer the door, my foot slipped on the scattered grains of sand that I had not stopped to clean up that morning. I caught myself before I fell, regained my balance, and opened the door.

Kent stood at the door, a sack of groceries in each arm and a broad grin on his face.

"Forget these?" he asked.

"Oh, no. I just hadn't had a chance to get back out for them. You must have been watching for me to get back, your service was so prompt."

"Well, I guess I was," he laughed. "Paul called and told me what happened and what he said to you, and I figured a peace offering might be in order."

"You don't need a peace offering. But it *was* kind of confusing. I guess misunderstandings always are. Forget it."

"No, I *won't* forget it. You deserve an explanation. Can I bring these in?"

"Oh, sure, sure. I'm sorry. Come on in. Watch out for that sand, it's slippery," I said, leading the way to the kitchen.

"What is it?"

"What? Oh, it was a flower arrangement. I think Freddy knocked it over, " I answered.

Kent made no comment, but I knew he could not imagine how Freddy would have done it, so I hoped he wasn't giving too much thought to my explanation. Apparently he didn't question it, for he was still talking about the unfortunate accident with the fuel. I told him to sit down while I put away the groceries and fed Freddy, and that I would listen to his explanation, though it really wasn't necessary.

"It *is* necessary. You have to understand that this wasn't intentional. From what Paul told you it would seem like a plot. Actually, neither Paul nor I would have ever dreamed of pulling such a prank. What happened was that I had asked Paul to refuel it, but apparently he wasn't listening. He has no recollection of the conversation at all. That happens sometimes with Paul. I think Denise mentioned it to you."

"Yes, she told me about Paul's past. But why did he say you talked to him his afternoon?"

"Because I did. I realized I should have checked the tank myself, and I was concerned that Paul might have forgotten. I hadn't know for sure that I would be using the boat, and I hadn't made too big a point of it. When I asked Paul if the boat had fuel, he didn't seem to know anything about it. It was as if I'd never mentioned it before."

"Well, it doesn't matter. No harm done. Like I said

before, just forget it. I really mean it."

"Okay—now that you know what happened. By the way, you haven't seen Denise, have you?"

"No, I haven't. Is *she* missing?" I asked, half-jokingly.

"Oh, no. I just wondered. I guess I'd better be going." The casual words failed to match Kent's vaguely anxious tone.

"It was really nice of you to stop over. I appreciate it, Kent. See you later," I said, as he left through the back door.

I felt somewhat soothed by the visit. In fact, I was quite touched by his concern for my feelings. It was hard for me to explain why I should be left with a lingering trace of doubt when Kent's explanation seemed so feasible. I pondered this question while I swept up the remains of the straw flower arrangement, but I could think of no reason to doubt Kent or to suspect Paul of any deliberate malice. It was just a feeling I had—something about it didn't seem right.

I wondered where Denise was. I could tell that Kent was worried about her. I had already sensed that Kent and Denise were so close that each of them would always expect to know where the other went, and what the other was doing. It obviously disturbed Kent that he didn't know where his sister had gone, and I hoped there was no real problem.

I felt sorry for Freddy since he had been shut in the house all day, so I took him out into the yard for some exercise. While he pranced about the yard, I watched a nuthatch cracking seeds on the bird feeder. Although it was getting late and I felt like relaxing in front of the television, I walked through the woods with Freddy. This time, however, I made certain he didn't get out of my sight.

The wind had risen quite a bit in the two hours since I had returned home. The clouds were now dark and threatening and the night came on rapidly. When I felt the first large drops of rain I called to Freddy and we went into the house together.

I turned on the television to see if there were any weather reports. The report said that severe thunderstorms were expected in the area from nine o'clock till midnight. It was five minutes to nine, and the thunder and lightning had already begun.

Chapter Four

Storms did not particularly bother me, and I soon found that, though Freddy liked to bark at the crashes of thunder, he was relatively calm about it. I got some cheese out of the refrigerator and put it on a plate, along with some crackers and seedless grapes, and went into the living room to watch television. I found a thriller on one channel that seemed to match the weather perfectly, so I sat and watched that, eating slowly, giving occasional bites of cheese to a comically anxious Freddy.

It was a rather lengthy movie that, when well filled out with commercials, would last nearly three hours. Just into the second hour, a little after ten o'clock, the haunting spirit in the attic was groaning and wailing, causing the young girl in the room below to shiver with fright. During a sudden silence of tense listening, I had a chance to hear some of the storm sounds from outside. The wind was howling and the repeated crashes of thunder sounded loud enough to crack the windows. I got up to look outside and heard a noise on the porch. I clicked off the television on my way to the window. The noise persisted. It sounded like a cat yowling or a baby crying, then rose in a sudden crescendo to a shrill scream. I ran past the window to the door without even pulling back the curtain.

As I flung open the door, a flash of lightning illuminated the porch for a brief moment. I rushed out the screen door and the wind caught it and held it open. A drenching rain blew into the hall, and in the few seconds it took me to pick up the sobbing child, I got nearly as wet as he was. I pulled the screen door shut behind us and soon had the torrents shut out of the house.

I walked through the house to the kitchen, Freddy trotting along at my heels. I set the child on the kitchen table and pulled a towel out of a drawer. I began drying the little boy's blond hair, then wrapped the towel about him and snatched another from the drawer. All the while I talked softly and reassuringly to a very frightened little three-year-old.

I was relieved to see the flow of tears begin to be checked, and I decided that I would probably be able to distract him with a few questions. I recognized him as the boy in the photographs, so I knew he was probably not lost at all, but just looking for Lily. I wanted to find out who he was and where he lived.

I wasn't sure if he would talk to me, since he was at a shy age and I was a stranger. I tried to win his confidence with patience and gentleness, but it was Freddy who finally drew him out of his frightened silence. When the big dog sniffed the child's dangling feet, no doubt tickling them, the little boy bubbled with laughter.

"Froggy!" he exclaimed, reaching out his little hand.

"Doggy," I corrected automatically with a smile.

"No, Froggy. Froggy-doggy!"

I gathered that the child's name for the dog was a combination of Freddy and Doggy, and I gave in with a laugh.

After this he was much more receptive to my questions, and answered me good-naturedly. I found out that his name was Timmy and that he thought his home was here, in Lily's house. He seemed to interchange the names Lily and Mommy quite freely, and I soon surmised that these terms referred to the same person.

He was worried about where she was, and in order to divert his attention I made him a cup of warm milk and told him about my adventure of the afternoon, leaving out the part where the boat had run out of gas.

The storm was still raging outside, and I thought to myself how fortunate it had been that Paul had come out to assist me. Though there had seemed to be no real danger at the time, this storm would have changed the complexion of the incident considerably.

When Timmy had finished his milk, I checked the back door and carried him with me as I locked the front door. When we went upstairs, Timmy pointed out his room, but the door was locked. I had not discovered this fact when I had first arrived and had been looking through the house for secret compartments, because I hadn't remembered any hiding places in the smaller bedrooms. I had noticed later that several of the smaller rooms had been closed off, but I had not felt that this was surprising at the time. Many people shut off unused rooms to save on heating bills, and I figured Lily would not have any particular use for them. Now, though, I knew I would have to find a way to open the locked doors—at least the one belonging to Timmy's room.

For the moment, I took the child to the room I had been using and dressed him in one of my sleeveless blouses. It was far from a perfect fit, but it would be adequate. I left his wet clothes drooping over the edge of the bathtub and soon had him tucked into bed beneath the yellow bedspread.

I turned off all the lights except for the night light in the adjoining bath, but this gave me enough light to straighten up the room a little as I watched Timmy drift off to sleep. As I carefully turned the knob I had pulled off the dresser drawer that morning until the screw threads caught and held in fresh wood, my eye was caught by a small glass hen. I recognized the object and remembered that, four years ago, Lily had laughed and said that the little hollow space between the milk-white halves of the dish was our own invented secret compartment. We had never used it, but I knew I should have remembered it. Of all the secret hiding places it was the one Lily would have been sure I would remember.

My hand shook slightly as I reached for the hen and the two halves rattled together with a clinking sound. I soon found that the dish was not empty but it contained a set of keys. I had hoped for a note but, fighting back the disappointment I felt, I slipped quietly down the hall and tried the keys in the lock of Timmy's door.

The fifth out of the six keys opened it, and I switched on a light as I stepped inside. To my surprise, the room was practically barren. There was no crib, and Timmy's toys and clothes were gone. Only the pictures on the walls and a circus lamp sitting on a chest of drawers assured me that this was a child's room. I looked in all the drawers and in the closet, but I found neither clothes nor information. I turned off the light and relocked the door, then hurried back to my own room and the sleeping child.

My clothes had dried as I wore them, but I was left with a damp, chilly feeling. This was the perfect culmination for a day that had been emotionally exhausting. None of my questions had been answered, and the new puzzles that had arisen left me feeling desolate. I was aware of my own confusion and uncertainty concerning Paul and Kent, but with the information available to me at the time, I had no way of sorting out facts from emotions. Almost everything I knew about Paul depended on my faith in Denise and Kent's honesty. Now, on top of everything else, was the child no one had mentioned to me, in spite of the many opportunities I had given to all of Lily's neighbors.

As I washed my face and arms, I savored the relaxing warmth, and began to turn off my thoughts. I knew that persistent thinking about these problems would have as its only result the unproductive effect of a sleepless night. I exchanged my damp clothing for a dry nightgown and robe, then curled up in the yellow chair beside the bed. The storm had settled into a heavy rain without thunder and lightning, and I listened to its steady drumming as I tried to sleep.

Because I was so tired, I slept almost immediately, and quite soundly. This lasted only a few hours, however, and I awoke about three o'clock. The rain had stopped. Freddy and Timmy were sleeping peacefully. I got up silently, stretching my cramped muscles as I crossed to the window. The moon lit the night with a pale glow, and I half expected to see a shadowy figure slip into the woods or move quickly around the corner of the house, but there was no one in sight. All the thoughts I had successfully avoided a few hours earlier rushed back into my head, and though I settled back into the chair, I knew there would be no more sleep for me.

I wondered what I should do about Timmy, whether anyone would step forward to claim him, and, if someone did, if I could be sure it was the person to whom Lily had entrusted her child. Someone would be worried when they discovered his absence—but where had he been? That was the one question I had been unable to get him to answer.

I wondered too where Lily could be, and what could be so important that she had not even had the time to give me a call. Of course, I had not stayed at the house around the clock, but I had been home in the mornings and evenings. Alice had not been contacted either, and I felt sure my departures from the house had not stopped any attempt by Lily to get in touch.

The absence of the crib and the clothes was encouraging, I thought. It was another indication that Lily had planned her absence carefully, providing care for the child I had not known existed. Perhaps she hadn't meant for me to know about Timmy even when she came back, and so she had locked the door to his room. I was a little hurt by this thought, feeling that, as a long-time friend, I had earned a little more trust than she was showing me. Whatever her problem was I could have helped much more effectively if only she had confided in me. As it was, I knew nothing, and could do nothing except wait for her to return.

If no one came to ask me about the child, I would be responsible for his care, and my activities would be curtailed. This didn't really bother me, because I no longer felt in the mood for light-hearted lunches or high-spirited beach parties. The uncertainty of Lily's situation was beginning to wear down my resistance.

I tried to think of a possible connection between Timmy, Lily's absence, and the pranks I had myself experienced, but I could only conclude that some vital piece of the puzzle was missing. I knew too little about the relationships between the three families, and even those opinions I had reached in the past few days were not facts but unreliable conjectures. On the face of the situation, no one would want to play tricks on me or withhold information about Lily from me. Yet I was sure that someone was doing both of these things.

By five o'clock I had a headache. I was glad to see that the faint pink glow of early sunrise was beginning to tint the eastern sky. I got up and took a couple of pills for my head, then put on some clean clothes. Timmy was still sleeping, but Freddy awoke when he heard me moving about, and I expected that Timmy would join us soon.

I was examining Timmy's clothing to see if it was dry enough for him to wear when I heard some frantic knocking at the door downstairs. Since the child was still asleep, I left him in bed to run downstairs. As I entered the front hall, I was alarmed by the violence of the pounding, and hesitated a moment before opening the door. When I finally did open it, I was instantly sure that my early visitor had come to claim Timmy.

Karen rushed past me, her cheeks flushed, her eyes bright with tears. I caught her arm to slow her down, and asked her what she wanted, though I already knew.

"He's got to be here!" she said shrilly. "Don't tell me he's not! It's the only place he'd come. You have to give him back!"

"Yes. He's here. He's all right. He came here last night, in the storm. I couldn't figure out who had been taking care of him, so I decided the best thing to do was to wait and see who showed up to claim him."

"Oh, no, of course you wouldn't know. I was so worried. Well, I'll just take him home. Where is he?"

"I hope you won't mind answering a few questions," I said quietly, not answering her inquiry.

"Oh, please. . ." she cried, becoming distraught once more.

"Timmy says he's Lily's child. I want to know why you didn't tell me."

"Does it really matter? Please, Kim—I'm supposed to take care of him. You weren't supposed to know."

"Why not?" I asked a little sharply.

"I can't say. Don't. . . Please, just be patient a little longer," she said beseechingly.

I could tell from her manner that she would tell me nothing. I knew that further persistence would be more harmful than beneficial, so I tried to become more casual as I relented. I told her that Timmy was sleeping upstairs and managed to persuade her to let him be. I invited her to have a cup of coffee in the kitchen, and as we sipped it, I told her of Timmy's arrival the night before.

I saw no reason why Karen should not be relieved to find Timmy safe, and begin to relax a little. However, as I talked on about the events of the previous evening, I realized that, though her initial panic was past, Karen was still very nervous and uneasy. She fiddled constantly with her spoon, scarcely listening to what I was saying. I had hoped that we might become friends, as Karen was apparently Lily's most trusted neighbor, but I could not seem to reach her at all. She was very distant, and wanted nothing more than to take the child and leave as quickly as possible. I had hoped to feel more reassured about Karen before placing Timmy in her hands once more, but I still had unsettled doubts. I decided to see how much resistance would arise if I offered to keep Timmy myself until Lily's return.

"Really, Karen, there's no reason why you have to take care of Timmy any longer. I'm here now, and he can stay here in his own house. You've been more than helpful, but I'm sure Timmy would be happier here at home. I guess last night proves that that's true."

"No, Kim, I insist. Lily put him in my charge. I must have him back. Please don't argue about this. What happened last night won't happen again. I promise!"

She was getting very excited, which made me more reluctant than ever to place Timmy in her care, but there was a look on her face which suggested that I had no real choice. Lily had trusted her, so I must too.

"I want to get him now," she said, rising from the table and heading for the stairs. I tried to slow her down by saying she would upset him if she did not calm herself, but she shrugged this off and ran up the stairs.

"Won't you stay for breakfast?" I asked hopefully from the doorway as she picked Timmy up from the bed. "I've got some cereal I know Timmy would like. There's really no rush, is there?"

"Thanks, Kim, but I'd rather get back home. Where are his clothes?"

I brought Timmy's nearly dry clothes from the bathroom. Karen took them and said she would return my blouse later. Then she hurried down the stairs and out the door. I followed and called goodbye from the door, but she scarcely turned her head in response.

Timmy seemed to like her; that much was reassuring. Everything else about Karen's behavior seemed odd to me. She acted as if something terrible might happen at any moment if she did not leave immediately. I had a very strong sense of being an ignorant outsider. Yet I was at a loss to think of a sure method to gather some reliable facts.

It was not yet seven o'clock, and though I was dressed, I felt exhausted. Any effect the coffee might have had was cancelled by the letdown of losing Timmy so quickly. I lay down on the sofa and tried to think of a satisfactory explanation for Karen's behavior.

A horrible idea presented itself, which I assured myself immediately was too far out to be believed. Still, the thought haunted me, and I could not shake it entirely. Was it possible that Karen had fallen so in love with Lily's child that she would stop at nothing to have him? What could she have done to Lily? Would she have been capable of murder, or was she keeping Lily captive somewhere? That was ridiculous. I had no reason to suspect anything like that.

Supposing, as I was fairly sure was true, that Eric was Timmy's father? Maybe Eric wanted his son, but he and Lily did not wish to marry. Perhaps the Norfolks were planning some trick to get custody of the baby. Maybe it was Mrs. Norfolk who wanted to care for her grandson.

None of these theories would indicate that I had put Timmy into danger, but they did not put me at ease concerning Lily's safety. I told myself that they were probably crazy ideas, highly imaginative ones at best, and that to allow such idle speculation to upset me was silly. Somehow, on this note of shaky optimism, I fell into a light sleep.

I must have slept more soundly than I had at first realized, because I had a very pleasant dream. Its theme was very unlikely and incongruous under the circumstances, but at least it was relaxing. In the dream, Kent and I were running a tour service. We were taking a group of passengers out to the island Kent had mentioned the day before. The *Betsy Ann* was as I had envisioned her, with fresh paint and varnish and new seat covers. Kent and I were both very happy, and Kent smiled at me and said that I had made his dream a reality.

From this point on, the dream became more confused and less happy. A little blond boy appeared on board the boat, and Karen swam up to us, begging me to throw him overboard. I told her I would not, because we were going to meet Lily on the island.

I woke up suddenly and found that the sun was shining brightly. The phone rang, and as I went to answer it, I noticed that it was a little after ten o'clock. I tried to become more alert before picking up the receiver, but I was not completely successful.

"Hello?" I said in a slightly muffled voice.

"Kim, this is Kent."

"Oh, Kent. Hi! I'm glad you called."

"I'm afraid it's not good news."

"Oh, really? What is it?" I was fully awake now, and imagining the worst.

"Well, we've all been worried about Lily, you know. I decided maybe something should be done. I just finished talking to the police in Harbor Center." He did not go on, but seemed to be searching for a way to say what was on his mind.

"Well, what did they tell you?" I asked reluctantly.

"I gave them a description of Lily, and they checked their records. Now, nothing is certain, Kim, but they did say that the body of a young woman was found in the bay last night. As far as can be determined over the phone, the description of that body is consistent with Lily."

"I see," I answered dully.

"The police need a close friend or relative to make a positive identification. I would offer to do it, Kim, but if it's a case of near look-alikes, I might not be able to tell the difference. After all, I really didn't know Lily too well."

"No. I guess not." My voice was a little shaky, and I fought to control it.

"Will you be able to go down there and see about it? I'd be happy to drive you. I'd rather not have you go

71

alone."

"That's really nice of you, Kent. Give me a half-hour, will you?" I hung up suddenly, and hoped Kent would not be offended.

I found my way to a chair and sat down. It was hard to believe that this was really happening, but even through tears of shock, I had to admit to myself that this conclusion had not been completely out of the realm of possibilities. Though I had not liked to think of it, I had been aware that there was some chance that Lily did not call me because she was dead.

There was no one present to see my tears, yet I buried my face in my hands, as if to hide my emotion. Freddy placed a sympathetic paw on my knee, and I hugged him. I saw the glitter of fallen tears on his furry neck and wiped them away. I knew I would have to control my emotions in the hours ahead, and that now was the time for release.

Gradually I began to tell myself all the things that would help me to calm down temporarily. I convinced myself that there was a good chance that Lily was perfectly all right. The police were not certain about the identity of the young woman found in the bay. The practical thing to do was to wait and see.

I hurried upstairs, dressed quickly in a navy blue skirt and jacket, snatched up my purse, and called Freddy to the back door. While I filled a bowl with water for the dog, I watched carefully to see that he did not leave Lily's yard. The half-hour was a few minutes past, so I called Freddy into the house and sat down by a window that showed the driveway clearly.

Kent's delay was probably a sign of consideration. He would know that I would be upset and that I would need more than a half-hour to prepare myself. He was right to think this, for it had taken me nearly twice as long as I had thought it would to get ready to go. But now that I was ready, I wished desperately that he would come immediately. Waiting with nothing to think about except things that distressed me would quickly destroy my shaky pretense of composure.

I had only a few minutes to wait before Kent drove up and walked onto the porch. I opened the door before he had time to knock, and I locked it behind me.

Kent seemed a little tense, but I could tell that he was trying, for my sake, to present a calm and unruffled front. He said he was awfully sorry to have to give me such sad news. I decided to let him know that he was dealing with an optimist.

"I think the sensible way to look at it is that the news isn't sad yet. Until we know, there's no point in assuming the worst."

An odd expression flickered across his features which seemed to be a mixture of scorn and pity. When he answered, his tone was gentle, but his words were a warning. "Maybe so, Kim," he admitted, "but it's also sensible to be aware that the worst is possible. It helps to soften the shock a little."

We got into the car. As we started toward town, neither of us spoke. The drive would take more than an hour, and I wished I could get my mind off of what I might find in Harbor Center. All I could think of was Lily and this body that fit her description. At last I asked Kent a question about his conversation with the police.

"Did they tell you how she died?" The words sounded abrupt and horrible as they broke across the silence.

"They aren't sure, but they did mention one possibility. They believe that the most likely explanation is a sailing accident of some kind."

"Oh, no," I said in surprise. If that was true, Lily's death was touched with irony. I realized that Kent would not know this, and I began talking to him about it.

"That would be a very ironic ending," I said slowly. "Ever since she was a little girl, Lily was afraid of sail-

73

boats. I think it began when she was about seven. She and Alice, her older sister, were out in the family's sailboat on one of the lakes in southern Michigan. Lily fell off the sailboat while it was still upright, and Alice had difficulty getting back to her. Alice was only eleven years old, and no expert sailor. Luckily, Lily was wearing a life jacket. Alice finally headed for shore without her to get help. The rescue took nearly an hour from the time she fell in the water. There was no real danger of her drowning, I guess, but she was awfully frightened.

"I didn't know she had ever got over that. Years later, Alice and I tried to talk her into another sail, but she would have no part of it. We just let it go. After all, it wasn't that important. We were sorry about it, but it never made that much difference. And to think that she may have died as a victim of a sailing accident. . ."

For a few moments I was lost in thought. Then I remembered Kent's presence, and glanced at him quickly. His expression was very grim, but when he caught my glance, he tried to smile reassuringly. I thought to myself—he cares, because I do. He hardly knew Lily. Kent's concern was for me, and I was grateful for it.

I made an effort to cheer up, and I happened to remember the *Betsy Ann*. I hoped I could encourage Kent to offer me another ride despite the unfortunate incident of the day before. I wanted to put him at ease about it.

"I never did see that island you were telling me about, Kent. I guess the gas ran out too soon," I said with a laugh.

"Oh, really? That's too bad. Well, I guess it will be better for me to show you some time. Actually, there are more than one. I wouldn't want you to have any more trouble with the boat."

"I think that's a good idea, Kent. I'll take you up on that offer. Thanks."

We smiled at each other, and I felt completely re-assured about Kent's part in the misunderstanding about the fuel. He was a person I could trust and rely on. I imagined that he sensed my feeling about him, and was pleased.

How glad I was that Kent had come with me. I was becoming increasingly apprehensive as we proceeded toward Harbor Center, and I appreciated his presence, both as a distraction and a reassurance. We talked very little, but Kent seemed to know when to speak, for when he saw me staring at the scenery for too long a time, he would ask me a question about the roads I had used to come north, or tell me about the local surroundings. It was a long drive, but he kept it from becoming unbearable.

As we entered Harbor Center, I suddenly wished for more time, more miles of travel. At a certain point, my confidence in the unlikely slipped out of my grasp, and I knew that there was no longer any point in pretense. I was terribly afraid of what I might find, so much so that I stopped really wanting to discover the identity of the dead girl. I wondered why I had felt so willing and eager to settle the issue. Once done, it would be horribly definite and final.

When we had parked in the lot by the police station, I could scarcely manage to tell Kent that I preferred to go in alone. How could I explain that I no longer could be sure of the strength of my reaction if the body was Lily's, that I would rather be hysterical before an audience of strangers than in the presence of the man who was beginning to mean so much to me? I did not explain it, but Kent seemed to understand what I was feeling. He squeezed my hand lightly before I left the car, but did not wish me luck.

As I climbed the steps to the door, I felt more frightened than I could ever remember feeling before in my life. Oddly enough, I thought as I opened the door, how dreadful I must look. I knew I was awfully pale, though my pulse was racing. It was strange that one's hands could be so cold, and yet clammy with perspiration at the same time. I could scarcely speak to the woman at the desk, for my mouth was dry, but she understood what I said and led me matter-of-factly along the proper corridor.

I do not remember very much about that building or about the people I saw there. Not much was really registering on my mind, because I was too concerned about Lily to notice things. There was a large clock on the wall, though, and its loud ticking somehow managed to penetrate. I saw that the time was ten minutes to one, and the fact acquired a significance beyond what it truly possessed, because it was the only calm thought in my mind. I remembered other clocks like that one, clocks I had seen in school, mostly. It was like being back in high school taking an examination, trying to force one's mind to work efficiently, but being able to think clearly only about the passing minutes, each one marked by a loud click.

It was not long before the woman pointed out a door and returned to her position at the front desk. I entered the room and stood before a large gray desk. The uniformed officer seated behind it glanced up from a stack of forms he was examining and motioned me to sit down. I waited a full five minutes, which seemed at least an hour, for him to set the papers aside with a decisive movement and turn his attention to me.

I remember the officer as neither pleasant nor unpleasant, simply interested in the facts in a detached, matter-of-fact way. He asked questions that demanded only short, mechanical answers, and I found myself able to answer these easily and without nervousness. When he rose to take me to look at the body, I followed as if in a trance.

At last the moment had come that would give an answer to my fears. I forced myself to look at the blonde head and to study the features of the face. At first, I glanced briefly and reluctantly, then I looked openly. My face must have revealed the shock of recognition and an unreadable mingling of regret and relief.

I recognized the girl I had seen so briefly in the Dipper Point grocery. The heavy makeup had been washed from her face, and I could see how pretty she really was, and also how very young. The girl could not be more than seventeen or eighteen at the most. The sight of her dead face was so tragic, yet I was overcome with happiness, because she was not Lily. I was caught between tears and laughter, and I could only turn away to hide my emotions.

"Is she your friend, then?"

I was aware that the officer had asked the question more than once. In spite of my still reeling emotions, I turned to him to answer. "No. No, she isn't Lily."

As if puzzled, he asked, "Are you sure, Miss Harris?"

"Oh, yes. There's no mistake. She's not Lily."

"Well, thank you, Miss Harris. Good news for you, I'm sure." Still he seemed to hesitate.

"Yes, it is," I said, managing a faint smile. Though I was delighted that the girl was not Lily, I did not feel any sudden surge of high spirits. I was sorry for the dead girl, and I still did not know where Lily was. If the officer had not been present, I would have sat down for a good cry, partly from relief, but also from a depression that had been building gradually since my realization that Lily was absent.

My hand was on the doorknob when the officer suddenly spoke again. "I don't want to detain you unduly, but I do have a few questions. Please sit down."

I did so, wondering what further questions he could have. He came straight to the point, and I realized I had been foolish not to tell him that I had seen the girl before. This could be the kind of omission that would appear suspicious.

"I couldn't help noticing a look of recognition when you first saw the body. Am I mistaken?"

"No," I said quickly. "I have seen her once before, in the grocery at Dipper Point. I didn't mention it, because I don't know anything about her, not even her name. It didn't seem important. I was so glad it wasn't Lily. . ."

"Of course. That's very helpful, though, because it gives us an idea of her recent location. When was it that you saw her?"

"Why, I guess it was only yesterday. Yes—late in the afternoon, yesterday."

"I see. And you're sure she is the same girl?"

"Yes, absolutely," I said, calming down now. "What a tragedy about the sailing accident! Was she caught out in the storm last night, do you think? Rather an unusual time to be sailing."

He looked a little surprised, and I supposed I would be told he wasn't free to answer that kind of question. Instead he told me quite frankly that there was no evidence that could prove it to be a sailing accident, that the cause of death had not been drowning, but a blow to the back of the head. He made no comment about the time of her death, but I expected that I had been right in placing it in the early hours of the night before. I explained that my friend must have misunderstood over the phone, and as there were no further questions, I left.

Kent did not notice my approach to the car, but sat staring gloomily into space, absorbed in thought. When I opened the car door, he straightened with a start, glancing at me inquiringly.

"Well, we still have a mystery," I told him with a slight smile. "It wasn't Lily."

Kent was totally unprepared for that possibility. He had been ready to comfort me, to offer consolation and share my griefs, but not to accept this good news. For several seconds he was silent, then said incredulously,

"Are you sure?"

"Completely. It was another girl. I'd seen her once in a store at Dipper Point. I told them that."

"You told them you'd seen her?"

"Well, not at first, but they asked, and of course I did then." I was a little bewildered by his reaction. He acted as if there was some reason I should not have mentioned knowing anything about her. He seemed more surprised than pleased, more perplexed than relieved. Just as this observation was beginning to trouble me, he seemed to shake whatever doubts were bothering him, and smiled freely.

"That's great! I guess I caused you a lot of worry for nothing. But we'd have heard about it on the news, I suppose, and wondered. Anyway, it's all settled, and not as unhappily as I was afraid it would be, either."

"Yes, it's a relief, all right," I agreed. "But of course we still don't know where she is. It won't be really settled until we do."

Kent started the car, but hesitated before pulling out of the parking place. "Well, what would you like to do? I didn't make any plans, of course. I mean, I thought we'd be going back home right away, if it had been. . . We could stop somewhere for lunch, if you'd like. Want to?"

"To be honest," I said after a pause, "I'm not hungry at all, but if you are, let's stop. It would be fun, anyway."

As we drove along the beachside road, Kent spotted an ice-cream stand, and we both decided that a cone would taste better than a complete meal. When we pulled in, Kent saw a pay phone, and said he would like to call Denise and tell her what had happened, since he knew she had been worrying. I bought the two cones while he called home, and we ate them as we drove back.

The drive back to the lake seemed shorter than the earlier trip to Harbor Center. Kent and I were both preoccupied with our own thoughts. Mostly, we relied on the radio to fill in the silence, yet there was nothing awkward or strained between us. I enjoyed the scenery and Kent willingly answered any questions I asked, once or twice volunteering his own comments, but we did not engage in a meaningless stream of small talk.

When Kent pulled into Lily's drive to let me out, I thanked him for his concern and for the trouble he had taken to go with me to Harbor Center. He assured me he would continue to help me in any way possible, and said he hoped he would be seeing me again soon. As he left, I was filled with gratitude and reassurance. I was relieved to have an ally and a friend, but along with all this, there was something else too. I believed that even if Lily had been home, even if I had not needed support in a time of uncertainty, I would have liked being with Kent.

A half-hour later, when I called Freddy back into the house and sat alone in the kitchen staring absently at the clock, this feeling of security and happiness was gone. I felt frustrated almost to the point of tears, and longed to call Alice, except that I was afraid of breaking down on the phone. I decided to call Karen Norfolk and ask about Timmy instead. After the phone had been ringing for five minutes, I set the receiver down and let my emotions spill over in desolate tears. A few minutes later, feeling completely empty and drained, left with a hollow peacefulness, I decided to call Alice.

Chapter Five

I knew the minute Alice answered the phone that it had been a mistake for me to call. Her voice was edged with worry and tension, and when I had nothing positive to tell her, she sounded bitterly disappointed. I had planned to tell her what Kent and I had been doing that morning, but I decided there was no point in upsetting her further. I tried to respond sympathetically to her worries without revealing my own. I must have sounded distant and indifferent in my effort to be controlled.

"Where were you this morning, anyway?" Alice asked, a note of frustration in her voice. "I tried to call you three times, just to see what was going on up there."

"That's too bad. Kent Robinson took me into Harbor Center." My indecision must have sounded like guilt.

"Oh, he did! Well, I hope you had a good time! I guess there's no point in worrying about Lily. After all, what's it to you if she's missing or murdered? What can you do about it? Don't you care at all? You just go ahead and enjoy your vacation!"

She hung up suddenly, giving me no chance to protest or explain. I tried to call her back but she wouldn't answer the phone. I sat staring at it for a few minutes, hoping she would call me back, and wishing that whatever I had said or done to create that impression could be undone. I tried again unsuccessfully to call her back, but it was no use. Perhaps I would be able to talk it out with Gary later.

My head was throbbing, I felt ill, and it was terribly hot in the house. I stepped outside to sit on the porch in the shade, trying to think of something positive to do. Like Alice, I was frustrated by my inability to help solve the problem. Lily must have wanted me here for some reason, but why? What was it she had thought I would be able to do?

I must have been sitting there for an hour or longer when the phone rang. I both hoped and assumed it would be Alice, and answered as quickly as possible in a tense, excited voice. Paul was on the other end, and I could tell he was a little surprised by my tone.

"Would you like to have dinner with me tonight, Kim? I thought we could drive to Dipper Point."

"No, I'd better stay here," I told him firmly. I was certainly not going to give Alice any more reason to be angry with me. Then, realizing I must have sounded rather short, I added, "Thanks for asking, though."

There was a hesitation on the other end before Paul tried once more to pesuade me. "I really wanted to talk to you. . . Are you sure you can't make it?"

"No, I have a headache and I would rather stay home tonight, anyway. Thanks for calling."

"All right. Maybe tomorrow."

I was sorry that I had felt obliged to turn him down. I wondered idly what he had wanted to talk to me about, but decided it probably had nothing to do with Lily. I wanted to be home if Alice called, and Denise had cautioned me about involving Paul in this trouble. I did not want to anger her by asking Paul questions which might be upsetting in some way. I concluded that I had done the best thing.

I tried again to call the Norfolks, but there was still no answer. I decided to walk past their house later in the evening to see if they were home.

Freddy was hungry, and after I fed him, I unenthusiastically made myself a sandwich, since I had eaten almost nothing all day. Then I went upstairs to change my clothes. The minutes dragged past slowly. I had made up my mind not to try to call Alice again until seven o'clock, when it was likely that Gary would be home.

Walking aimlessly about the house, I found the little totem pole I had bought for Lily still in its sack. I set it up on the mantle where she would be sure to notice it when she came home. I crossed to the front window as if to watch the drive for her arrival, pretending I expected her at any minute.

I wanted to call Kent, to ask him if there was something else we might do to find Lily. It would have been reassuring just to hear his voice, to know I was not alone after all. Somehow, I felt that this was something I should not do. I had no reason to think I could depend on him to solve this difficulty which scarcely interested him. He had already done more than could be expected.

It was time to try to call Alice again. Gary answered, as I had hoped he would, and said that Alice was a little embarrassed about what had happened earlier. I explained about the body that had been found in the harbor, and the request made by the police that I should go to identify the girl.

"I'm sorry I didn't just tell Alice straight out. But I was afraid it would be upsetting to her to think I had thought Lily was dead. Then she got angry and hung up before I could explain it to her. I'm awfully sorry. This has been one rough day all around."

"You're sorry! Don't be silly. It's just one of those misunderstandings. I'll tell Alice about it, and it'll be all right. Don't you worry about that. I can't imagine where Lily is, though."

"That's the real problem, all right. Do apologize to Alice for me. I know she was awfully upset and I'm really sorry about the whole thing. If anybody has any suggestions, I hope they're not holding out."

"Suggestions? No. We'd tell you if we did. I just hope this doesn't go on much longer."

"That makes two of us, for sure. Keep in touch, okay? Bye."

"Right, Kim. Bye."

It was a relief to have that settled. I tried the Norfolks' number again but there was still no answer, so I called to Freddy and locked the back door behind us.

It was a lovely evening with a gentle, cool breeze. The evening light was an intense, a clear golden color, making the green of the trees look a shade brighter than usual. The birds called to each other in the treetops, sensing that night was not far away.

I walked slowly down the drive to the road and called Freddy to me before turning to follow the road toward the lake past the Norfolks'. As we walked past, I could see no sign of activity. No one was inside, the front door was closed and the car was gone. It was probably not dark enough for inside lights yet, and it was still possible that either Karen or her mother might be home, but I could see no indication that this was so.

I continued along the road, having decided to walk back through the woods. I was sorry that I could gain no reassurance about the child, but there was no reason to panic. They simply were not home. There could be any number of explanations for that.

I proceeded very slowly through the dusky privacy of the woods, not because the shadows obscured my vision, but because I was trying once more to piece together what I had learned about Lily and her neighbors since coming north. I had not yet discovered any coherent connection between the many fragments of fact and conjecture that had been presented to me, yet somehow I felt that, from what I knew, I should be able to figure out much more about Lily's situation than I had so far.

It seemed to me that I had never given full significance to the fact that Eric was also gone. No one had said they left together, but it was an interesting coincidence, particularly in view of the child. I wondered if I was right about Timmy's parentage. What could this sudden and secret departure mean? Had they finally decided to get married? Maybe so—and wouldn't it be a relief, if that was all there was to it! But why the secrecy? Why wouldn't they want me to know? It was far from clear in my mind, but it was the most optimistic answer I had yet hit upon. I decided it might help Alice if I shared this idea with her.

As soon as I got back to the house I called Alice. As before, Gary answered the phone, but he sounded vaguely excited and pleased about something. I could hear talking in the background, so I hesitated, not sure I should disturb them any further.

"Listen, if you're busy, it's not that important. I was just going to try to cheer up Alice, but it sounds like you're having a party. Don't mention I called."

"No, wait a minute. She'd like to talk to you, I think. Just a minute. . ."

"Hello, Kim? I'm so glad you called. I'm really sorry about this afternoon—"

"Oh, forget it. I didn't call to hear you apologize! I just wanted to be sure you weren't upset about anything. I've been thinking about Lily, and I'm pretty sure everything is all right. I hate to say anything definite, but it seems to me that there's probably a very simple explanation."

"Why—what do you mean? I'm glad to hear you're so optimistic—but why?"

"Well, it's kind of complicated, and I'm not sure, but it seems possible that Lily and Eric Norfolk have gone away together. You see what I mean? I'm not nearly so worried as I was."

Alice laughed strangely. "Oh, that *is* good news."

"What's so funny?"

There was a pause on the other end, and I thought I heard Alice ask someone else, "Can I tell her?"

"What's going on?" I asked good-naturedly.

"They're here! They just got here after you spoke to Gary before. Together—just like you thought!"

"Oh, great! I'm so glad! But what's been going on? Do you know?"

"Not really. Listen, they'll be home tomorrow, and they'll tell you about it then, okay?"

"Sure, sure. Okay, Alice. Goodbye, then."

I was elated but still puzzled. I discarded hastily all my doubts and questions and hurried over to the Robinsons' to share the good news. I was too excited to keep it to myself, and I knew that Kent and Denise had been concerned about Lily.

The Robinsons' living room was well lit and clearly visible to me as I walked up the porch steps. The plaster walls were painted a soft blue-gray, and the carpet was a medium gray, like weathered driftwood. The wooden furnishings, three tables and a bookcase, were made of rich, dark mahogany. Two chairs and a loveseat were of the same heavy wood, cushioned with pale blue crushed velvet. The large davenport and two ottomans were upholstered in a flowered material, deep blues and greens against ash gray. A bowl of yellow roses brightened one of the tables and a sunny autumn landscape provided a pleasing note of color in the subdued elegance. Without these touches, the room, for all its lushness, would have been too somber for me.

Kent and Denise were playing a game of chess, and Paul sat with his back toward them, listlessly stroking Shag. When I touched the doorbell he stood up slowly, letting the cat slide gently to the floor, and came to answer it. He seemed surprised to see me, but very readily invited me into the living room and asked me to sit down. Kent and Denise stopped their game a moment to greet me, and I could wait no longer to tell them.

"I've had some great news! I just talked to Alice, and Lily and Eric both showed up at Gary and Alice's house about an hour ago. I've no idea what all this has been about, but I guess there's no problem. They'll be home tomorrow."

I heard Denise say "Great!" and was dimly aware of Kent's echo, but my attention had been caught by something in Paul's expression as I mentioned Lily and Eric being together. What had it been? Shock, anger, apprehension? I could not be sure, but it made me feel uneasy. It had been a very fleeting reaction, quickly covered by a slight, set smile, but nonetheless it was unsettling. Perhaps it was simply because we had so carefully avoided involving Paul in the problem that he had been surprised to hear of it. Surely that was all there was to it—nothing more.

"Well, I won't stay and keep you from your game. I just thought you'd like to know. I really hadn't intended to stay long," I said, moving toward the door.

"Whatever you like," Denise said pleasantly, "but don't rush off on our account. I'm glad you came over to tell us. It's been on all our minds. After that horrible experience this morning, it must be a relief to have the whole thing resolved."

"Oh, yes, a great relief. Well, I think I'll be going. Good night."

Paul's expression had deflated my happiness a little, and I suddenly remembered that I hadn't locked the door when I left the house. My hasty departure might have seemed strange to the Robinsons and their cousin, but I still did not know the source of the odd pranks that had been played on me every time I was careless enough to leave the door open, and I was anxious to cut short the length of time I left available to the prankster.

When I entered the house, however, Freddy met me in the hall, wagging his tail unconcernedly. There had been no trouble, and for that I was grateful.

I pushed aside the nagging feeling that everything was not after all completely explained, and set about straightening and cleaning the place. As I dusted the mantle of Lily's fireplace, I smiled to myself at the thought of this strange role reversal that placed me in the position of welcoming hostess instead of visitor. I was satisfied with my work after a litle more than half an hour and, being tired, decided to get a good night's rest.

Though I had gone to bed early, I did not awaken until the sun was streaming through the window with near-mid-morning brilliance. I dressed quickly, feeling happy and relaxed. Freddy bounded down the stairs ahead of me and we shared a couple of fried cakes before leaving the house. I had no definite idea about Lily and Eric's planned arrival time, and it was a beautiful morning. I decided to walk past the Norfolks' on my way to the lake to see if anyone seemed to be there.

Though I had many reasons still to feel worry and suspicion, it was remarkably easy—too easy—to push all of these aside now that my main concern over Lily was settled so agreeably. It was as if the other problems that had bothered me since my arrival were mere imagination. The discovery that Lily's absence was no mystery at all took away the dark meanings I had been attaching to those baffling incidents and left them their inexplicability but no longer their sinister quality. I felt almost as freely optimistic as I had on the day of my arrival.

As I walked leisurely down the drive, I listened to the cheerful voices of the chickadees and watched the acrobatics of some young ones on a small pine tree nearby. The little birds were tame, almost friendly, and they watched me with bright, curious eyes. Their parents flitted past close to my head, seemingly unaware of my presence and certainly undisturbed by it. I remembered Lily mentioning in a letter that some of the chickadees would perch on her camera while she was setting up outside to take pictures. I could believe it.

As I walked along the road I was half lost in a vague, pleasant daydream about the weeks ahead mingled with snatches of childhood memories. When I reached the Norfolks' drive, I decided impulsively to share the good news of Lily and Eric's coming arrival with Karen and her mother. Or, if they already knew, we could all share the wonderful feeling brought about by this turn of events.

Freddy stood sniffing some bushes by the side of the road as I turned to walk up to the house. I saw no indication that anyone was there, but I never reached the house to find out definitely whether the Norfolks were home or not. When I was about halfway up the drive, I heard a car accelerating on the main road, the thud of impact, and Freddy's cry of shock and pain. I whirled and ran back toward the road, but the car did not stop. I only caught a glimpse of red through the trees as it followed the road toward Dipper Point, still going at a high speed.

I was afraid to look at the dog, but I rushed over to the thick grasses into which he had been thrown. As I got there, he was just beginning to struggle to get up, but I could see that both of his left legs were injured. I placed my hand on him to hold him still while I tried to think how I could best get him into the car and to the veterinarian.

As I contemplated this, I stared unseeingly at the tire tracks that swerved across the soft sand of the road's shoulder. Freddy was far too heavy for me to carry, yet I didn't want to leave him alone while I went to get my car. I wasn't sure if I would be able to lift him into the car if I went to get it, but I knew it was the only way I could possibly manage.

As I stood up reluctantly to go for the car, I heard the sound of someone running along the road, and thought with relief that Kent was coming to help. When I looked up it was Paul I saw, not his cousin. Paul brushed past me without speaking and knelt down by Freddy's side.

"Go get your car," he directed with just a trace of impatience.

His words jarred me into action and I sped off toward Lily's house. Once again I had neglected to lock the door, but I gave no thought to that as I bolted up the stairs to get my purse, which contained my car keys. I fumbled through it on my way down the stairs, but couldn't find the keys. I paused for a moment, glancing vacantly about the living room, while I tried to remember what I might have done with them.

A fragment of freshly splintered wood caught my attention, and I crossed to the mantle. The small totem pole I had bought for Lily lay in a neat pile of smashed pieces. My car keys had been set on the mantle beside it. I snatched them up quickly and hurried to my car, pausing to lock the door as I left.

I realized as I pulled out of the driveway that this last incident revealed something more about the prankster than had the others. Could it have been a coincidence that the one article in the house I had bought recently had been the one selected for the prank? It hardly seemed likely, but if this had not been chance, it meant that whoever was responsible for these strange tricks was intimately acquainted with Lily's house. Otherwise they could not have so readily picked out an object which had not been there before my arrival.

My earlier feeling of security and exhilaration was completely shattered. I was tense now, frightened. I had no idea how serious Freddy's injuries might be, but whatever their severity, I knew I was to blame. I should have kept a tighter control over the dog. He was my responsibility, and I had not been cautious and concerned enough about that.

He knew better than to stand in the road, I thought to myself, but that was no excuse.

Paul had watched for the car, and as soon as he saw me pulling out of the drive he picked up the dog and carried him to the other side of the road. I brought the car to a stop next to them and leaned across the seat to push open the door. Freddy was quite heavy, even for

Paul. I was thankful that he had come to help me. I couldn't have done it alone.

"How bad do you think it is?" I asked as we started toward Dipper Point.

"Hard to tell," he replied shortly, then continued more encouragingly after a pause. "I think he'll be all right, thought."

"I can't understand it. He never stays out in the road where he would be in danger of being hit. He always stands to the side. Whatever would have made him—" I broke off, remembering the pattern of the tracks across soft sand, the speeding red car heading toward Dipper Point, and realized that to hit Freddy the car had had to cross the other lane and even go off the road.

My expression must have revealed something of the shock I felt when I realized that this accident was no chance hit-and-run, but quite deliberate. Paul glanced over at me when I stopped talking so abruptly, and asked me sharply what was wrong. For a few seconds I didn't answer. I was driving as fast as I could, and some of the turns in the road required my attention.

"What is it?" he repeated. "Are you all right?"

"Yes," I answered slowly, trying to decide if I should tell Paul what I was thinking. "It's just that I'm not sure this *was* an accident."

He was silent for a moment, then confirmed my assessment of the situation with a question. "Because of the tire tracks, you mean?"

"Yes. I think whoever hit Freddy had to swerve off the road to do so."

I glanced at Freddy as I spoke. The pain was unmistakable in his eyes, but he noticed my eyes upon him and moved his tail slightly. The blood had seeped into the beige material of Paul's jeans, and I fixed my attention quickly on the road.

"It's not that bad," Paul told me quietly, but I kept looking straight ahead and said nothing, waiting for him to comment on my suspicion that Freddy's injury had been intentional. I wondered why he had acknowledged my theory with such coolness and apparent lack of interest.

Paul gave me directions as we went, since I did not know exactly where the vet's office was. It wasn't long before we arrived there, and I hurried around the car to help Paul manage the doors. When the woman behind the desk saw us come through the door, she motioned two other pet owners into seats and led us back into one of the examination rooms.

"The doctor will be with you right away," she said, and left us to inform the doctor of the emergency. Paul set Freddy down on the examination table and stroked his head gently while we waited.

The veterinarian stepped quickly through the door and began to examine Freddy. Dr. Winslow was a middle-aged man with a calm, gentle expression. He asked no questions, but set about his work with a quiet efficiency and competency. After a few moments he looked up, as if noticing us for the first time.

"I can see nothing here that shouldn't mend in a few weeks' time. The left hind leg is broken, but not in a way that should cause any permanent damage. The front leg is sensitive, but not broken, and the surface wounds should heal up in a few days. It would be best to leave him here at least overnight, though. You don't need to wait while I set the leg and clean up the other injuries. It will be safer if he is here, so that if any sign of internal injuries should show up, corrective measures can be taken immediately. I don't believe there will be any problem. I'd say he was pretty lucky. I'll take him out to the surgical room and fix him up right away."

We thanked him and went back out to the desk, where we were told we could pay when we picked Freddy up and that, if we called later in the afternoon, they would give us a progress report. I hated to leave him there, but it seemed necessary. I hoped Lily would not be too upset when she came home and found Freddy gone, and that he would heal as smoothly as the doctor had indicated, with no further complications.

I felt miserably guilty and angry with myself for letting such a thing happen, and I was filled with uneasiness. I knew it had been no accident. When I stepped out of the clinic into the bright sunshine and clear air, it was as if I woke from a nightmare only to find that the dream was real. The seemingly disjointed and unrelated incidents of the past few days suddenly fell into a terrifyingly logical pattern.

Someone had been against my coming and had tried several times to frighten me into leaving. Twice earlier the person had entered Lily's house while I was away to leave disturbing messages for me to find, and now he or she had gone so far as to take the car keys from my purse. How did the incident with the boat fit in? Was that another prank, or just an honest mistake? I couldn't be sure.

I realized that I should have been alarmed by the death of the unknown blonde girl, though at the time I had only been relieved that she was not Lily. But whoever had struck her from behind might have believed that she was Lily too. The police hadn't been all that sure that her death was an accident. I should have seen long before this that my friend was in very grave danger.

It had taken the shock of the obviously deliberate injury to Freddy to make me realize that something was seriously wrong. This no longer seemed to be a threat, but rather an angry, spiteful action, directed more against Lily than myself. Yet I did not blind myself to the fact that my friendship with Lily was enough to make my position uncertain, just as Freddy's connection with her had endangered him.

I tried to puzzle out who might be behind this. Who would have felt threatened by my presence, and why? What could have caused anyone to hate Lily so much? Was the same person responsible for all of these incidents, or were there several different motives operating?

What about Mrs. Norfolk and Karen? The motives might be very strong where Mrs. Norfolk was concerned. Perhaps she was angry because she felt her son had been trapped into marriage by an unwanted child. She had certainly resented my presence. But Karen had been frantically concerned about Timmy, possessive and frightened. What was the source of her fear? Her mother's actions, Lily's return, or something entirely different? If she was afraid of Lily's return and her own loss of the child, she might be a suspect. Either one of the Norfolks could have been familiar enough with Lily's house to have picked out the totem pole as a new object.

I tried to remember where I had been when the three instances of entry to Lily's house had occurred. Once I had been walking in the woods with Freddy. Anyone could have done it that time. The second time I had gone over to the Robinsons' because Freddy had been chasing their cat. I had seen both Denise and Paul. Neither of them could possibly have been responsible for the message in the sand of the spilled flower arrangement. This third time, again it might have been anyone. I had not seen either Karen or her mother for some time.

I knew that Paul was not responsible for Freddy's accident. I was troubled by the glimpse of the red car I had seen through the trees, because Kent Robinson's car was red. Yet I didn't know anything about the Norfolks' car, and there was always the possibility that someone else entirely had hit Freddy, someone who was simply enraged by the sight of what would have appeared to be a stray dog.

I tried to think of possible reasons why either Kent or Denise might be angry with Lily, but nothing I had seen or heard indicated that they felt very strongly about her one way or the other. Both of them had been very friendly and helpful to me. I was quite sure that Paul was also uninvolved. This narrowed my suspicions down to the Norfolks. Yet something failed to ring true.

I had walked to my car in preoccupied silence and begun to drive home, only dimly aware of Paul's presence, as I tried to sort out my thoughts. I glanced over at him, realizing that my long silence must have been disconcerting. I would have liked to talk with Paul about all this, but Denise's warning held me back. Because of this cool reserve between us, I felt that I knew little about Paul's true thoughts and feelings. I had never even discussed Lily with him.

Paul must have noticed my glance, for he stirred uneasily as if he had been caught with his mind far away.

"Well, I guess it was pretty lucky about Freddy. I mean, that he's going to be all right, and everything. I would have felt terrible if it had been any worse. He's my responsibility. I feel bad enough as it is," I rattled nervously.

"I know," he said thoughtfully. I realized he was not thinking about my feelings of guilt, but reliving his own, and I could have kicked myself. I tried to think of something to say to turn the conversation onto a more pleasant track, but before I could come up with anything, Paul continued. "It's a mistake to blame yourself for things that go wrong when you never intended them to happen. We just do the best we can. Sometimes later we see that we might have done something differently, but what difference does it make later? It's too late to change anything. And probably, by being preoccupied with past mistakes, we just make it all the more likely that what we do in the present will be open to self-criticism later too."

"Yes, I suppose so," I answered with relief. Though I had nearly made a distressing blunder, it was clear that the scar tissue on that particular wound was no longer sensitive. I was glad for Paul, grateful that he would try to draw from his own painful experience to help me. "I'm glad Lily's coming home today. Then we'll just have to wait for Freddy to get out of the hospital and maybe things can get back to normal."

"I hope so," Paul answered, but he sounded as if he had serious doubts. I looked over at him questioningly, but his eyes did not meet mine, and I knew he had no desire to comment further.

I wished now that I had warned Lily. I was not sure what would happen when she arrived. Was it possible that attempts would be made on her life? There was reason enough to believe so, and I began hoping that she and Eric had not arrived while I was gone. I wanted to talk with them about this right away before anything could happen.

The horrible thought occurred to me that perhaps Freddy's accident had more purpose than mere spitefulness. Suppose it was one last attempt to get me away from her house—if not permanently, at least for a short while? Perhaps they had gambled that Lily would arrive during the morning while I was gone and that they would have a chance to do whatever it was they wanted to do to her before I could warn her.

I pushed the accelerator a little harder, and Paul asked with mild surprise why I was hurrying. I smiled and shrugged off the question, but I maintained the faster speed. If my suspicion about this plot to get me out of the way was correct, did that mean that Paul was involved? Not necessarily. He might have acted purely out of concern for Freddy. Yet he had been so prompt. . .it was an unsettling thought.

I was relieved to see that there was no other car in the driveway and no sign that anyone had been there in my absence, though I could not be sure just from driving by in the car. I drove to the Robinsons' to let Paul off, thanked him for his help, then returned to Lily's house. Even after close inspection, it appeared that all was well. I would have a chance to warn Lily after all.

Chapter Six

I had checked all of the open rooms in the house, because now that I knew of the close relationship between Lily and whoever was trying to frighten me away, I could no longer be confident that this person would not have a key to the house. There was no sign of any trouble, no indication that Lily and Eric had arrived and left again in my absence.

I stood at the back door and looked across Lily's back yard to the woods, but I did not unlock the door. I had locked the front door behind me as I came in. I wanted to be very sure no one entered the house when I was not aware of it, especially now that Freddy was gone. If the person had a key it was possible that this precaution would not be very effective, but there was a good chance I would hear the key in the lock.

I went upstairs to comb my hair and freshen up a little, then hurried to clear up the remains of the little totem pole before they arrived. Then I sat down to wait, trying to think of how best to explain all that had happened since my arrival. I wanted to put across to Lily a feeling of serious suspicion without frightening her unnecessarily. I was convinced that she was in danger, and I could only hope Lily would have some clearer ideas about why this had happened and perhaps be able to pinpoint the source of the trouble.

As I sat watching the driveway, I suddenly remembered Paul's unexplained phone call of the night before. What had he wanted to talk with me about? If only I had remembered to ask him that morning! I was sure he hadn't told me about whatever had been on his mind.

I didn't have the opportunity to brood long on my unfortunate forgetfulness, because Lily and Eric soon pulled into the drive. I ran to the door to unlock it before they reached the porch, so that I could explain my fears later and more gradually than would have been the case if they had immediately seen such dramatic evidence of my concern.

"Lily! It's so good to see you! And Eric—hi!" I was making every effort to sound natural and as if everything was all right—perhaps too much of an effort.

"Kim! I'm so glad you're here! I hope you haven't spent the whole time worrying. We should've let you know— But where's Freddy?" Lily brushed past me into the kitchen. "Hey, Freddy, what's the matter? Aren't you glad to see me? Where is he, Kim? Out in the woods? What's this door locked for? Hey, Freddy!"

"Listen to me, Lily," I said uneasily. I was feeling uncomfortable about having to tell her about Freddy's accident, and had seen no urgency in the situation. If only I had known what the results of this delay would be, I might have been able to stop her and make her listen. As it was, I was in no hurry. She pulled open the back door, exuberant over her homecoming, and I went after her, followed by Eric.

Lily began to run down the stairs, shouting, "Freddy!" Suddenly she fell forward and down, hard.

"Lily!" I shrieked. "What is it? Are you all right?"

"Oh, God!" Eric muttered. I was ahead of him on the steps and I could see that one of her feet had gone right through the second to the last step. Her leg was caught by the splintery wooden board. That was why she had pitched forward so violently.

I stepped over the broken stair and was beside her in

an instant. She had been stunned by the fall, but by the time I knelt down she was struggling to straighten herself up. Her face was twisted with pain, but she was making a valiant effort to keep the tears in her eyes from spilling over. For a moment no one said anything as Eric helped her to a sitting position on the step above the broken one. I pushed on one half of the board until there was a clear space for her foot to pull back up through.

"What hurts?" Eric asked at last.

"Everything!" she exclaimed with a high-pitched giggle. The tears were streaming down her cheeks now, but she was laughing as if the whole incident was hysterically funny.

"Is anything broken, do you think?" I asked cautiously.

She was beginning to calm down, but I could see it was too soon to tell. She shook her head doubtfully, then said, "I don't know."

Eric went inside to phone the doctor, and I brought a clean dishcloth and a pan of warm water out to the porch for Lily. Her arms had been scraped when she fell, and I knew she would want to have the blood cleaned away as quickly as possible.

"What a silly thing to have happen!" she commented shakily.

"Why, it's terrible. I can't imagine how that step broke like that. I've been up and down those stairs a dozen times since I've been here, and it seemed perfectly sound."

"Ouch! Oh, that hurts! I wonder if it's broken."

"Maybe I'd better wait till the doctor looks at it," I said, trying to ease her right arm back down to a comfortable position.

The fall had distracted Lily temporarily from her desire to find Freddy, but now that the shock of it was passing, I knew it would not be long before she began to ask questions again. She rubbed her slightly swollen ankle for a few seconds, then straightened up suddenly.

"But where can that dog be?" she asked anxiously.

"It's nothing to worry about," I began carefully. "Freddy is perfectly safe. This wasn't his day, either, though. He had a little problem with a car and he's at Dr. Winslow's clinic now. But Dr. Winslow says he'll be fine real soon. I'm awfully sorry that happened, Lily, and now this on top of it."

"Oh, no! Are they sure he'll be all right? Why did he have to stay if it wasn't that bad? Was his leg broken? How did it happen? He's so good about the road!"

"I think it was just a routine precaution. Besides, I expect they'll take some x-rays. One of his legs was broken, but Dr. Winslow said it would probably heal completely in a few weeks."

"Maybe it'll take me about that long to get back in one piece myself. We can hobble around together," she laughed.

Eric appeared at the back door looking a little bit exasperated. "How do you feel now?" he asked with concern.

"Oh, I'll live," Lily assured him. "But I can't tell what's broken and what isn't. It could be just sprains, I suppose, but my right arm and ankle sure feel—well, terrible."

"I thought you'd need a doctor. I tried to get Dr. Jacobs to come out here, but it isn't possible. He said if you can get into the car, he'll take care of you right away when we get to the clinic. Do you think you can?"

"I certainly hope so. Let's try it. Ah, wait, maybe you can pull the car in closer," Lily said, trying to get to her feet, then settling back down.

Eric went to bring his car. I asked if mine was in the way, but he said he could pull around it. I tried to help Lily, but she was unable to put any weight on her right foot, and since her right arm was also injured, she couldn't balance well enough to get to the car. Eric finally picked her up and set her gently on the front seat. I told them I would stay behind so that they need not delay to lock up.

I felt horribly alone as I watched the car pull out of the driveway. I hadn't even had the chance to share my suspicions with Lily.

I turned back to the house, wondering what could go wrong next and fighting away such speculations. I stopped to reexamine the step that had broken. Because of all the other suspicious incidents which had occurred, I was ready to assume that, again, this was no accident. I fingered the wood along the broken edge and found it hard and firm. Why would it have broken when there was no sign of weakness in the board? I lifted it to see it more clearly, and found that just beneath the splintered surface the break was clean and smooth. Someone had used a saw on it, but from below, so that the damage would not show to the casual observer. To do that, it seemed to me, one would have had to remove the step from the staircase temporarily. On one end of the board I could see the marks where someone had used a tool to pry the step loose. There could be no doubt now. Someone had done this deliberately, probably during the time I had been away with Freddy.

I still could not be sure who had done this and why. Was someone trying to kill Lily? A tampered stair would not very likely have resulted in her death. Besides, whoever had devised this had no way of knowing who the victim would be. It could just as easily have been Eric or myself. Perhaps I was wrong to assume this this injury had been specifically intended for Lily. What if all these unsettling episodes had been planned with me in mind? In that case, Lily would know nothing that could be helpful, and until I left they all would be in danger. I made up my mind then that I must talk to Lily as soon as she came home again, no matter what arose to interfere with what I had to say. Few things could be more important. I mustn't allow myself to be delayed again.

It would be hours before I would get a chance, though, and I could scarcely face another afternoon of waiting. Surely there must be something to be done in the meantime, but what? I made a pitcher of iced tea and drank half a glass while I tried to think. Was there anyone I should tell about this tampered step? Perhaps Kent, I thought, but couldn't make up my mind.

I had just decided to call Mrs. Norfolk to inform her of Lily's accident when the phone rang. Denise was calling to find out if Lily and Eric had arrived yet.

"Yes, they were here," I told her, "but they've left again already. Lily fell on the back porch steps and Eric thought she ought to see a doctor."

"What a shame! I certainly hope it's nothing serious." Denise sounded genuinely worried.

"I don't think it is, but she may have broken her ankle. It was hard to tell. It'll be awful if she has to wear a cast all summer."

"Terrible," she agreed. "Well, I'll call back some other time—maybe tomorrow."

"Fine. I'll tell her you called."

I had dialed all but the last digit of the Norfolks' telephone number when the front doorbell rang. I set the phone down and hurried to the door, thinking that perhaps Mrs. Norfolk and Karen had decided to come over to see Eric and Lily. I wanted to watch their reactions to this last episode very carefully. I had almost come to the conclusion that in some way they were behind the things that had happened, though I was not yet clear on the details. I was nervous about talking to the Norfolks, but glad for a chance to test my theory.

When I opened the door, however, my visitor was Kent. My face must have revealed my surprise, because Kent asked if I was expecting someone else. Because I could not be sure if he had also detected a measure of relief, I didn't mention that I had been thinking of the Norfolks, but simply said that I had not been expecting anyone. I asked him in, but I noticed as he came in the door that he held one hand behind his back. There was a teasing little smile on his face, so I laughed and asked, "What is it?"

He brought his hand slowly from behind his back to reveal a lovely bouquet of roses of many different colors, ranging from pure white to deepest red, with intermediate shades of yellow and pink.

"Fresh from the garden!" he said, laughing at my obvious delight.

"They're gorgeous, Kent! Thank you so much! Let's put them in water right away. I just love them."

"I'm glad." He smiled, then added jokingly, "Of course, they're really for Freddy, but I thought you'd appreciate them better."

We laughed together as we looked for a vase. I found one and was filling it with water when Kent asked about Lily and Eric.

"Where have they gone off to so soon? Denise said she saw Eric's car drive in. But surely they can't have come and gone already!"

I sighed. "Yes, they have. Lily fell on the back porch steps and had to go see Dr. Jacobs. She thought perhaps she'd broken her arm or her ankle. Maybe both."

"How awful for her."

"Well, these will cheer her up. They're beautiful, Kent."

"I'll be glad if Lily likes them, Kim, but remember—they were meant for you."

I glanced up quickly at the sound of his voice, which was no longer teasing, but gentle and sincere. His eyes met mine only briefly, but I could see he was no longer joking, but quite serious. There was kindness in his eyes, and something else, as well. Was it concern? How much did he know about what had been going on?

"That's nice of you, Kent. I will," I answered, thinking to myself, if only I could talk to him. If only I could be sure.

"Is anything troubling you, Kim? I can understand that these past few days have been upsetting, first with Lily gone, then Freddy's accident, and now this, but is there anything else?"

"What makes you ask?" I countered defensively.

"Well, for one thing, questions like that. You seem nervous or something. But it's not really you so much as Paul. I know he's worried, but he doesn't talk to me so I can't tell why. It could have nothing to do with you, but I've gotten the impression that it has."

Maybe Kent can help me, I thought to myself, fighting my indecision. But what if he was involved with the pranks? I could tell him nothing he did not already know. If he really knew nothing about it, maybe he would be able to guess who was behind it, once he was informed. I offered him some tea, which he declined, and we went into the living room to sit down.

I began carefully with the less serious offenses, avoiding speculation about who might be responsible. I watched Kent closely as I talked, and thought that I could read genuine shock in his face while I told of the entries into Lily's house and the strange messages that had accompanied them.

"I would say someone wanted you to leave," he commented after I had described the broken totem pole.

"It seems that way—but why? Who would care?"

Kent was shaking his head slowly, clearly puzzled. He drummed the arm of the sofa absently and said, "I can't say."

I wanted desperately to go on talking. to tell him everything I knew and everything I suspected. The longer Kent sat so absorbed, puzzling on the problem, the less resistance I felt against discussing it with him.

He turned to me abruptly and asked, "But isn't there something else—something more to go on? Are you sure you've told me everything?"

"I'm not sure how much I should say," I told him with tortured candor.

"What do you mean? What—oh, because you don't know. . .I see. Kim, believe me, the only way to work this thing out is for you to tell me everything you know—or even *think* you know. I know all the people here. I'm in a better position to guess at their motives. You know what they've done. Together we can figure it out."

"I hope so," I said lamely, still hesitant.

"Do you really doubt me that much? Do you think I'm behind this? You want me to help you, but how can I? You've got to trust somebody."

"I know. I know. But, how do I know you're the one?"

Kent stood up and crossed to the window. "All right," he answered quietly. "Perhaps it's better if you talk to Lily first. I can see the spot you're in, hardly knowing any of us. If it isn't Denise or Paul or me it would have to be the Norfolks, and you probably can't believe that's the case because of Eric. I know what you must feel. I only hope it'll all work out this way, that's all."

I could not see his face, but I was moved by this unexpected understanding, and also by the fact that, beneath his rational acceptance of my position, I could tell that Kent was hurt by my doubts. I crossed the room to stand beside him, but he did not turn to look at me. He made no effort to change my mind, but simply waited silently for my answer.

"I'd like to talk to someone about all this," I said cautiously. "I really do want to tell you."

"Then do," he said gently, turning to smile at me. "There's no reason to be afraid to talk to me about it.

Believe me. I don't want to push you, that's all."

"I appreciate that," I answered warmly. "Let's sit down again. There's a lot to tell."

I was filled with a sense of relief as I began to explain to Kent some of the more serious reasons for my fear. I told him first about the afternoon when I had seen the blonde girl in the grocery and had mistaken her for Lily, and reminded him that this same woman had been found dead in the harbor less than twenty-four hours later.

"But she didn't drown," I said significantly.

"No?" Kent seemed surprised. "How did she die, then?"

"She died as a result of a blow to the back of her head."

"But it still might have been a sailing accident. Maybe she was struck by the boom as it swung around unexpectedly," he suggested.

"Maybe," I conceded, "but they don't know. Suppose it never had anything to do with a sailboat. Someone might have killed her. Someone who had mistaken her for Lily—as I did."

"That's incredible, Kim! I don't believe it! But go on. I can see there's more to come."

"Well, then there's Freddy's accident. He wasn't standing in the road, but to the left of it as you face Dipper Point. And the car that hit him was going in that direction. I saw it through the trees. The tire marks swerved across the shoulder. There's no way that was an accident."

"You saw the car?"

"Only the color, that's all. Does anyone around here have a red car besides you?"

"Red? Oh, I see why all the hesitation! No. Not that I know of. Maybe it was someone passing through, I don't know."

"And then this last incident," I said with a note of finality.

"Lily's accident? What about it?"

"Someone fixed that step to cause her to fall. Or to cause *someone* to fall."

"You're sure?"

"Completely. I can show you."

"I'd like to see."

We went out to the back porch and Kent studied the broken step with grim amazement. "Yes, it's just as you said. But why?"

"I was hoping you might know. Was there trouble between Mrs. Norfolk and Lily or anything? I mean, do you know how Eric's mother felt about the baby?"

Kent looked startled. "You know?"

"What do you mean?"

"About the child—about Timmy."

I hesitated, picking my words carefully. "I haven't been told anything, but I have seen him, but it's not too difficult to guess who his parents are."

"That's true. But where did you see him?"

"One night he ran away and came over here looking for Lily."

"Oh, then he's with the Norfolks?"

"That's right." I was puzzled by Kent's obvious interest in this matter, and disappointed by the lack of helpful information I had received. It seemed to me that the conversation had been far more informative for Kent than for me, and I was beginning to have doubts again.

Kent must have read the discontent in my face, for he said quickly, "But now to get back to the real problem—"

"Yes. Well, you've heard it. Any suggestions?" I tried hard to keep the note of chill disapproval from my voice. I knew it was unreasonable to blame Kent because he did not know how to solve this problem, but I felt as if the difficulties were magnified when he could offer me no help. I had hoped that sharing this with him would have helped to ease my fears, but they were only increased.

"I don't want to suggest a name at this point. Too much is uncertain," Kent told me firmly. "What we need to do is decide what action to take now. I would discourage you from repeating all the details of that story to anyone else—even Lily. If you feel you must warn her, do it as discreetly and vaguely as possible. I don't think you should discuss it with anyone else."

"But why not?" I asked, surprised, yet already beginning to feel more at ease. Kent was putting forth some definite ideas, if not solutions.

"We don't want to put any pressure on this person, force him or her to feel hurried in any way. I may be able to pinpoint the source of all this trouble before the next incident is staged, if the person is in no hurry. It's our best chance to stop any seriously damaging action. We must try to make things go on as smoothly as possible."

"Well, that's certainly true," I admitted, though I was far from convinced that his choice to keep the matter secret was the right one. "But why are you so sure that the way to accomplish it is by saying nothing? I would think if this person knew we were suspicious it would slow him down, maybe even discourage him from attempting anything more."

Kent considered this for a moment, but I could see in his expression a determination to convince me that he was right. He was clearly reasoning the matter out very carefully in his own mind before committing himself any further. At last he began to explain his reasons and I could tell that he was completely sure he was right.

"I can understand your point," he began tactfully, "but look at it this way. Whoever is doing this knows that you are quite aware that something strange is going on. He's made that obvious to you. He wants you to know it. That means he isn't concerned about arousing suspicion. In fact, that's part of the plan. But he doesn't want you to know who he is, and so far we have no way of guessing. If we knew who was responsible I wouldn't suggest keeping quiet—but we don't. If we open this thing up, the person will know he's running a great risk of discovery. He'll be doubly careful, and probably act as quickly as possible. We may never be sure who is behind this in that event. No, I think we should let the person go on feeling relatively secure just a little longer. It will give us just a little time to try to work this out. Are you with me?"

"All right," I assured him, "to a point. I want to discuss this with Lily. I'll explain your reasoning to her so that it'll go no further. But I think *she* has to be told."

I could not understand why that compromise appeared to make Kent uneasy. He said that would probably be all right, but I could tell that something troubled him about my insistence that Lily be told. However, he did not try to persuade me again to keep this startling information from Lily, but seemed to accept my decision to be open with her as final.

"It's dangerous to leave that step as it is," Kent commented, as an afterthought. "Why don't I at least pull it off and throw it away for you? Eric can put on a new one as soon as he can. Make sure he does."

"Thanks, Kent," I said, as he stuffed the board into the trash can that stood beside the garage.

Kent followed me into the kitchen, but said he had to be going. I walked with him to the front door, where he turned and regarded me searchingly. "You did the right thing to tell me, Kim. I only hope I'll be able to help you and that everything will be all right now. I'm sure I'll be able to find out more about this very soon, and as soon as we are sure who's doing these things, the person can be stopped. It'll all work out. Don't worry. Just hang in there."

"Thanks so much, Kent, just for listening to me. I feel better about it now that I've talked to you. I'll be very watchful and careful. Maybe one of us will see something. Let's keep in touch about this. Anything I find out, I'll tell you right away, and you'll tell me, won't you?" I was talking just to keep Kent from leaving. I didn't want to be alone. I knew the assurance he had given me would begin to fade as soon as he left. I could not say why I felt so much less apprehensive as long as Kent was with me, but this was so. After that one horrible moment when I had been afraid that I had confided in the wrong person, every word and action of Kent's had worked to dispel my lingering doubts and to increase my confidence.

"Of course I will. The moment I learn anything new, maybe before. You can count on it." He smiled reassuringly.

"What about Denise?" I asked suddenly. "I know you're close. I suppose you'll be telling her about this, won't you?"

"I haven't decided yet," he answered. "Unless I tell you differently, no one else will know of this from me. If I decide Denise should know I'll tell you first. All right?"

"Of course. Whatever you think is best. You don't have to tell me first, just let me know sometime."

"I will. Now don't worry," he said, taking my hands in his. He looked into my eyes, and I thought he was going to kiss me, but instead he squeezed my hands gently before releasing them, and said lightly, "Take it easy."

"Yes. You too. 'Bye," I said, a little wistfully, as he descended the stairs.

I watched him until he reached the road, but he did not turn back. I shut the door and listened for a moment to the empty stillness of the house.

"What have I done?" I whispered to myself. Had it

been a mistake to be so open with Kent? It was as if two different people answered the question. Of course it was the right thing to do. Kent would be helpful; I could stop worrying. But another voice, a more self-reliant one, disagreed. It had been foolish to bring him into this on the basis of emotions. How much more sensible it would have been to consult Lily and Eric first.

I traced the green-and-white floral print of the davenport's upholstery while I considered this matter for several minutes. Then I pushed myself to my feet with a sigh, dismissing it. There was no point in having doubts now. I had made my decision and acted upon it. It had been taking a chance, I supposed, but it might also have been the right thing.

I called Dr. Winslow's office to inquire about Freddy. After a moment's consultation with the veterinarian, the receptionist told me that it was as the doctor had expected—one broken leg, but otherwise only bruises. Freddy would be all right in just a few weeks. He was young and would heal quickly. There was no reason at all to worry. We could pick him up about ten o'clock the following morning.

I was immensely relieved. It would have been a blow to Lily to lose him, I knew, and I felt responsible. With the dangers that seemed to be rising up on all sides, it was important that her spirits be kept high, especially since her physical condition was going to have suffered because of the fall. If she came home with a cast, or was unable to walk on a sprained ankle for a few days, how could she help but feel vulnerable? I was glad that no other serious problem would be added to her already complicated situation.

I had been about to phone Mrs. Norfolk before Denise had called and Kent had come over to see me. I decided I should still tell her what had happened to Lily that afternoon, if for no other reason than that her reaction might be interesting.

The phone rang five times before Mrs. Norfolk answered it. I knew from the tone of her voice that she was still on edge, and I wished I could find out more about her.

"Mrs. Norfolk? This is Kim Harris. I thought you'd want to know about Eric and Lily."

"Oh, yes. I've been waiting for them to call. Eric said they'd be here today. Has anything gone wrong?" she asked anxiously.

"They got here a short time ago—"

"Where are they now?" she interrupted impatiently.

"Well, Lily fell on the back porch steps, so Eric has taken her to see Dr. Jacobs. It happened almost immediately after they arrived."

"I see. Well, something was bound to happen. Tell Eric to call me as soon as he can. I suppose it'll be an inconvenience, but I really must talk to him right away," she said, sounding vaguely piqued.

"Oh, I don't think so at all," I said quickly. "I'm sure he'll want to call you. I'll tell him you're anxious to hear from him. Maybe he'll come over."

"I don't imagine so. But please tell him. Goodbye."

I wasn't sure what conclusions could be drawn from that conversation. Something was wrong between Eric and his mother, but exactly what, and how serious the problem was, I had no way of guessing. As for Lily's accident, Mrs. Norfolk had not bothered to pretend any surprise or concern. She had seemed annoyed or disgusted, perhaps, but it was almost as if she had known it would happen. How could she have known unless she was the one who planned it? But if that was the case, why was she so obviously displeased? I was as puzzled by her reaction to this as I had been by my other encounters with her.

I was surprised to hear Eric and Lily at the front door so soon, but when I glanced at a clock on my way to the hall, I realized that more time had passed since they had left than I had thought. I was after four-thirty, and they had left just before one o'clock. I had lost all track of time while I was talking to Kent.

Eric carried Lily up the steps, and when I opened the door for them, he continued to carry her until he set her on the couch. I must have looked alarmed, because Lily smiled at me as convincingly as she could.

"I won't be helpless for very long," she told me quickly. "We've got crutches in the car and I'll start using them tomorrow. But for tonight, I'm supposed to rest my arm. Nothing's going to need a cast. Just an Ace bandage for my ankle. I should be walking on it in a couple of weeks. I sure hope so."

"So nothing's broken. That's lucky," I commented, then, remembering Mrs. Norfolk's request, I turned to Eric. "I called your mother just a few minutes ago. She's very anxious for you to talk to her."

"Oh, really?" he sounded surprised. "Well, I'll go call her, then."

He stepped out into the hall. I decided to waste no more time before informing Lily about the strange incidents which had been occurring. I wanted to know whether she thought Eric should be told before mentioning anything about it in his presence.

"Lily, before you left, did you notice anything strange going on here? I mean suspicious?" I began uneasily.

Had I failed to notice how pale Lily was when she first returned from the clinic, or did my question frighten her? For a second she said nothing, then she laughed. "Why, no. I can tell you why we were gone— to be married. Eric and I just got married!"

"That's wonderful," I said unenthusiastically, "but it's not what I mean. Strange things have been happening ever since I arrived, and I want to know if you know anything about them. I think you're in danger, Lily."

"That's ridiculous. But let me tell you about the

honeymoon. I know you must be put out with me, not being here, and all, but don't be. It's so exciting and romantic—''

"And I want to hear about it. But not now. Why aren't you paying attention to what I'm trying to tell you? Believe me, I'm completely serious about it, no joke. Can we talk with Eric about it?''

"No," she said sharply. "I'd rather not talk about it at all. But if you must know, there have been a few peculiar events. I know I have to be careful. Some time when we have more time—but not to Eric.'' She almost whispered the confession that she was aware of what I was talking about, and I could hardly believe she would be so secretive, especially considering that Eric was her husband now.

"But do you know someone may be trying to kill you, Lily? A girl was killed while you were gone—a girl who looked a lot like you. Don't you see? I have to warn you!'' I persisted in a lowered voice.

"No, no," she said angrily. "I can't believe that's true. Don't go on about this. Please, Kim.''

Eric's conversation was drawing to a close. I was stunned by Lily's reaction, but I had no choice but to respect her wishes, at least for the moment.

"We must talk later," I said quietly. "I'll drop it for now, but you know I can't just let it go—not suspecting what I do.''

She made no answer to this, but smiled her easy smile and asked what I thought about her surprise marriage.

"A little unconventional," I replied with a teasing grin, which made her laugh.

"Like almost everything I do?" she suggested light-heartedly.

"The thought crossed my mind," I admitted, and we laughed together. There was no point trying to force Lily to consider her problem seriously, if she was set against it. It seemed important to her that Eric did not sense that anything was wrong. I had no choice but to go along with her and watch for the next opportunity I would have to speak to her alone.

Eric entered the living room and smiled when he heard our laughter. I was curious about his conversation with his mother, but there was no casual, natural way to ask him questions about it, as he began to talk of the recent marriage immediately.

"So Lily's told you the happy news?"

"Yes! I'm so glad for both of you. Very clever of you, Lily! You never gave me the slightest hint."

I wanted to ask her why there had been such secrecy, but I hoped she might volunteer something in response to some less obvious probing. Surprisingly, it was not Lily who responded to the remark, but Eric.

"It's too bad, in a way, that we didn't let anybody know. But we didn't want a lot of fuss."

"I can imagine," I answered sympathetically, but could not help feeling disappointment. There had been a flippant look on Lily's face, and I knew she would have answered my implied question with a joke. That would have been unrevealing, it was true, but I would have been free to pursue the matter further. Eric's answer was less obviously an evasion, but still, he had not told me anything. It was the kind of answer that invited no more discussion.

"Well, are you at all hungry?" I asked. "I can get us something for supper if you like, and you can tell me about your trip."

"I could eat something—maybe some soup," Lily answered.

I had bought some cream of shrimp soup, because Lily liked that, and I served it with crackers, cheese and fresh peaches. I had put a bottle of Lily's favorite black raspberry wine in the refrigerator to chill. I hoped that would give this occasion a feeling of celebration in spite of the undercurrents of tension I was sure existed for all three of us.

It was a very pleasant meal. I found myself feeling almost relaxed and happy. Lily and Eric had a great deal to tell me about their honeymoon trip to Canada, and I was content for the moment to listen to their descriptions of scenery and cities. Those days, as they described them, had been a time of perfect joy. I was glad for them both, for I knew these memories would be with them for all the years to come, and I also suspected that they had been a well-earned reward after some very trying times. I could only guess at what their past troubles had been, but at least there seemed to have been a happy ending.

They obviously loved each other very much, I thought, as I listened to their dreamy remembrances. There were times when they were, I knew, talking more to each other than to me. But perhaps I was too sentimental, I could not stop myself from thinking. Did Lily really trust him and love him, or was it all an illusion? She was already keeping secrets from him, and even I was not showing what I felt. I was making an effort to keep my doubts and worries from tarnishing their evening. Was their mood an effort and a pretense as well? But they were married, I reminded myself. Surely that had to mean something.

If Lily noticed my preoccupation, she asked no questions. Perhaps I concealed my uneasiness completely enough that she did not notice.

Inevitably, there were questions about my stay. These began with Lily's observation of the roses I had put in the center of the table.

"Such lovely roses, Kim. Where did you get them? Not from my garden, I can tell. Mine aren't that big and beautiful."

"Kent brought them over. I told him you'd like them," I answered.

"Oh, but he wouldn't have brought them for me. Did

he?'' she asked, surprised.

"Not exactly," I admitted. "They were for me."

"You must have seen quite a bit of the Robinsons while we were gone," Eric commented.

"They've been very friendly and helpful. Paul too."

"Well, I'm glad," Lily said quickly. "Have you been to the lake yet?"

"Oh, yes. I've walked over there several times, and Kent and Denise gave me a tour in their boat. It was really lovely. Lots of wildlife."

"How nice of them," Lily murmured. "So you weren't bored, waiting for us?"

"Hardly," I laughed, but decided not to elaborate, not to tell them that one of my excursions had been a visit to Harbor Center to identify what I had believed to be Lily's body. Whatever I had been during their absence, it wasn't bored.

"Well, good," Lily said with a note of finality. I knew she hoped I would not continue.

I offered them some coffee and cookies, but Lily assured me she had eaten more than enough already. The doctor had given her a sedative to take if she had trouble sleeping, but the wine, she said, had made her drowsy. She was tired and looking forward to a good night's rest. Eric declined the offer too, saying that he would begin getting their room settled right away.

As I cleared the table, I could hear them talking together in lowered voices whenever I left the room. I had just begun to feel that this was rather rude when Eric left to get their suitcases from the car. I helped Lily to a more comfortable chair in the living room before completing the kitchen cleanup. It was a good opportunity for us to talk, but Eric was in and out with the luggage, and I knew how uncomfortable it made one feel to be given the impression that secret negotiations were going on just out of earshot.

There was one question I could ask in Eric's presence

with complete innocence. It seemed that because I was there and they were not aware that I knew of his existence, they did not intend to bring Timmy home. There was no reason to delay because of me, and I wanted them to know it.

"Aren't you going to bring Timmy home? I know he's anxious," I said casually, as I joined them in the living room. Eric had apparently finished their unpacking just as I completed the kitchen chores.

They both turned to me in surprise, but to my relief it was only seconds before Lily was laughing. "How in the world did you ever find out, Kim? Here Eric and I have been trying to think of a way to explain the situation without offending you. I mean, you must think I'm not a very trusting friend. . .but you already know! Of course we'll bring him home. We were just going to talk to you about it. I'll call right away and Karen can bring him over. We won't fuss with his crib and everything tonight, but I want Timmy here. Oh, you call, Eric. It's easier."

We watched in silence as he crossed to the hall door, then listened for him to pick up the phone. There was so much I wanted to ask Lily that it took me those seconds to reduce it to one question.

"Why didn't you tell me?"

"How did you find out?"

We spoke simultaneously, though Lily quickly added, "I asked you first."

I shrugged my shoulders and said briefly, "He wandered over here one time looking for you. But, Lily—"

"He what? You mean he crossed that road? He crossed it by himself? How? What in the world happened? When was this?"

"Now, don't get excited. He's perfectly all right," I reminded her before answering. "It was one evening after they thought he was asleep. He missed you and thought he'd find you here, that's all. It was really lucky that nothing happened, but I'm sure it wasn't their fault. Karen was frantic."

"You were here and heard him outside somewhere? So you brought him in, and he told you who he was?"

"Eventually, yes. Karen came for him early the next morning. He wouldn't tell me where he was staying."

I had omitted the details of the storm to save Lily's nerves. Lily's personality was, by nature, vital and lively. I had often admired her spontaneous charm and sparkle, but now there was something different about her. I had never seen her quite like this. I had never known her when she was truly afraid. The word that came to mind as I pondered this difference was volatile. I had always been the quieter one, the one who could, at least, appear calm in a trying situation. Somehow I felt that this problem of Lily's was larger and more difficult to handle than anything we had ever faced together before. I was concerned for her, and about her, and totally unsure of how I could help her.

"How could they be so careless? I can't understand that! Not knowing where he was. Gone all night. He could have been— What if—all night long dead on the road—I'll never leave him again, never!" Lily declared shrilly.

"He's a beautiful child," I commented gently. "You must love him very much."

"Oh, I do. More than anything," she said vehemently.

"But, Lily, things like that happen to kids all the time, and since there were no ill effects, there's no need to get so worked up over it. He's fine, and he'll be here any minute. But why won't you tell me what's really gone wrong here?"

For a moment Lily was thoughtfully silent. Then she said softly, "You're right, of course, that there's more to it than just what you've told me about Timmy wandering away from them. There's so much I want to tell you—''

Her green eyes met mine candidly, and I felt the old bond of friendship strong and sure between us, but just at that moment Eric entered the room. She smiled across at him and asked about Timmy as if she had not been speaking to me at all. Any confidences, it was clear, would have to wait for another time.

Lily reminded Eric that she was very tired, and asked if he would help her upstairs while I waited for Karen to come with Timmy. I stood alone by the window, watching the driveway, as I had done so many times during the past few days. A week earlier I had anticipated none of this. I had known nothing of the marriage, the baby, or the danger. I had never sensed anything strained or faked about Lily's letters. She had given convincingly concealing performances at Christmastime when we met at family parties. Yet, in some ways, we knew each other so well; I had thought, too well for successful secrecy. There must have been a powerful reason behind it.

The sight of Karen and Timmy walking up the drive interrupted my speculations. They came along slowly, because Timmy stopped to look at grasshoppers or beetles every step or two, but Karen held his hand firmly and tried to hurry him a little. Karen carried a paper sack in her other hand. I assumed she was bringing back a few of his clothes.

It was a warm evening. Even though the sun was well below the trees and the light was beginning to fade, there was a feeling of freshness in the air rather than coolness. It had been a beautiful day, though it had slipped past me unappreciated.

Karen smiled with pleasant remoteness and asked me to say hello to Lily and Eric for her. I invited her to come in, but she was in a hurry to return home, especially since Lily and Eric had already gone upstairs. I thanked her for bringing Timmy to the house, and she was down the steps before I had finished my sentence.

Timmy was anxious to climb the stairs when I told him his mother was upstairs. I paused only long enough to lock the door before following him. I carried him up the stairs and when I set him down again at the top, he ran as fast as he could to Lily's room. The door stood open, and soon he was in her arms.

Lily's face was the perfect reflection of radiant happiness. If there was still any pain in her right arm, she did not show it. Eric greeted Timmy enthusiastically, but while the child's response showed that they were not strangers, there was still a trace of shyness in Timmy's behavior when his father spoke to him. He smiled adorably at Eric, but clung to his mother when Eric reached out to take him from Lily.

Lily looked across the room to where I stood in the doorway. I stepped in to hand her the package of Timmy's clothes. I felt that I was intruding in a way so I moved back toward the door.

"Thanks, Kim, for everything," Lily said when she saw I was leaving. Then she yawned delicately. "Oh, I'm so sleepy. I guess I'll get Timmy ready for bed and then get some sleep myself."

"Good night," I said, and closed the door behind me.

I had had no opportunity to do more than warn Lily in a vague, unspecific way, but at least I had done that much. Kent would have been pleased by the way things had gone, but I felt a little let down and disappointed.

I decided to call my parents to inform them of recent events, since I had told them about Lily's absence the day after I had arrived at her house. They were, of course, glad to hear that she had returned, and shared my surprise to learn that she had married Eric Norfolk. I did not mention Timmy at the time, but hung up, saying that I was not sure what my plans for the next few weeks would be. Then I checked the doors to be sure they were locked and remounted the stairs.

I had just stepped into the second-floor hall when I heard Eric's voice raised in anger. "You shouldn't have asked her to come!"

"But I did!" Lily answered, then continued more softly, so that I could not hear what she said.

I hurried silently to my room and shut the door noiselessly behind me. I'll leave, I thought to myself. They don't want me here. But then I remembered that it was Eric who had expressed disapproval, not Lily, and it was Lily I was there to see. She had been genuinely glad I had come, I thought. Still, I would ask her in the morning if she wanted me to go.

I watched the sky darken and the stars come out while I tried to resolve away the sting of Eric's words. At last I undressed in the dark and slipped into bed. It must have been another hour before I slept.

Chapter Seven

I awoke early the following morning. I wanted time to think. Eric's remark, which I had overheard the night before, had distracted me from Lily's real problem, and I hadn't even tried to fit it in with the rest of what I knew. I had been hurt, and I had not stopped to think about the strange circumstances that surrounded it.

What I had learned was that Eric had been against my coming to visit at this time. At last I had a clear indication of one person who wished I wasn't there. How much more likely it seemed, in the face of this new evidence, that the prankster who had tried to make me leave from the beginning must be one of the Norfolks. I no longer had any intention of asking Lily if she wanted me to leave. Obviously Lily wanted me there—even enough to oppose her new husband over the issue. She was in danger, and somehow she trusted me to help her more than she trusted anyone else.

I watched some young black squirrels chasing each other around the base of Lily's feeder while their mother sat in the box eating sunflower seed. The early morning haziness was lifting, and when it cleared, the brilliance of the sun surprised me. It was later than I had thought, after eight o'clock. I quickly slipped into denim cut-offs and a sleeveless blouse and hurried downstairs to prepare breakfast. The wooden heels of my sandals clicked lightly on the stairs, and as I reached the bottom, I heard Lily's rapturous "Good morning, Timmy!"

I had time to set the table, put the coffee water on to boil, place some breakfast rolls in the oven, and stir up a pitcher of orange juice from frozen concentrate before Lily triumphantly reached the bottom of the stairs on her crutches, Eric and Timmy preceding her. One glance told me that Lily's mood had reverted to the unconcerned lightheartedness of early the previous evening. I was glad, because it made it easier for me to conceal the fact that I had overheard them talking about me the night before.

"Well, how's everybody this morning?" I asked from the kitchen.

"Oh, never better, almost," Lily told me.

We passed a pitcher of steaming water around the table and mixed instant oatmeal in our bowls. Lily exclaimed enthusiastically about everything from the hot honey pull-aparts to the instant coffee. I knew she felt sorry that all the kitchen work had been turned over to me because of her sprained ankle. I really did not mind doing it for her, but I thought to myself wryly that at least I would be useful as a maid and babysitter if nothing else. Eric and I were both rather quiet, but Lily made up for it, as she was particularly animated that morning. Timmy was also in a sunny mood, due to his mother's return from her short vacation.

"There's a place I want to show you, Kim," Lily said as we sat drinking our coffee, waiting for Timmy to finish his cereal. "I've taken some knockout landscapes up there. Fantastic view. Maybe we can drive over this morning, if you'd like to see it."

"Sure, I'd love to." I managed some enthusiasm. "I'll hurry and clear this up so we can."

"Help her, will you, Eric? I feel awful seeing her work all the time. What's it like being a maid?"

"Sit still," I said to Eric. Raising an eyebrow at Lily,

I countered, laughing, "What's it like having one?"

"Heavenly," she sighed. "I'll have to sprain the other ankle if service is going to be this good."

"Don't count on it. I've been on my good behavior," I teased her as I disappeared with a load of dishes.

It was not long before the four of us were in the car, headed for Dr. Winslow's office, since Lily wanted to pick up Freddy before going to the scenic lookout. Eric drove and Lily sat on the front seat beside him with Timmy in her arms. Normally there would have been bags of camera equipment beside me on the back seat, but Lily had decided not to bring her things along because of her injured ankle.

This did not, however, prevent an animated discussion of exposure factors, lighting techniques for close-ups of birds and animals, and the other technical aspects of Lily's profession. Over the years I had learned enough to follow what was being said, at least in a general way, but I was pleased and surprised that Eric entered into the conversation, showing both interest and knowledge. They talked of pictures they had taken together, and I was able to surmise that many of their happiest times had centered on cameras and tripods.

I realized how little I knew of Eric Norfolk, and felt a bit guilty about my suspicion concerning the Norfolk family. Yet I could not dismiss them entirely from my mind. Was it possible that Lily was a problem to them, one they had tried to eliminate? If so, then I was another obstacle, because I was her friend and her ally. How much easier it would have been for them to cause her "accidental" death before I had come. She had no close friends here as far as I could tell. The Robinsons seemed neutral, uninvolved. I was the only one who would care what happened to her, who would suspect any further trouble should it occur. There were good reasons for them to wish I had not come.

But who exactly were "they?" Was I to include Eric?

There had been plenty of opportunities for him to kill Lily if he was the one who wished her dead. They had been alone together for the days of the honeymoon, and he had not acted. If only for that reason, I was reluctant to conclude that he was behind the murder of the blonde girl who resembled Lily. Yet he had said that I should not have come. Was it simply a desire for privacy? But why wouldn't Lily tell me, if that was all there was to it? Perhaps Eric had felt as he did because he knew what difficulties his mother or sister planned for Lily and would have preferred to handle them by himself. Now he had two of us to consider instead of one. That had to be the reason. I could see no way out, if Eric was not to be trusted.

We arrived at Dr. Winslow's clinic, and Eric went in to pick up Freddy. During those minutes, while Lily and I were alone together, I had hoped to try to find out why she did not discuss her threatened position with Eric, and, unless she should confess that she did not trust him, I intended to try to convince her to bring the matter out into the open. Before Eric was two steps from the car, however, Lily turned to face me across the back seat and began talking earnestly about another, less complex problem which had arisen because of her injury.

"Kim, I hate to ask another favor of you. You've been so patient with all my difficulties, and such a help to all of us. I really do appreciate it, and if you want to say no, I suppose they'll understand. But this is the problem. I promised Eric's mother and Karen we'd get together this evening for supper. Maybe a hot dog roast would be fun, or something like that. But now, with this ankle, so much would be left up to you. It isn't fair to ask it."

"Yes, it is. It's all right. It'll be fun," I said, feeling slightly panicked at the thought of a party made up of all those I most feared. But what could I do? There was no way to refuse to help her without appearing to be less than a good friend. If only Kent could be there too. I asked, almost before thinking, "Why not invite the Robinsons too? I know they'd like to see you. I'd like to ask Kent—if it's all right with you and Eric, of course."

"The Robinsons?" she asked slowly, clearly surprised. "Why, I hadn't thought. . . But why not, if you want to? Sure, we can ask Kent."

"I guess we should include everybody. That way no one will feel left out," I suggested.

"Yes, I suppose so. Well, great. I didn't know you'd be so enthusiastic," she said, looking at me strangely.

I knew she must be puzzled. I had always been just a little too quiet, a little too reserved, to enjoy large parties the way Lily did. I preferred a smaller group of close friends to a larger number of acquaintances, and Lily was well aware of this. I would have liked to explain my suspicions to her, to tell her why I preferred the larger group, but there was no time.

Eric was bringing Freddy out to the car, so it was impossible for me to find out from Lily any of the things I had wanted to know. Our conversation stopped abruptly as we watched Freddy galloping toward the car on three legs. He was overjoyed to see Lily and his injury scarcely slowed him down. Lily opened the car door so she could reach out to pat him, then Eric gave him a little boost up onto the back seat, since the cast on his hind leg was cumbersome. Freddy was so glad to be with us that he did not seem to mind the inconvenience.

Eric told Lily what the vet's comments and instructions had been as we drove toward Lily's special scenic spot. It seemed that everything was very well under control, where Freddy was concerned. I stroked his head absently, only partly aware of the blur of passing scenery.

There were so many things on my mind that I found it impossible to concentrate on anything. One minute I was hearing a snatch of conversation about the dog's cast, then I was wondering about the menu for Lily's supper party, which made me worry about what could be done if Kent could not accept the invitation at such short notice. That possibility so upset me that I found myself looking for road signs and watching the route we were taking rather than seriously considering an alternative should Kent turn me down. Then I would try again to listen to what Lily and Eric were saying, before my mind jumped on to something else.

It was not long before we pulled into a small, unpaved parking lot surrounded by pines and oaks. The car had been gradually climbing a gentle slope and I guessed we were near the crest of a hill. A short walk from the car I saw a staircase which had been built to make the last few yards of steep ascent easier.

Lily was looking at the stairs too, and I could imagine she might not feel like climbing them. She turned to me with a sigh. "The best views are from up there, of course. I thought I'd be up to the climb. Maybe I can make it."

"I'm sure you could, Lily," I said reassuringly, "but it really isn't necessary. I can go up by myself and save you all that strenuous climb."

"Do you mind?" she asked, obviously relieved.

"Of course not. I'll go take a look."

"Don't you want to go, Eric?" I heard Lily ask.

"No, I'd rather stay with you," he told her quickly. So I did not hesitate before beginning to climb the steps.

Because it was a long flight of stairs, there was a landing halfway up, and I stopped for a moment to watch some rose-breasted grosbeaks feeding their young from a tray of sunflower seed that had been placed among the trees on the hillside. The males, especially, were a colorful sight, with their sharply contrasting black-and-white wing feathers and the rosy chests from which they get their name. I heard a woodpecker rapping at a tree trunk and looked for it as I continued to climb, but I never saw it.

At the top of the steps was a wide platform built on the same level as the top of the hill but extending perhaps twenty feet over the downward slope. I walked out to the edge and leaned on the rail, taking in the view, which, as Lily had said, was terrific. The hill dropped steeply to the shore of the bay, and I was looking over the tops of tall trees at the bright blue water. Another outcropping of land protruded into the bay in the distance, looking gray-green in the softening haze. Seagulls dipped and soared, luminously bright as they reflected the morning sun. I could hear their cries across the water and the sound of waves breaking below. Looking directly down, I could see the spray as the water met the land, slapping against large boulders and huge blocks of cement which had been used to prevent the erosion of the sand from about the sturdy pillars that supported the platform. A sandpiper teetered on stilt-like legs, then ran across the rocks to the sandy beach. It looked small from such a height, and I realized this lookout must be the equivalent of three or four stories from the rocks below.

I felt the sensation of height then, not altogether unpleasant, but slightly dizzying. I closed my eyes and found myself smiling into the cool, moist wind which blew off the bay. The air smelled fresh and clean, and I breathed deeply, relaxing. It was such a quiet, beautiful spot. I could have wished time to stand still for a few moments then. I had found a minute's peace. My mind was almost blank.

I was called back to reality by the sound of light, quick footsteps on the stairs. I turned to face the steps, a little apprehensive at the thought that Karen might be coming. It was absurd to expect this person to be anyone I knew, yet somehow Karen had come to mind, I suppose because she was the person I least wanted to see. I was afraid she would sense a strangeness in my behavior towards her and she might realize that I suspected her.

Just before she came into view, I turned back to survey the scene below. I would glance briefly at whoever it was who joined me by the rail and not unnerve some stranger by staring at her arrival.

"Kim!" she exclaimed. It was Denise. "I saw Lily and Eric in the parking lot. They said you were up here."

"What a surprise to meet you here. Isn't it a wonderful place?" I said enthusiastically.

"Delightful. Not really such a coincidence, coming here at the same time. Since Lily found this spot, it's been a favorite of all her neighbors too. We drive up here pretty often."

"I can see why," I commented.

"Yes," Denise said absently, leaning over to examine one of her shoes. "There's something in it, I think."

I expected her to balance against the rail, but instead she placed one hand on my shoulder for support. The extra weight applied so suddenly and unexpectedly pushed me forward slightly, and I caught the railing to steady myself. I felt a splinter prick my palm, but I said nothing, feeling a little ridiculous for being so easily knocked off balance.

Denise said quickly, "Oh, I'm sorry! I'm so clumsy. There, it's fixed now."

"Not at all. That's good," I said, embarrassed. It was an awkward moment, because Denise lingered apologetically over the incident instead of letting the matter drop. I was relieved to hear Paul calling to Denise as he ran up the stairs, since it ended her profuse apology.

"Hello, Paul." I greeted him warmly as he joined us. "Lily wanted me to see this view right away. It's a wonderful place, and a beautiful day to see it too.

Denise was telling me how often all of you come here.''

"Oh, yes, very often," he said a little breathlessly. I wondered what had been in his mind as he hurried up the stairs, calling to his cousin. Whatever it was, he did not share it with us now.

I realized that I had a good opportunity to extend my invitation to the supper party, and I did so, explaining that Lily had promised her mother-in-law that they would get together as soon as she and Eric returned. Since I was to be the hostess of the party, I had decided to include all of Lily's neighbors if they wanted to come.

"And was that all right with the happy couple?" Denise asked with a little laugh.

"Of course. I hope you can make it. Kent too.''

Denise hesitated a moment, turning to look across the bay. "There's a sailboat," she commented, pointing toward the horizon. Paul looked slightly uneasy and began to make some excuse for the evening, but Denise cut him off with a smile. "Oh, don't be silly, Paul. Of course we can go. After all, people don't get married every day of their lives. We ought to be on hand to congratulate the newlyweds. Kent will be delighted to come, I'm sure.''

"I'm so glad," I said. "Be sure Kent knows he's invited in case I'm not able to get in touch with him before this evening.''

"Is it going to be casual?" Denise asked.

"Oh, yes, I think so. It's very much a spur-of-the-moment thing. It's so nice of you to accept on such short notice. Are you going to come, Paul?" I asked, wanting to give him a chance to make his own decision.

"I wouldn't miss it for the world," Denise put in.

"Yes, I'll be there," Paul said, but I was aware of a note of reluctance in his voice.

I left them on the platform, staring down at the bay. I was very pleased to have met them and settled the matter of the party. It was one thing I could stop worrying about. There could be no danger to Lily in a group of that size.

I was beginning to look forward to seeing Kent again, and wondering if he had discovered anything. The sense of urgency I had felt immediately after discovering the tampered step had somewhat dissipated, however. I was able to start planning the party almost as if there was nothing more to it than assuring the guests of a good time.

Because of my general feeling of satisfaction, I almost failed to notice the flush of color in Lily's cheeks and the grim set of Eric's mouth. I had approached the car full of what I regarded as the wonderful news that Denise had accepted our invitation to the party, and had convinced Paul to come, as well. I was about to continue with the marvelous probability that Kent would join us, when I paused to ask as an afterthought what had caused their disturbed expressions. This inquiry was met by a stony silence, so I stopped my chatter and took my place in the back seat of the car, much subdued.

"It certainly is a beautiful view up there," I ventured timidly after a suitable pause.

"Yes, isn't it, though," Lily managed stiffly, not turning to face me.

Timmy seemed not to have noticed the tension which had built during my absence. He took our silence as an opportunity to tell us about his pet chipmunk, which he had not seen for days, because it lived in Lily's back yard. He imitated its noises and movements with childish innocence and enthusiasm, and gradually won Lily back to a semblance of easy good humor.

"We'd better stop at the store and let Kim pick up a few things for tonight," she told Eric after fondly assuring Timmy that his chipmunk would be waiting for him.

I wished I had some notion of the cause of the obvious trouble I had just witnessed. Had they quarreled while I was gone, perhaps over my visit? It was a shame if that was the case. Or was there something more fundamentally wrong between them? What sort of a marriage had Lily made, anyway? I remembered the remark she had made the previous evening concerning her feelings for Timmy. She had said she loved the child more than anything. It was true that she had been nearly hysterical with concern for her son at the time, but there had been little enough provocation for that state. She had just married the child's father, yet whatever feeling she had for him did not seem to compare with the depth of devotion she felt for her son.

By the time Lily had discussed her menu ideas with me, we were at the grocery. I hurried in to buy hot dogs, rolls, and relishes, plus potato chips, cola, some special salads from the delicatessen, and three different kinds of marshmallows. Lily and I both hoped that this would be a supper party that was fun for everyone from little Timmy to his grandmother. It seemed to me that standing around the glowing coals feeling their rosy warmth and watching the food plump and brown as it was twirled slowly above the fire was an experience that would cause wonder and joy in a childish heart and never lost its charm with the passing years.

The clerk who checked out my order was the same person who had accepted my money in payment for the cigarettes Lily's look-alike had taken. He remembered me right away and seemed anxious to talk. I guessed that he was in his fifties, as I noticed his thinning hair that had once been a light brown color, but now was mostly gray. He watched me with unsettling curiosity through thick-lensed glasses.

"Police have been in here asking questions. Have to do with you, I think," he said with thinly concealed excitement.

"Oh, really?" I answered carefully. What sort of questions were they asking? I had to find out. But how could I ask without risking the possibility that he would hold back if he saw my curiosity? "About that girl, I suppose? I told them I'd seen her here."

"Yes. She died, you know. I told them how scared she was when you spoke to her, and how you paid for the cigarettes so I wouldn't raise the cops. They were real interested. But you say they've talked to you already, have they?"

"Yes, I've talked to them. They know everything I know about it, so I expect they won't be questioning me again. I really had very little to tell them," I said calmly. He must not guess how his words had startled me. What he had told the police must surely raise a new suspicion in their minds. What other suspect was there? There had to be another person who knew much more than I did about the girl, but that person would not come forward. How would they ever find out what had really happened? That's their job, not yours, I told myself fiercely as I walked out the door. There was surely no cause for me to worry just because an imaginative shopkeeper had tried to solve a mystery with but one tiny piece of circumstantial evidence. I could easily explain what had happened if it came to that. That was all there was to it.

I had not been able to conceal my feelings from Lily very successfully for a long time, and even four years apart had not changed this. She took one look at my face as I slipped into the back seat and asked, "Is something wrong, Kim? What happened?"

"No, of course not. What could be wrong?" There was an unpleasant edge to my voice which I disliked but had been unable to control. Lily did not press the issue, but she gave me a quizzical look across the back of the seat, and I knew she was not convinced. I would have liked to tell Lily what had happened, but I sensed that this was not the time. It would only upset her to hear the details of what had happened to the other young woman, and I certainly did not want to burden her with this ridiculous new problem of mine.

We were not far from home when we passed a red Volkswagen headed in the opposite direction, and Eric honked the horn lightly as a greeting. The man and woman in the other car waved and smiled. I wondered who they could be.

"Who was that?" I asked.

"Sally and Dick Blair," Lily told me. "Dick is the storekeeper's son—the one in the grocery where we just were. He and his wife do a little work for the Robinsons now that their parents have taken the regular staff to Europe with them."

"Regular staff?" I asked.

"Oh, sure. The maid, the cook, and the gardener. Paul does the gardening now. He enjoys it. But Dick helps with the heavy maintenance work. Denise didn't want a live-in maid with her mother gone. She'd rather do the light work herself and have the extra freedom. Sally goes in once a week to clean."

"How nice. I've never met them," I said, but I was thinking very different thoughts.

There was another red car—one Kent should have known to tell me about. Didn't he realize that their car was red? Or had it simply slipped his mind? Why would he protect them when he knew how important it was to Lily and me to discover in which direction the danger was lying? Maybe he wanted to question them himself, find out what their involvement was before insinuating to me that they were responsible. That would have been an effort to be fair to them, and I could not fault Kent for that. He might even tell me about it at the party.

Dick Blair, the clerk's son, I thought. It will not be long before they all know what's being said about me. Maybe Denise already knows, or Paul. Would they believe what Mr. Blair was thinking? What would they think when they heard that I had frightened that girl and that she had died? I could not be sure what their reaction would be, but I did know that Kent would not suspect me. He would know it was not true.

Almost immediately upon our arrival at the house, Lily decided that we should prepare lunch so that it would not interfere with our preparations for the evening. While I heated some canned macaroni and cheese, set the table, and made a pitcher of lemonade, Lily perched on a chair by the sink and cut the tops from a box of strawberries, rinsed them, and scooped them into dishes. Eric was busy not far from the back door, getting ready to fix the step.

"What did you tell Denise about tonight?" Lily asked over her shoulder.

"Well, I said it was a casual supper, kind of an informal celebration of your wedding. I said to come about six or so. Is that what you mean?"

"Yes, I guess so." Lily sounded a little jittery. "I was wondering what to wear."

"I told her casual so that's no problem," I assured her. It must be her ankle that made her so anxious. I had never known her to worry over a party before. Undoubtedly she was worried about the impression she would make on her mother-in-law, though, after four years, it would hardly be a first impression.

We ate a quick lunch, and the conversation mostly involved the preparations to be made that afternoon. Lily was preoccupied with thoughts about her clothes, and Eric made several suggestions, too many to help her indecision. Then he told me about a method he had worked out for starting quick hot charcoal fires. It involved an electric starter and a fan.

"We'll leave the entire charcoal business to you," Lily said, flashing him a smile. She turned to Timmy then, the smile still lingering on her lips. "And what are you doing with that macaroni, Timmy? Not eating it, I can see."

"Making a picture," he said sheepishly.

136

"Well, let's see. What is it? A squirrel? No? A raccoon? Not quite right yet? I bet I know. It's Freddy!" Lily joined in his game good-naturedly.

"Aren't you hungry?" Eric asked him.

Timmy shook his head no, and looked at each one of us appealingly. Lily pushed his dish of strawberries a little closer to him and encouraged him to eat some of them.

"He's excited about the party," she explained to me. "It's no use trying to get him to eat when he doesn't feel like it."

Eric left the table to finish fixing the step, and I began to clean up from the lunch, while Lily sat with Timmy. By the time I had finished in the kitchen, Eric had completed the repair on the porch, and I helped Lily and Timmy out to the yard.

It was a beautiful afternoon, sunny and warm. Eric brought a lawn chair from the garage for Lily, and Timmy sat in the grass beside her, looking for a four-leaf clover. The time passed quickly while Eric and I set up Lily's lawn furniture, hosed it clean, and patted it dry with some old bath towels. The redwood picnic table was set beneath a huge oak tree, and other chairs were placed in groups of two and three about the yard. We expected that the guests would rearrange them as they chose, as the chairs were very light aluminum frames with yellow, orange, and green plastic strips woven to make the seats and backs. The yard looked pretty when we finished, with all the bright colors.

When Eric had wheeled the grill from the garage and put the charcoal in it, and I had organized the food and dishes in the kitchen, it was nearly four o'clock. There was nothing more to be done but to change our clothes, and Lily was anxious to have plenty of time for that.

I was glad to have a little time to myself before the arrival of the guests. I felt the beginnings of an excitement and tension that I knew would build throughout the evening. Part of it, of course, was the simple desire to see my friend's party come off smoothly, especially since I had had a hand in the planning of it. I knew Lily's happiness would be much more secure and complete if she could please her mother-in-law, and I hoped she would. As her best friend, the impression I made could be helpful in attaining this goal, if all went well. I was naturally anxious that this should be the case.

The thought of Kent's presence at the affair contributed its share to my state of mind. I did not deceive myself. I was looking forward to seeing him again, and part of my keyed-up feeling was this anticipation.

Had these been the only considerations running through my mind, I would have felt happy in a vaguely electric way. As it was, though, I was more than a little apprehensive. The thought I was fighting to keep at the back of my mind was that one of our guests could possibly be Lily's enemy—and I was not yet sure which one. Was I really sure that our plans were safe? As the time drew nearer, I knew I was not.

I had tucked my hair up in a shower cap and stood for a long time under a cool spray. I knew what I was going to wear and that I could be ready in a matter of minutes after stepping out of the shower. When I finally did so, I was thoroughly chilled, nearly to the point of shivering, but in the heat of the afternoon that did not last long. By the time I had pulled on my brown corduroy jeans and slipped into my favorite sunset-colored long-sleeved jersey blouse, I already felt warm. I had just finished combing my hair and putting on a touch of makeup when Lily tapped at my door.

"Come in!" I called, setting down my compact with a sharp clack, and turning to face the door. Lily pushed it open and came in slowly on her crutches, a tenuous smile playing uncertainly about her lips.

"Oh, Lily! That looks perfect. It's just right. You always were the one with a flair for the casual."

Lily had finally settled on her favorite denim jeans, worn just to the point of softness and embroidered lovingly about the hems of the legs and on the pockets. Her blouse was a trim-looking green-and-white checked cotton, with short sleeves that buttoned just above the elbows and puffed out slightly about her upper arms. The green check accentuated the color of her eyes attractively, just as the eye-catching macramé belt she wore cinched about her tiny waist emphasized her slimness.

"I do hope so," she said almost petulantly, dropping into the yellow chair. "Oh—you look fine. That blouse is quite becoming."

"Thank you," I answered serenely, confident that this was so. It was a long blouse, rippling gracefully over my hips and pulled in at the waist by a belt of the same gold-and-orange material. I always felt wonderful in it.

On impulse, I crossed to the dresser and picked up a brass ring to slip onto the third finger of my right hand. It was a little heavy, but the five petals of its laboriously crafted rosette were almost even. One of the boys I had known in high school had made it for me in shop class.

"A ring?" Lily perked up with interest. "Let me see it."

"You already have," I told her, smiling at her surprise as she recognized it.

"What? You still wear that?" she asked incredulously.

"You mean to say you don't like it?" I countered, teasing. "I always thought it was nice."

"No, that's not what I meant to say!" she laughed with me. "I was just surprised, that's all. I thought you and Charlie were finished years ago."

"Who said we weren't? Of course you're right. The

ring has nothing to do with him anymore—not really. It's just sort of symbolic." I hesitated, unsure how to explain, and finished lamely, "Of something."

"Of your many loves?" It was Lily's turn to tease.

"No," I said, seriously, "certainly not. Not that there haven't been two or three others since. But that's not it. It's more like—don't laugh—the quest for the ideal relationship. I mean, this ring kind of represents all the things you think about love when you're very young, and realized later how lucky people are who really find them."

"And you still hope to?" she asked quietly.

"Oh, sure. Why not?" I answered flippantly, a little uneasy at our seriousness.

She regarded me wisely as I stretched out on the bed, propping myself up on one elbow to look at her. "You wouldn't say it that way if it was true," she commented.

"Maybe not. But there's no reason not to hope. I know that. Look at you, Lily. You think you've found it, don't you? And once I thought I had, but I was wrong. Still, I think I was fairly close to it. I'm not discouraged."

Even as I said this to Lily, I knew it wasn't really the truth. I had never felt strongly for any of the men I had met in college. Once or twice I had pretended to myself that I had been in love, but though I had accepted dates occasionally, I had never allowed myself to get seriously involved. I was embarrassed to admit that to myself, let alone to Lily. I had spent years of my life wrapped up in books and study, never taking the time for love. I had never acted on my emotions, but rather had ignored them. This thought startled me, for I had never seen myself in this light, but though it was something of a revelation, I forced myself to return my attention to Lily and her problem.

"It's far too soon to know where I'm concerned," Lily was saying thoughtfully. "A marriage certificate

140

isn't everything."

"Why, no, I realize that. I just thought you probably had some feeling it would work out, or why bother? That's all."

"Well, that's so. But it's still much too early to be sure."

"Well, I certainly hope it works out well for you, Lily. You know I mean that."

"I know you do, Kim. What would I do without you?" Her eyes had a misty look.

"Oh, you'd do well enough, I should think," I said quickly. "You're already well established in the work you like best, you have this beautiful old house, a wonderful son who loves you, and the man of your choice. I'm pretty dispensable in that picture, don't you think?"

"Oh, you're such a kidder!"

"Well, someone's got to keep you on track. We've got a party coming up."

"Yes. I thought we might talk, you know, about some of the things that are going on here. But maybe it's not the right time," she hesitated.

"I know what you mean. We need to get into it, but it's a bad time to get upset. Is there anything I should know before tonight?"

Lily straightened in the chair and leaned toward me slightly, which I took to be an affirmative answer, but before she began her confidences, we heard Eric and Timmy coming down the hall.

"Mommy, Mommy!" Timmy cried shrilly as he ran through the door ahead of Eric. His father had just dressed him in clean clothes for the party, and they both looked triumphant.

"How's my peppermint?" Lily cooed, lifting him onto her lap. "Your daddy did a good job, didn't he, Timmy? And you helped a lot too. That's my big boy."

"I almost tied my own shoe!" Timmy exclaimed

proudly, and Lily hugged him. He looked adorable in a red-and-white striped shirt, short red pants, white socks, and red gym shoes. He scrambled down from his mother's lap and began running about the room singing a little song about tying shoes and roasting hot dogs. He was excited and happy. Freddy galloped into the room, his cast clumping on the floor. When he saw Timmy playing on the floor, he began to bark and bounce about the room after the little boy.

"Shush!" Lily told the dog affectionately, putting out a hand to quiet him. Freddy sat down by her chair and Timmy stoped running around and went to sit by the big dog.

Eric stood in the doorway, smiling across the room at his wife. "Now that the entire delegation is ready," he said lightly, "it seems the appropriate time to make a motion to adjourn to the back yard, where the arrival of our guests seems imminent."

"Just look at the time! I'll second that, Eric. Let's go," Lily said, rising to her feet. She winced slightly, because she had put some weight on her injured ankle, then picked up her crutches and started for the door.

We had not been settled in the back yard long before we heard Mrs. Norfolk and Karen coming up the drive. Eric hurried around front to meet them, and I guessed by the tone of their voices as they greeted him that, whatever Mrs. Norfolk's reservations or true feelings about the marriage, tonight the mood was to be conciliatory. When they rounded the corner of the house, I rose from my chair beside Lily and took a few steps toward them, then waited. I wanted to appear friendly and yet avoid leaving Lily out of the second round of greetings. After all, she was the bride, and this was her party, not mine.

Mrs. Norfolk and Karen hurried over to where Lily was sitting, smiling a brief but pleasant hello to me as they stepped past.

"And how are you feeling after your fall, Lily? Better, I hope." Mrs. Norfolk expressed her concern.

"Oh, yes, there wasn't much to it," Lily assured her. "I'll be okay in no time."

"Just imagine, Lily, we're finally sisters. Isn't it exciting?" Karen exclaimed warmly, and Lily nodded, beaming.

"How's my favorite grandson?" Mrs. Norfolk asked, taking Timmy from Lily's lap into her arms, much to his delight.

It seemed a warm, congenial family gathering, and I was both relieved and puzzled. They seemed such a close group that I was conscious of a sense of being an outsider. Lily did not leave me out of the conversation for very long, however.

"But really, we all should thank Kim! She's been so much help with all the preparations for tonight! What would we have done without her?"

"Don't be silly," I laughed, embarrassed. "It's not that elaborate a party, and I've loved doing what little there was to do."

"Always modest," Lily murmured, and I could have kissed her, but instead I simply changed the subject by telling Eric's mother and sister about the drive we had taken that morning. Mention of the lookout brought back happy memories to the newlyweds, and the conversation drifted back to their wedding.

Perhaps because of Lily's preoccupation with clothes earlier that afternoon, I was sensitive to what Mrs. Norfolk and Karen were wearing. Karen wore worn blue jeans, old blue tennis shoes, and a tight short-sleeved sweater of a tannish-pink shade that, in my opinion, did nothing for her. Her mother was dressed casually too, but her brightly colored dress was fresh and attractive. I felt, if anything, a trifle overdressed, but I realized I had been thinking more of Kent than anything else when I had made my selection.

When he heard footsteps on the drive, Lily asked me to go meet the Robinsons and Paul, making it clear that they were my guests at the party. I could see that Eric's mother and Karen were surprised to hear that there were more people coming, and I hoped it would not spoil the evening for them. It would have been a good idea to inform them earlier, I realized, but it had not occurred to me.

Kent smiled at me warmly when we met, and Paul said hello very pleasantly. I was surprised that Denise was not with them, but Kent hastily explained that she would be along any minute. I led them around to the back yard, saying how glad I was that they had been able to come on such short notice.

A silence fell over the Norfolk group when the three of us came around the corner of the house, and I felt a twinge of uneasiness. The awkwardness persisted only a moment, however, before Kent and Paul were welcomed by all, if not warmly, with a suggestion of relief, especially in Eric's expression, which I could not understand.

Eric and Paul began to start the fire, and Kent pulled a chair over between Mrs. Norfolk and Lily. Karen came with me to the kitchen to help carry out the food. She seemed a little quieter and more pensive than she had been when they first arrived, but I could not help feeling that my earlier suspicions were incongruous considering the obvious affection for Lily which both Karen and her mother had displayed. As we filled trays to carry out to the grill and the table, I tried cautiously to find out why the Norfolks had taken such trouble to keep the marriage a secret from me.

"It must've been quite a surprise to you and your mother when you heard Lily and Eric were married. Or did you know it all along?"

"Well, we didn't know, exactly," she murmured with some embarrassment. "I mean, we weren't sure how it would work out. But we did know they left together. I feel a little guilty about letting you worry all that time, but Lily didn't want anyone told. If it hadn't been for Timmy, Mother and I probably wouldn't have known either.''

''I wonder why,'' I said, but Karen refused to show any interest.

''I imagine Lily was glad to see Timmy last night,'' she said, changing the subject.

''Oh, yes—extremely. And he was happy to be home.''

''Did you have to tell her what happened—I mean, about Timmy crossing the road that night?'' she asked uneasily.

''Well, it did come out,'' I admitted hesitantly. ''I played it down as well as I could, though.''

''Oh, I'm sorry she had to find out about it. I hope she's not too upset.''

''She was a little at first but I'm sure everything's all right now,'' I soothed automatically. Karen looked troubled and said nothing. I felt sorry, since I was responsible for telling Lily about the incident, but the thought that it would be better for her not to know had never really occurred to me.

When we started down the back steps with our trays, I nearly upset mine by running into Karen's back as she stopped suddenly ahead of me. A plastic mustard container teetered precariously then began to settle back on the tray, before I looked past Karen to see what had surprised her so. I had missed Denise's arrival by a few seconds, but I watched in amazement as she greeted Mrs. Norfolk with a quick hug and a tearful kiss on the cheek. A stifled sob distorted her words, but even from my place on the steps I caught fragments of her sentence. ''Mother, darling. . .so afraid. . .never the same again.''

Mrs. Norfolk patted her uncertainly on the shoulder,

a stricken look of concern and compassion on her face. She cast a quick, accusing glance at Eric, then flushed slightly in guilty embarrassment as she gently extricated herself from Denise's tearful embrace. Denise turned quickly away from her the instant the older woman pulled back. Her eyes were bright with tears as she looked from one astonished face to the next. For those few seconds, she had completely captured the attention of everyone present.

"You're all staring at me!" she admonished us in a high, soft, breathless voice. "What are you looking at?"

I immediately glanced guiltily away from the theatrical figure standing alone in the middle of the yard, but the others continued to watch her. Undoubtedly they understood more fully the meaning of the emotional scene. Eric's look was one of shock and anger, Kent seemed faintly puzzled and fascinated, while Paul's expression was grimly reserved. Lily's color had fled from her face, and her knuckles were white as she gripped her crutches tensely. All these reactions I noted in a matter of seconds before I once again centered my attention on Denise.

It was no wonder we all stared at her, for her appearance alone would have attracted attention, even if the scene with Mrs. Norfolk had not taken place. She stood in the center of the yard, tall, slim, and graceful, dressed in an elegant pale blue velveteen pantsuit of a style suitable for evening wear. Her dark hair flowed over her shoulders in soft waves, and her eyes flashed in accusation as she looked around the circle of astonished faces. Gems glittered at her throat and on her right hand, diamonds and sapphires, which I had no doubt were real. Her lips parted in a strange little smile, half triumphant but trembling slightly with some other deeper emotion. It was as if she held us motionless with a spell. Then suddenly she moved quickly to Eric's side, asking wordlessly for his protection.

Lily's husband stepped away from the jeweled hand that would have rested caressingly on his arm, but her eyes demanded something of him. As he looked away, he reassured her softly, "If anyone was staring, it was because you look so beautiful, I'm sure."

Eric had made this comment in a very low voice, I supposed with the hope that Lily would not hear it. But, even if she had, there would have been nothing in the statement to upset her, for it would have been impossible for anyone to say those words with a more total lack of feeling. In spite of this, Denise laughed delightedly and exclaimed in a silvery voice that carried very well, "You always say the sweetest things."

"Let's go," I whispered to Karen. She started, as if I had awakened her from a dream, and proceeded hastily down the stairs. She set her tray down sharply on the table between Eric and Denise, then turned quickly and crossed the yard to Lily's side. Lily was fumbling with her crutches, her face flushed crimson. I knew that, unimpeded by her injury, she would have flown into the house where her emotions might be vented in privacy. As it was, she was in an impossible position, and I could do nothing to help her. Denise had turned to me immediately, and I hoped that, if I talked with her, Lily could compose herself before Denise gained the satisfaction of knowing that her flirtation had struck home.

"It was nice of you to come," I said nervously, in a feeble attempt to ignore the last two or three minutes and start the party over at the point of Denise's arrival.

"That's tactful of you to say, but I'm sure it's not what you're thinking. I'm sorry to make such a scene, Kim, when everyone should be happy. It was wrong of me to come." Her red eyes brimmed with tears again, but she smiled triumphantly.

"What is it, Denise? What's wrong?" I asked, unable to make any sense of what was taking place. Something must have gone terribly wrong in the past few hours; she must have received bad news of some kind, to upset her so.

My words seemed to surprise her, and she uttered a little nervous laugh that ended in a sob. "You really don't know, do you?" she asked brokenly.

Something in my obvious confusion dissolved our embarrassed guest to tears, and she sobbed softly against my shoulder as I awkwardly offered her what comfort I could. I could not imagine why neither Kent nor Paul were making any effort to explain what was wrong, but I also realized that I was the only one who seemed not to understand it.

When I looked up to see if Lily might offer me some explanation, I was surprised to see that she was hurrying to the back door on her crutches, Karen beside her. Lily glanced over at me, a look of reproach and anger that startled me sharply and filled me with guilty bewilderment.

Kent came to my rescue by slipping his arm around Denise's shoulders and guiding her gently to a chair. He spoke to her softly and rapidly, and before I had finished arranging the food on the picnic table by the grill, Denise had stopped crying and was even laughing shakily at some joke her brother was making. Eric had disappeared into the house and I would have liked to follow, but Paul pointed a fork questioningly at the hot dogs.

"We might as well get started, I suppose," I commented uncertainly. "Would you like to roast some hot dogs while I get a few plates ready?"

"Good idea," he assented, then added helpfully, "Denise likes cole slaw; Kent, potato salad; Mrs. Norfolk and the rest a little of both, I think."

I filled plates according to these specifications, watching the back door apprehensively for the return of the other members of our party. When I had finished pouring drinks, the hot dogs were nearly done, and I told Paul I would just step into the house long enough to tell Lily, Eric, and Karen the food was ready. I ran lightly up the steps and slipped quickly through the door into the kitchen. I heard voices in the living room, so I continued through the house. As I approached the door to the room, I saw an old ball of Freddy's which had been left on the floor, and stopped to pick it up and move it underneath a small table so no one would trip over it. As I paused to do this, I could not help hearing the conversation from the next room, and I was stopped short by what I heard.

"—dressed like that on purpose to humiliate me! Your mother, Eric, that's what I'm thinking of! You know how she feels, and Denise plays on that—she does it deliberately!" Lily's voice was high and strained, expressing her frustration and anger.

"It doesn't matter," Eric said firmly, a cold quietness concealing whatever emotion he may have felt. "What worries me is Kim. If Paul is right, we've made a mistake. I don't trust her, Lily. How can we?"

"I won't believe—" Lily began weakly.

"You can't be too careful," Karen warned.

I stood awkwardly near the door, my cheeks hot with embarrassment, the reason I had come into the house completely evading me. Paul had found out about the dead girl and the suspicions of the police and he had lost no time in telling everyone. I tried to move away from the door without being seen, but I turned too quickly, and the floorboards protested under the shifting weight. Eric looked up immediately, and I had no choice but to continue into the room.

There was a strained silence during which I would have been wiser to pretend I had not heard what was said, but the accusation in the words stung, and I could not stop myself from trying to deny and explain.

"It isn't true! I would never do anything to hurt you!

You have to believe that!'' I insisted.

Lily would not meet my eyes, and the cold silence disheartened me. I turned to leave the room, then remembered suddenly what it was I had come in to tell them.

"The food is ready," I murmured awkwardly. "That's what I came in to say."

"Thanks, Kim. We'll be right out," Lily answered me, and there was a tone of reassurance in the words meant to help me, I knew, but somehow it was a little too late. It could not obliterate the impression I had received that even Lily no longer trusted me. The evening had been ruined as far as I was concerned. The heady sense of anticipation I had felt earlier was gone, and the next few hours seemed an interminable stretch of time. As I returned to the back yard, I longed more than anything for the night to come quickly and for this fiasco of a party to be over.

Chapter Eight

By the time I rejoined the party, Paul had already served the first plates of food, and Denise had regained enough poise to help him. There was lots of talk and laughter, which made it easier for me to hide my emotions. Paul looked up as I descended the stairs. He watched me steadily, and I felt self-conscious as I avoided his eyes, but none of the others paid any attention to me.

Mrs. Norfolk was sitting with Timmy. Denise smiled charmingly and stroked Timmy's blond hair with long, graceful fingers as she offered his grandmother a glass of soda. Mrs. Norfolk thanked her, then motioned Denise to sit next to her. It was clear to me that Eric's mother liked Denise Robinson very much, and I could understand Lily's anxiety and jealousy.

"Everything okay inside?" Paul asked as he handed me a plate.

"Yes, thanks," I answered stiffly, and turned quickly away from the table. I was angry with Paul for turning the others against me while pretending to be so calm and supportive. I wanted to talk to Kent, to find out if he believed Paul's story too. It mattered to me terribly that Kent should still believe in me.

He stood just apart from the rest of us, watching his sister and Lily's son. Although he saw them, there seemed to be a distant look in his eyes, as if his thoughts were far beyond the scene before him. I could see how much he loved his sister, but I saw also a deep concern. I longed to ask him what was wrong, but as soon as Kent noticed me, his smile dispelled all suggestion of trouble.

"I wondered what became of you, though I'll admit you were only missing for a minute or two," he said lightly.

"Absence makes the heart grow fonder?" I asked, laughing.

"Sometimes," he smiled. "But stick around. I'm just as glad you're back."

"Well, that's what I like to hear," I answered quickly, concealing the flood of pleasure I felt behind the flippant, easy words.

I found that those few seconds had drastically altered my outlook on the evening. I was still embarrassed and apprehensive, but somehow Kent's presence made it all seem much less important. As long as he was on my side, I felt that nothing could really go wrong, that the rest did not matter. I began to relax and allow myself to be distracted by the pleasure of Kent's company.

Kent and I had chosen a couple of chairs apart from the rest. I did not notice for several minutes that Lily, Eric, and Karen had come back outside, and when I finally realized it, I could not help feeling a jolt of surprise at how much fun I had been having with Kent. One look from Lily turned that surprise to guilt, and I stood up abruptly, upsetting a nearly empty glass onto the lawn. Kent and I both reached for it, and I giggled nervously, my cheeks flushed with embarrassment.

"Oh, how clumsy of me! Lucky it was outside," I sputtered unhappily.

"No harm done," Kent said quietly, taking one of my trembling hands in his. "Relax, Kim. Everything is going to be all right."

Our eyes met briefly over the empty glass, and I knew in that instant that Kent knew everything and that he still believed me and understood what I was going through. I longed to sob out my relief on his comforting shoulder, but the others were watching. I whispered my thanks to him as I took my hand from his and passed it in a smoothing motion over my hair. Then, smiling uncertainly, I crossed the lawn to see if Lily needed someone to take her a hot dog or something to drink.

I soon discovered that my assistance was unnecessary, for Eric and Karen had already brought Lily what she wanted. In fact, when I joined their little group, I could not help noticing the slightly awkward silence and the way Lily looked at her plate when I tried to catch her eyes.

Paul and Eric began a discussion of the environment and energy research, and this technical talk filled what had promised to be an uncomfortable gap in the conversation. Kent soon joined his cousin and Eric in the discussion, and Mrs. Norfolk followed Timmy when he came over to be with Lily. Denise stayed where she had been sitting, merely turning her chair to face us instead of moving a few steps closer. I decided to let her alone. I felt myself to be an outsider in some ways, and I disliked the feeling. I wanted to spend enough time with Lily to dispell it.

Freddy sat at Lily's feet, and Timmy threw his arms around the big dog's neck. Although Freddy's injuries were undoubtedly still painful and the cumbersome cast interfered with his normal lively romping, nothing stopped him from washing Timmy's ear with his huge, affectionate tongue. The little boy crowed with delight and brought smiles to the faces of all five of his feminine admirers.

"It's wonderful what children and dogs can do to make the heart feel young again," Mrs. Norfolk remarked, offering the last bite of her hot dog to an eager Freddy. "I hope you'll bring Timmy to see us often and let him stay with us sometimes. He's a beautiful child, Lily, even if I am partial."

"Or course—living so close, we'll see each other a lot," Lily responded, beaming.

"You should take some pictures of Tim and Freddy together. Commemorate the cast," Denise put in with a little hard laugh. There was a slight pause due to the ambiguous tone of this suggestion, and I thought that Lily and her mother-in-law were made decidedly uneasy by it.

"I saw some of your slides of Timmy, Lily, while I was straightening the darkroom. Very nice," I contributed, hoping to smooth over Denise's remark by this superficial response.

Mrs. Norfolk seized the comment gratefully. "Oh, and there are many others. An album of prints. You'd love them. Karen, honey, why don't you get Kent to go with you and bring back that book of pictures for Kim to see."

Karen looked clearly unhappy about this obvious matchmaking. I would have expected an embarrassed smile, but it was obvious that this proposal really annoyed Karen very strongly.

"Oh, Mother, really!" Karen grumbled. "I'm perfectly able to go by myself, and I'd far rather."

I was sure Kent had heard this exchange, and I felt that it had been very rude, but Kent gave no sign that he was paying any attention. Denise laughed softly as Karen hurried away, and Mrs. Norfolk blushed slightly in embarrassment.

"That girl!" she exclaimed unhappily. "I'll never understand her, I guess."

Lily smiled at her feebly, and I noticed she looked quite pale. I supposed her ankle hurt her, and that this party was simply too much on top of everything else.

"Why don't we go ahead and toast some marshmallows while we wait for Karen to come back?" I suggested, then continued more softly to Lily. "Then you can get into a more comfortable chair inside. You look tired.''

"Oh, I'm all right," she answered automatically, then added more honestly, "but that's a good idea. I'd love a marshmallow, and it wouldn't hurt to get my foot up pretty soon."

While we stood about the grill, the conversation touched on politics, the weather, and the baseball season. Mrs. Norfolk helped Timmy toast his marshmallows, and I gave her some of the ones I toasted. Eric took several over to Lily, who grumbled good-naturedly about her inability to cook for herself. Paul and Kent offered one or two to Denise, who sat languidly back in her chair and told them not to bother any more about her. We were just finishing when Karen brought the album, and Mrs. Norfolk proudly showed me a few of the pictures while her daughter ate.

As Eric put the hot coals in an old metal potato chip can, the rest of us went inside. Karen and I each carried a tray as we went in, and I quickly put away the things that needed refrigeration, leaving the rest on the counter by the sink to clean up later. Mrs. Norfolk had more pictures to show me, and Paul and Kent helped Lily into a comfortable chair.

The light was quite dim in the house, though the sun had not yet set completely. The tall trees around the house cast long shadows and blocked the sun, causing evening to fall more quickly there than at the lakeside. The birds twittered in the uppermost branches of the trees, settling themselves for the night. I pulled the drapes across the front window slowly, reluctant to shut out the last faint glint of natural light, then, turning briskly to the inside scene, quickly brightened the room with the warm glow of electric light.

Mrs. Norfolk reopened her album beneath one of the lamps, and I stepped over beside her. "Oh, this one is one of my favorites," she told me enthusiastically, pointing to a picture of Timmy sitting in a baby's swing, the type with built-up sides and a bar across the front. "That was Eric's swing too, when he was a little boy. How they both loved that swing! Timmy is so like his father."

"An adorable picture," I remarked sincerely, though I was trying to keep track of what the rest of our guests were doing.

Karen was talking with Lily, and Paul sat near them, helping Timmy build some stacks of blocks on the floor. Kent and Denise had retreated to the far side of the room from this domestic scene, and were talking rapidly in low voices. I caught a couple of Kent's phrases, though I was unable to distinguish very much of what was being said. From the words I heard, "doing so well," and "over soon," I supposed that Kent was trying to persuade his sister not to leave the party early.

As we came to the end of Mrs. Norfolk's picture album, she told me that there were also quite a number of slides of her grandson, mostly taken on his birthdays and around Christmastime.

"I'd love to see them some time," I assured her, wondering to myself how Lily had managed to attend all the Christmas festivities back in our home town and still share that special season with her son.

As Mrs. Norfolk closed the album and tucked it down between her purse and the chair in which she was sitting, I heard the kitchen faucet running and realized that Eric was washing the charcoal smudges off his hands before rejoining us. I had been waiting for him to come in before serving the coffee and cookies, so this was my cue to stand up and ask them all if they would like some. The offer was greeted with approval, and I hurried to the kitchen. As I was leaving the room, I heard Lily announce that it was Timmy's bedtime, and Karen and Denise both quickly volunteered to take the child up to bed.

"Finished with the fire at last?" I asked Eric with a

smile, setting bags of cookies from the cupboard on the kitchen table.

"Yes, and you have to admit we scarcely needed it for warmth tonight. The air is just beginning to cool off and feel pleasant. A shame to come in, almost, on an evening like this."

"I know what you mean. It's the kind of night for fireflies and crickets and stars. Mosquitoes too, though, I suppose." We laughed together, and he turned to leave the kitchen and join the others.

Eric and his sister confronted each other head-on at the doorway, which precipitated a quick Alphonse-and-Gaston routine before they finally slipped through the door simultaneously. Eric administered a brotherly pat to the seat of Karen's pants, which elicited the predictable soft squeal of laughter followed by a quick look of mild annoyance. She joined me at the kitchen table, slightly flushed but totally unsmiling, and asked in the most dignified manner possible if there was anything she could do to be of assistance.

I kept my eyes on the pale pink cut-glass plate which had been a gift from Lily's grandmother, and carefully placed a chocolate covered marshmallow swirl amidst the iced raisin bars, chocolate chips, and peanut butter cookies already arranged on the plate. The warm pressure of suppressed laughter subsided and with what I hoped was only a faint trace of a smile I asked her to put out a few more of the swirls while I started some water boiling for the coffee.

While we waited for the water to boil, Karen and I arranged cups and saucers, spoons and paper napkins, on one end of Lily's dining room table. I found a cream pitcher and sugar bowl set in Lily's best dish cabinet and took it to the kitchen to be filled.

Karen seemed very quiet to me. Other than a polite remark about the appearance of the plate of cookies and the table, she had said nothing at all. I had made two feeble attempts at conversation concerning Timmy's pictures and the Norfolks' geranium garden, but the truth was that I felt very little like talking myself. I was glad when the kettle steamed and whistled and the coffee could be made. The minutes seemed to pass slowly, and I was beginning to feel a little tired and edgy.

"You and Lily seem to have become good friends," I said, to break the silence.

"Yes, we've become close; especially this past year," Karen responded enthusiastically.

"How nice for both of you," I said, but even to my own ears the remark sounded forced and stiff.

"Does it bother you?" Karen asked quickly. Then, realizing how blunt this question sounded, she blundered on hesitantly, "I mean, you don't seem very happy—"

"Don't be silly," I began a little sharply. "Of course it doesn't. Why should it? There. Everything's ready. Let's tell the others."

I knew I had sounded abrupt and defensive. The question irritated me because a completely open answer on my part would have contradicted this sharp denial. It was difficult for me to sort out my feelings, to see them clearly and accept them. Somewhere deep inside I was hurt and shaken, because no matter how I tried to ignore it, Lily and I were no longer really best friends, no longer really even close. The years had gone by quickly, and I had been totally unaware of the many changes in Lily's life. She had permitted so many things to come between us, things we should have shared but which she had kept from me. It was far more than her new friendship with Karen Norfolk. It was Timmy too, and Eric—her whole new life, of which she had told me nothing. In all the letters, all the phone calls, even the Christmas visits, there had been not one word of all this. Yes, it bothered me that she had shut me out, had turned to others for support and sympathy and love.

But this was far more than I could reveal to Karen, even had I understood these feelings clearly. But I had not articulated them even to myself. I only knew that deep inside I was hurt, vaguely unhappy, a little jealous, and it seemed very unreasonable and childish.

Karen poured a cup of coffee and selected two cookies, which I recognized as Lily's favorites, then crossed to Lily's side. Lily took the coffee from her with a grateful smile, and the other guests stood up and came over to the table. I poured coffee for them all, a frozen smile on my lips but no true happiness inside me. I found it difficult to laugh at their jokes, to listen to their conversation with an interested expression. Kent did not come to talk to me, and I felt ill-at-ease, standing there alone.

"Where is Denise?" Eric asked suddenly.

There were a few seconds of silence while we cast startled looks about the room and at each other, then Karen said calmly, "She's upstairs putting Timmy to bed, I think."

"I thought someone went with them!" Lily exclaimed, stricken. "Go, Kim! See if it's all right."

There was urgency in her voice and fear in her eyes as they met mine across the room. Mrs. Norfolk and Karen began to soothe and question Lily, but I did not stop for that. I remembered that Lily had thought both Karen and Denise were helping her son, and that I should have realized earlier that Denise was alone with the child. Denise's mood had been strange all evening. I could understand why it frightened Lily. Yet Karen had not hesitated to entrust Denise with the child.

My heart was pounding as I reached the head of the stairs, but I ran toward Timmy's room, not stopping to think how shaken and out-of-breath I would appear when I arrived there. I pushed open the door quickly, not bothering to knock. Denise looked up from the story she was reading to the little boy, a cool, faintly malicious smile playing about her mouth.

"Is there some problem?" she asked with a hard, humorless laugh.

"No, no," I faltered, feeling the full disadvantage of my flight up the stairs. "I just came up to see that you weren't having any trouble." I was still breathing quickly, and my voice sounded thin.

"Now what trouble would I be having?" she asked softly, laughing silently at me. She closed the book slowly and set it on a table as she rose to join me. "Go to sleep, Tim, like a good boy," she said, and drifted past me to the door. "Nerves of steel," she whispered contemptuously as she left me alone with Lily's son.

Timmy complained that the story had not been finished, so I sat beside him looking for the page where Denise had stopped. The tips of my fingers tingled and trembled slightly against the edges of the pages, but I read on to the end of the story and Timmy smiled his drowsy approval. I kissed him lightly on the cheek, flicked off the light, and pulled the door silently shut behind me as I left the room.

By the time I rejoined the party downstairs, Paul and Denise had gone home and Karen and Mrs. Norfolk were just saying good night. They did not stop to speak to me; in fact, they almost seemed to hurry away as they saw me approach the front door. Lily still sat with her foot propped up on an ottoman, and in a glance I could see how tired she was. She returned my smile weakly, but I knew something was still very wrong, even though our concern about Denise had been an embarrassing false alarm.

Kent had waited for me to come downstairs, and I was surprised and pleased when he not only thanked me for including him in the evening but asked me to go with him for a walk in the woods. I accepted, relieved that my suspicion of his sister had not angered him, and delighted with the prospect of some time alone with him.

It was like a night out of a love poem or a romantic dream, complete with a full moon and glittering stars spread across the clear blackness of the sky. The moon was bright enough to cast a criss-cross of shadow branches across the drive and the lawn, and I knew the darkness need not hinder us from taking the path to the lake. I longed to see the reflection of the moon on the rippled surface and to hear the soft rhythm of the water against the sand. I took Kent's hand in mine impulsively as we turned across the grass, and said softly, "Let's follow the path to the lake. It's so beautiful tonight."

"Anything you like," Kent answered, a little distantly.

I gently let go of his hand, for I was aware that the warm, firm fingers suffered my touch passively, offering no responding pressure. I glanced up quickly at his face, but Kent was not looking at me, and there was little in his expression that I could read. We walked along in silence for a few moments, crossing Lily's back yard to the point where the path entered the woods.

"A night like this is so special for me," I said, trying to reopen communications between us. "At home, in the city, I rarely notice the stars. They seem so much brighter and more lovely away from the buildings and streetlights."

"I suppose so," Kent assented.

The penetration of the moon and stars was not so great as I had imagined once we had moved several steps beyond the clearing and into the trees. Kent seemed to know the path well and moved easily along it. I tried to keep pace, but my feet hit against roots that bulged up in the path, and I even brushed my arms against unseen tree trunks in the nearly total darkness.

"Let's go a little slower," I reluctantly suggested at last.

Kent stopped ahead of me and reached out an apologetic hand. "I'm sorry. Let me help you."

I took his hand gratefully, reassured by the tone of his voice and steadied by the touch of his hand. When we came to the stream and the stepping stones, he drew me a little closer to him and guided me carefully across. As soon as we reached the opposite bank, though, his hand fell from my arm, and he walked along the path ahead of me almost as quickly as before. I was disturbed by these quick changes in Kent's attitude. One moment he would seem so considerate and gentle, the next as if he hardly knew I was there. I followed him as rapidly as I could, but I felt a quickening of my pulse beyond what a fast walk would explain. I was uneasy and suspicious, only a few more silent seconds away from fear.

"What was wrong with Denise tonight?" I blundered nervously into the horrible, still darkness. "She didn't seem like herself at all. Do you know what's upsetting her?"

Kent laughed shortly, a cold, hard sound. "So she's become number one on the list of suspects, is that it?"

"No, I didn't mean that!" I protested quickly.

"Maybe not, but you'd be more honest if you did. I saw the way you hot-footed it upstairs when Lily thought her precious little boy was alone with Denise. What were the two of you afraid of?" There was an ugly, sarcastic edge to his voice, but I nonetheless blushed hotly with apologetic embarrassment.

"I—I'm sorry. It's just—well—you know what's been going on. It wasn't that I don't trust Denise, exactly. I was just afraid. I could see Lily was afraid." I floundered helplessly. "Oh, please, Kent, can't you see how it was?"

"Yes—that's just the trouble!" he retorted angrily.

We had come to the water's edge and we stood very still, an arm's-length apart. I trembled slightly from the chill wind which blew off the lake, and in reaction to Kent's anger. The stars were bright above us, but my vision blurred with the hot tears that welled up in my eyes, and I could not bear to look at them. The moonlight seemed too harsh and white, unscreened by the trees, and I turned away from Kent because I did not want him to see that I was crying. I heard him move very close to me, and I took an uncertain step away from him, wanting to escape the rough hand that I knew would force me to face him, force me to see the bitter hatred in his eyes. I was afraid, but more than that, I was torn by the sudden, painful knowledge that I loved this man and that I had hurt him deeply. His fingers were hard and painful as he gripped my arms and turned me toward him. I tried weakly to pull away from him, but he did not release me, and when I looked up into his face, the tears I had fought to conceal spilled over uncontrollably.

"Why are you crying?" he asked me sharply, his voice hard and full of anger. "Do I frighten you? Is that why you're crying? Answer me!"

I no longer tried to stop my tears or to pull back against him. He was strong, and I knew he would not let me go. And yet my tears were not from fear. I relaxed beneath the pressure of his hands, shaking my head wordlessly, fighting for control.

"No," I whispered brokenly. "No, it isn't like you think. I'm crying because—because I love you!"

I had scarcely managed the words, but he had understood me, and the anger melted out of his hands. He pulled me gently to him and I sobbed quietly against his chest. He stroked my hair with one hand, holding me close to him, and repeated over and over, in a soft, shaken voice, "I'm sorry, so sorry."

I had never known such a tender, soothing caress, and as I relaxed against him, all the tensions, worries, and fears of the past days poured out of me in fresh tears of relief. We must have stood so together in the moonlight for several minutes before my tears subsided and I could at last draw an almost steady breath. When I lifted my face from his shoulder and pulled back against the comforting pressure of his arm, he let me go silently.

I walked slowly away from him along the shore of the lake, studying the moon's reflection on the water. My eyes were still warm from the tears, but I felt calm and peaceful inside. Kent was following hesitantly behind me, and I stopped beneath a tall tree and waited for him to come up beside me. He stopped a step or two away from me, and I smiled faintly, encouraging him to speak.

"Can you forgive me?" he asked awkwardly, his troubled eyes meeting mine briefly, then skipping away. "I mean, the way I acted. I—"

I shook my head gently, saying quickly, "No, no, there's nothing to forgive. I understand how you felt. It's all right."

I reached out my hand tentatively for his, and he accepted it, moving a little closer. We both stood watching the brilliant glitter of the moon on the lake, the pale glow touching everything with a special charm, making it all seem not quite real. I thought I had never seen so many stars, never been so acutely aware of the beauty of the night.

I sighed deeply, and said at last, "I'm so glad we came here tonight. I wouldn't have missed this for anything."

Kent smiled at me tenderly, then suddenly released my hand and said in a cool, businesslike tone of voice, "It's getting late. We'd better go back." Without waiting for a response, he turned and started toward the path through the woods. I followed him unquestioningly, although deep inside I was hurt and confused. I wondered why Kent had asked me to go for a walk with him in the first place.

I managed the path more easily on the way back, and did not have to ask Kent to help me or wait for me.

When we reached Lily's house, I told him again how glad I was we had gone to the lake together, and he agreed pleasantly. But I could not help feeling that he was hiding something from me, holding back something I needed to know. I hated to push him about it, but I was also afraid to leave it alone.

"Are you sure there isn't anything you can tell me?" I managed at last, with difficulty. "I mean, I know Lily's very worried still, and you're the only one I can turn to for help."

"There's nothing to tell," he said shortly. Then he continued more gently, "Don't worry. I won't let anything happen. Everything will be all right."

I was soothed by this momentarily. "Thanks, Kent. Good night." I smiled up into his eyes, and felt a little thrill of pleasure at the warm response there.

"Good night," he said, squeezing my hand lightly, and I stood at the door watching him disappear into the shadows along the driveway.

As I entered the front hall, my thoughts went back to those wonderful moments by the lake when, out of my grief, I had spoken the secret of my heart. Until that moment I had not been sure of my own feelings, but there in the moonlight, despite the anger and the pain, it had all become very clear to me, very simple and beautiful. I loved him, and nothing else mattered. Some painful, restless thing inside me had found peace.

I moved toward the stairs in a sweet, sad dream, almost not hearing the voices that came from the living room, almost escaping the bitter sounds of the real world. And yet, I heard them, and I stopped to listen.

"I hate to believe that's true, Paul," Lily objected.

"I tell you, if she's attracted, it's to his money," Paul stated cynically.

"What difference does it make? I'll talk to her. But I don't believe it. Not of Kim," she repeated.

"You're thinking of a girl you knew long ago. It was

four years ago and things have changed.''

"No, you never knew her. You're wrong. I'll talk to her tonight, Paul.''

"If you like, Lily. But I'm warning you, be careful about how far you trust her.''

Why did he hate me so? I wondered. He had come back to Lily to plant doubt and suspicion in her mind against me. For what purpose? Why did they care what my feelings were for Kent? It did not concern them. What was Lily thinking of, to sit there calmly listening to Paul's wild insinuations, denying them halfheartedly, with no anger or surprise.

I had gone halfway up the stairs before I remembered that I had neglected to clean up the kitchen after the party. I reluctantly retraced my steps, my former euphoria completely shattered and replaced by a nervous irritation that I scarcely trusted myself to control. I had no desire at all to see Paul or to speak to him. I scarcely even wanted to face Lily. I slipped quietly to the kitchen, my lips pressed together in a hard, angry line, and tackled the chores with a vengeance.

At some time, under cover of the rumble of the dishwasher or the roar of the garbage disposal, Paul went home and Lily made her way upstairs, for when I turned off the kitchen light, the lower floor of the house was totally dark. I waited for my eyes to adjust, then headed upstairs to my room, most of my emotional turmoil drained away into the inescapable routine tasks of existence. It suddenly seemed to have been an incredibly long day, and I wanted to sleep, to dream, and to forget.

When I wearily pushed open my bedroom door, the light startled me, and I stood still in the shadow of the door. Lily sat waiting for me in the bright yellow chair, her blonde hair shining in the lamplight and her marigold-color nightgown intensifying the color, so that it seemed that she was the center of a golden glow that dominated the room. Her green eyes flashed at me, a challenge and a reproach, while she smiled and urged me to come in. I stood where I was, strangely reluctant to move closer to her, as if by stepping into that yellow light I would be giving up something, placing myself at a disadvantage.

"The party went off fairly well, I think," I remarked from the shadows by the door.

"Better than I expected. Why are you standing there like that? Come here. We need to talk."

Lily leaned forward, away from the lamp, and gestured for me to sit on the bed next to her chair. The illusion that had struck me so powerfully when I first opened the door was dispelled by Lily's movements, and I stepped quickly into the room, closing the door behind me softly. I crossed the room without meeting Lily's eyes and flopped down nonchalantly on the bed, allowing one arm to fall across my tired eyes, blocking out the light.

"Tired out from your long walk with Kent?" Lily asked wryly.

I rolled over and propped myself up on one elbow, forcing myself to meet her eyes steadily. "Hardly. It was a beautiful, cool, relaxing evening."

"Are you speaking of the weather or your companion with such enthusiasm?" she laughed gently.

"Both. . .neither." I waved the question aside with an impatient gesture. "Why?"

Lily was still smiling, but a vaguely worried look had crept into her eyes. "You were always so defensive when you thought you were in love."

"Is that a fact?" I bristled.

"Yes," she said, smiling serenely.

"Well, why you or Paul should care is more than I can imagine," I said flatly.

"So you did hear us! No wonder you act so strange.

How much did you hear? 'Fess up!" she coaxed.

"How about if *you* tell *me* how much was said, and why?" I parried, but the annoyance had seeped out of me.

"Aw, c'mon! No fair! Tell me what's bugging you so I can fix it up!"

"Well, it was Paul, really, not you," I admitted.

"I know that much! I know what I said, and not a word against you, I can swear!" she reassured me.

"Well, that's nice to know," I acknowledged briefly, looking away from her to avoid the easy charm that could tease me into good humor in a matter of minutes if I did not guard myself against it. "But then you surely also remember what Paul said to you. About being attracted to money, and how you weren't to trust me."

"And you think I believe that? Don't I know you better?"

I could feel her smiling at me, but I would not look.

"Do you?" I asked darkly. "Do you really know anything about me any more? Maybe the money was part of the charm. I didn't think so. But I did know about it."

"Hey, don't!" she reached over and gave me a little shove on the shoulder. "You're not at fault here, Dummy!"

The old nickname from our high-school days brought a burst of delighted laughter to my lips. No one else had ever called me that, only Lily, and only in private. I had always been a good student, and I had had the grades to show for it, but Lily knew my weakness. I was too serious, too sensitive, too easily hurt by things that never should have been taken to heart. I suffered because of this, and she knew it. She would call me "Dummy" when I interpreted things in unnecessarily painful ways. It was a code word, a signal of affection.

I could not hold out against her any longer. I turned to meet her eyes, and the worried look in hers disappeared when she read the laughter in mine. "All right! That's enough. You win," I told her, smiling.

Suddenly Lily's face became very serious, and I noticed for the first time the thin brown spiral notebook she held in her right hand, slapping it absentmindedly against the arm of her chair.

"What is it?" I asked encouragingly, looking at the book.

"This?" she held it up. "This is the story of my life, at least of the part you don't know so well. I need you to know it now, Kim. Tonight."

I sat up and took the little journal from her. Our eyes met, and somewhere deep inside her I knew Lily was afraid. It startled me, and I wanted to question her, but she was picking up her crutches and getting up out of the chair. I reached out my hand to touch her arm, uncertainly.

"But, Lily—" I began.

"Read it tonight, Kim. All of it. I have to go now. Eric is waiting."

"I will," I told her, stepping ahead of her to open the door.

"Thanks," she said, and I thought she meant merely for the small service I was performing. Then she turned her eyes to mine and added, "For everything."

I had the distinct impression that this included something larger than anything I was yet aware of, something that lay ahead of us. It was an unsettling feeling, and I would have liked to call her back, but Lily hurried down the hall on her crutches, not even pausing to return my uncertain "Good night."

Chapter Nine

When I turned back to the room, pushing the door closed behind me, it seemed that all the warmth had suddenly gone out of it. I shivered slightly as I crossed to the open window, tossing Lily's book onto the chair she had just left as I stepped past it. I hesitated only briefly before shutting out the cool night air and pulling the curtains against the desolate blackness that stretched out beyond the glass. This was the first night I had shut myself into the room this way, and I felt annoyed with myself for giving in to an uneasy impulse. As I had crossed to the window, the faint, ghostly reflection of the empty room and my lonely image against the blank darkness had disturbed me. It was like seeing my soul mirrored there, familiar and normal on the surface, but expanding out mysteriously into the unknown.

I paced about the room briefly, kicking off my shoes beside the bed, hanging my blouse on the closet door-knob, slipping restlessly into my nightgown, hardly conscious that I was doing any of those things. I longed to know what answers were in store for me in Lily's book, but I was too keyed up to sit still in the chair and read it. I picked it up and flipped unseeingly through the pages, then twisted the heavy ring off my finger and crossed to the dresser to set it down. At last I was beginning to relax a little. I sighed deeply and returned to the yellow chair, tucking my cold feet up beneath my body and settling back to read. The journal began as a long letter written to me.

Dearest Kim,

Well, it's all on paper now, the great events that have happened to me these past four years and their consequences. Much of this will hardly be news to you any longer, since you've been here a while, but at least I can explain how all this came to be, and help you understand what's behind the sense of threat a perceptive girl like yourself just couldn't have escaped noticing. It's funny. This story, which was once so impossible for me to tell you, is now something I eagerly want you to know, and the hard part is explaining why there ever was such secrecy at all! Have patience! I want to explain it. I want you to understand. So here goes!

In the beginning, I couldn't shake this feeling that I'd made some pretty dumb mistakes. Haven't you ever kept a bad grade at school from your parents or neglected to tell them of some small failure that years later seems very petty, but at the time is painfully embarrassing? When you care about what someone thinks of you, when their opinion really matters, it can be so difficult to let them see where you've been wrong, so tempting to cover it up if you can. How often I wanted to tell you my problems, yet how much I was stopped by pride from letting you see how I had failed. I always wanted you to think well of me, and I know now I was wrong, that real friendship and love means sharing both the good and the bad. Yet it seemed like things just kept getting worse! I would be on the point of telling you something, and then there would be a further turn of events to mortify me more! You'll see.

Anyway—I give you this account with a heart full of trust and gratitude. There have been moments when I've doubted you could understand and accept this apology, but I think those doubts are unfair to you. They stem from a bitterness planted in me by others. All I have to do to overcome them is think about you for a while. Then I remember what it is to have someone to rely on.

There's one last thing you must know, and I hope it can in some small way make up for the rest.

My love is yours forever.

Lily

My heart went out to Lily as I read this letter, for I could see how much my friend had suffered, how one secret kept had led to another yet more painful to conceal. I could see how her natural trust had nearly been destroyed by these terrible lonely years, and how she had at last cried out to me for help. I longed to go to her, to comfort her, to assure her of my love and understanding, no matter what was said in the remaining pages. I sighed deeply and turned the page to read on.

Well, I think it should come as no shock to you that after you left here four years ago to go to the university, the Norfolks and I continued to become the best of friends. You knew how much I liked Eric that summer, and as the fall progressed we came to know each other even better. I can't tell you how many sunny September afternoons we spent together, taking pictures of wildflowers and butterflies, talking and laughing as we worked. At first Eric just loafed around, sitting back on the grass and watching me, while we talked about our childhoods and our dreams for the future. It wasn't long, though, before he began to take a more active interest in my pictures. He borrowed my camera manuals and magazines and asked me questions while I set up for pictures. He learned quickly and became very helpful to me. I soon trusted and respected his judgment on many aspects of my work from meter readings to suggestions for picture compositions.

He also began coming over in the evenings to help me process my film. Sometimes he would bring over something for supper. I remember once he brought some fried chicken and another time, some hot chili in a big thermos bottle. Other times I would heat up some soup for us, or if I knew ahead of time that he was coming, I would have egg salad or tuna salad in the refrigerator.

It was all very exciting and lots of fun. I had never had a friend like Eric before, a man who spent so much time with me, who filled my thoughts with plans for the next day and my life with happy little moments.

Yes, Kim, I was happier than ever before in my life. Small things could fill me with almost unbearable joy. The way he would pluck a daisy from the meadow and smile as he tucked it in my hair, or simply the way he would look at me as we sat by the fireplace sipping hot coffee after a long, chill October afternoon outdoors.

We loved each other. Soon after meeting him, I knew it was true. Yet we never spoke of it at all. It was just something we knew deep in our hearts—and we said nothing. We were friends. We were happy; neither of us wanted anything to change or to be spoiled.

Oh, there were times when I wished that Eric would put his arm around me as we walked home together from the lake at sunset, moments when it would have been the most natural thing in the world for me to turn to him with a kiss. But he rarely touched me, and when he did, it was always impulsive, I would almost say involuntary, for he would draw his hand back from my arm very quickly when he realized it rested there. I didn't understand this restraint, but I was too happy to push or to ask questions. I would never pry into his life where he did not offer it freely to me.

During September and October I also came to know Karen and Eric's mother fairly well. I would usually spend three or four days a week with Eric, but I also saw his family from time to time—about once a week, I guess. Karen and I liked each other right away. We were friends even before you left at the end of the summer, and sometimes she would drop over in the morning to talk while I worked in the garden or hang out clothes to dry. Sometimes Mrs. Norfolk came with her, and once in a while I would take them some cookies or some lilies from the garden and they would ask me in for coffee.

Mrs. Norfolk and I never became very close. She seemed to like me well enough, yet, she was always cool and formal. At the time, I accepted it as her way, but I didn't understand her then.

Besides helping me set up and process my pictures, which I appreciated mostly because of the time it meant we could share, Eric also helped me to sell my work, and this was a service for which I felt genuinely indebted to him. The only pictures I had sold were some I had framed myself and taken to an arts-and-crafts store which handled sales for local artists. I knew, though, that if I seriously hoped to support myself by my photography, I would have to contact some nature magazines and persuade them to pay me for my work. I knew nothing about dealing with magazine editors and publishers, and it scared me a little to think of it. Eric took all those worries away from me.

The first picture he sold was of a Queen Anne's lace with a bumblebee on it. You may remember the one, because it was taken in August when you were still here; in fact, you were with me. Anyway, he sold that one to a local nature club, and they used it on the back page of the October issue of their monthly newsletter. I'll admit they didn't pay a very impressive price. After all, they were a relatively small group without lots of funds. But I was thrilled.

When Eric brought me the news that the picture had been accepted, he also brought along a bottle of champagne. Talk about class! It was the first champagne I had ever tasted. We sat together on the back porch steps and drank it out of paper cups. I will always remember how tingling and sweet that first sip was, and how we laughed as we shared that special moment of my first success.

A few days later I received the check in the mail from *Nature Tales*, and I rushed out and spent it on a thick sirloin steak and a bottle of the best wine available in Dipper Point. I added some of my other money to what little was left and bought the most beautiful hostess pajamas I've ever owned.

The Norfolks came over to celebrate with me the next evening. I thought everything was very elegant and perfect. I didn't notice at first how quiet Karen was and how her mother looked disapprovingly at my expensive new outfit. I had only one thought in my mind—Eric thought I was beautiful. I could see it in his quick glances and little smiles. He was happy for me, and I was in a dream.

During dinner, I became suspicious that everything was not as smooth and wonderful as I had believed. Mrs. Norfolk and Karen were both quiet and polite, but their coolness and formality vaguely disturbed me. Eric seemed not to notice, but I became self-conscious in the strained atmosphere. Mrs. Norfolk was cutting her steak carefully into small pieces with the utmost concentration. I hesitated to interrupt her by asking for the butter, so I reached for it instead, since it was only a few inches beyond my range. Unluckily, my hand hit my wineglass as I brought it back toward my plate, trying to conceal by speed a slightly unladylike stretch. The red liquid poured onto my new outfit and showed dreadfully on the pale blue, green, and gold floral pattern. I was, as you can imagine, totally mortified.

"Oh, dear!" Karen commented uneasily, but her mother didn't let me off that simply. She watched her son gallantly dabbing at the ugly spot with his handkerchief, and there were icicles in the look she gave me.

"Well, let's hope it doesn't stain," she said in a scolding, pessimistic tone. "The least you could do is be more careful with expensive clothes and wine if you can't be more careful with your money."

"Mother, really!" Eric admonished her, but I hurried away from the table to the kitchen without making any answer. I stayed there at the sink for a long time, trying to wash out out the wine and to calm myself. By the time I went back to the dining room, Mrs. Norfolk and Karen had gone home. Eric sat waiting for me, a glass of wine in his hand. He offered this to me as I sat down, and I took it, but my eyes brimmed with tears before I could drink it.

"What did she mean, Eric? What did I do wrong, in your mother's eyes?" I asked him.

For a few seconds he was silent while his mouth worked angrily. Then at last he said, "You did nothing wrong. Just don't pay any attention. Do you hear me? Can you forgive and forget?"

"Sure, Eric," I said in a high, trembling voice. "But if only I understood—"

"Leave it alone, Lily. Let it pass," he whispered gently.

"If that's best," I sighed unhappily.

"It is." He nodded grimly. "Well, I hate to eat and run, as they say, but I guess I'll be off."

"So early?" I asked, alarmed by his mood.

"For tonight, yes. I think so. Good night."

And he was gone. I cried myself to sleep that night after cleaning up from the party alone. I was totally

176

miserable, but when I awoke the next morning I did my best to forget that unpleasant incident entirely, and actually made the party into a happy memory in my mind. My love for Eric was so deep and powerful it made me forget the pain. It also helped me to ignore the fact that I saw much less of Eric for the next two weeks or so.

In fact, the next time I saw him for more than an hour at a time was well into November, past the middle of the month. That was the day we drove into Dipper Point together before dawn. The pictures we took that morning were good ones, dramatic and haunting. I wanted to catch the little marina at sunrise in the cold white light. The water was a hard steel-gray and the masts of the moored boats loomed out of the mist, black against the sharp, white sky. I shivered in the light wind, waiting for the sun to climb a little higher. Eric offered me his gloves, as my fingers were red with cold, but I shook my head, oblivious to all but the stark beauty of the morning and the warm joy deep inside me because we were together again.

A few days later, Eric came over late in the afternoon, his eyes alight with excitement. I asked him what had happened but he wouldn't tell me. He made me wait until we were sitting at the kitchen table with steaming cups of tomato soup in front of us. Then he laughed and said, "I have wonderful news for you."

"I knew it!" I cried. "What is it?"

"I've sold your picture of the monarch butterfly, the one where the sun came through the wings like a stained-glass window."

I could see he was teasing me with this long description, and that there was more. I prompted him eagerly. "Well?"

"This time it's to a national magazine with a fairly big circulation. They pay very well."

"Oh, that's fantastic! I'm delighted! How can I

thank you?" I jumped up from my chair to throw my arms around him, but he waved me back, still smiling that provocative smile.

"Wait. I'm not finished," he told me calmly. "Have you got any crackers?"

"What? Have I— Oh, you!"

I hurriedly pawed through the cupboard until I came up with a box of crackers, because I knew he'd never tell me until I did. He had me on the edge of my chair while he slowly crumbled a cracker into his soup.

"Aren't you going to tell me?" I asked at last.

"I thought you'd never ask!" he laughed. "Well, the best part is, it isn't only the one picture. They've agreed to set up a sort of contract, so that they will consider your work, and in fact almost certainly publish it, every month. Kind of like you are one of their staff photographers. It's a real break for you, Lily. It may not make you rich and famous, but it's steady, and your name will become known in the circles that count. It could lead to other, bigger things in time."

I was completely overcome, caught between tears of joy and jubilant laughter. This time, when I flew around the table, he stood up and caught me in his arms.

"You're wonderful!" I gasped at last. "I'm the luckiest girl in the world!"

I can remember that afternoon as clearly as if it were yesterday. Tears come to my eyes when I think how simple it all seemed then, how happy I was. You probably remember getting short notes from me once in a while, Kim, when I would say I'd sold a picture and mention how much I was enjoying my new life and what a good friend Eric was to me. But I never took the time to really explain to you how things were. I want you to see how our relationship developed—how much he meant to me.

The days passed quickly. Eric and I were together quite a bit, perhaps not as much as earlier in the fall, but

I loved him, and what time we did have seemed even better. We were still taking pictures even though the snow had come. We photographed snow-dusted pine boughs and icicles in the sun, evening grosbeaks and slate-colored juncos perched on an old stump near my bird feeder.

I was constantly busy in the darkroom. When Eric wasn't with me, I worked on the Christmas present I had decided to make for the Norfolks. I was making an enlargement of one of the harbor scenes we had taken in November and framing it for them. For the Robinsons, whom I had hardly gotten to know, really, I decided to make a smaller enlargement of a blue jay picture that I liked. And, of course, you know of the ones I made for you and the family back home. I was very busy and the time passed quickly.

I remember you called me on Thanksgiving that year. It was so good to hear your voice. That was one day when I really was a little down, because I had hoped Eric and his family would ask me over for dinner. I didn't hear from Eric that whole day, and I ate a frozen turkey dinner all alone. When I told you that when you called, there was a sad pause, then you laughed and tried to cheer me up. Do you remember? I do.

But I was mostly very happy. Early in December, Eric drove me into Harbor Center to do some window shopping. We walked up and down the long main street, stopping at each window and going into the larger department stores and an occasional small shop. Eric bought a lovely matching scarf and gloves set for Karen's Christmas present and a beautiful sterling silver locket for his mother. We ate dinner at a little restaurant on one of the side streets and went to an early movie. When we came out of the movie, all the Christmas lights were on.

It was a beautiful sight. On the way back to the car, we walked briskly in the clear, cold air. Delicately shaped snowflakes drifted slowly down through the circles of light surrounding the street lamps. When we turned the corner to go to the parking lot, we stopped to look up at the huge spruce tree set up right in the middle of the street and circled with electric lights of every color.

It had been a perfectly wonderful day, and as we stood there side by side gazing at that beautiful tree, I reached out for Eric's hand and took it in mine. He smiled down at me, a smile of surprise and, I thought, of love.

"I love you," I whispered, an answering smile trembling on my lips. His hand tightened on mine, and he kissed me lightly, our first kiss. Then we walked quietly to the car, and we drove home in a silent dream.

I hardly slept that night. I wanted to live over every moment of that precious day again and again, until it would be indelible in my memory. I could still feel the thrill of pleasure at the slight pressure of his lips on mine, and emotions stirred in me, stranger and deeper than I had ever known possible.

Eric was away from home for a few days after our trip to Harbor Center. I missed him terribly, but I kept myself busy taking Freddy for long walks, wrapping gifts, baking cookies for the Norfolks, and, of course, working in the darkroom.

Karen invited me over one afternoon to help them decorate their Christmas tree. The ornaments they had were so lovely. Some of them were of hand-blown glass, and one set I liked especially had beautiful paintings of birds on them—cardinals, chickadees, nuthatches.

I wanted to talk with Karen about her brother, confide in her something of my feelings for him, but I could not quite bring myself to do this. Our conversation was mostly superficial, but I was still pleased that Karen had thought to ask me over. I did manage to find out that Eric would be back in only a few more days, and it was an enjoyable afternoon.

On the day of Eric's return, I could hardly wait for him to call or come over. When the phone rang about two o'clock, I pounced on it after the first ring. Eric asked me to go for a drive with him and said he would pick me up in an hour. That was one of the longest hours of my life. But, at long last, the two of us were together in the car, and we headed down the peninsula toward Harbor Center. I realized that though Eric and I had spent countless hours together, this was only the second time that we had been together and really alone, without either Freddy or my camera equipment or his family.

There was something different about Eric that day. I sensed it immediately when I got into the car. He was keyed up, excited, and somehow freer than usual. He reached over for my left hand and gave it a little squeeze while he laughed and told me how wonderful it was to be back. I was surprised and delighted.

"There's one last Christmas present I'd like to get today, and I want you to help me pick it out," he told me when I asked where we were going.

I tried to find out what it was, or who it was for, but he wasn't going to tell me anything. All he would do was smile.

It was a soft gray wintry day, a quiet, sleepy, peaceful day. It was almost a surprise to see the activity of children skating on a pond or sliding down a hill. The countryside was so still and so at rest. Eric and I were quiet and comfortable together. From time to time we would sing softly together with the car radio, and we talked a little, but mostly there was a new harmony between us, something we felt inside but could not express.

This time, when we walked along the main street of the town, Eric slipped his arm about my waist and led me quickly past the shop windows until he stopped quite

181

suddenly before a small but very lovely jewelry store. Our unaccustomed closeness felt so good and right. I smiled up into his eyes as we stood before the window, and he bent his head to kiss me. For a moment I was overcome with the heady exhilaration of his nearness. Then I opened my eyes and let them wander over the display of engagement rings before us.

"This is the place," he remarked matter-of-factly. "I want you to pick out one of those."

"Do I know the girl?" I asked him teasingly.

"Fairly well, I think," he laughed.

"Then that will make it easier. Who is she?"

"Well, I'll tell you. She has little hands, just like yours, and I know that if the ring fits your finger, she can wear it."

"Oh, you're such a tease!" I said, pulling away from him, but he held my hand as I stepped back. Our eyes met, the laughter replaced by a sudden seriousness. "Do you mean it?" I asked him simply.

"There's nothing in the world I want more than to hear you say you'll marry me."

His voice was gentle but a little rough with longing and doubt. I knew he was sincere. I threw my arms about his neck and kissed him impulsively. "Then I will. Of course I will!"

We went inside the store and the jeweler helped us select the right ring. The diamond we chose was not a large one, but it was exquisitely cut, very white and fiery. The jeweler was proud of its high quality and told Eric that it was a splendid selection. The setting was delicate and simple, with two tiny diamond chips set on each side of the perfect gem. I adored it, and Eric said my eyes shone more brightly than any of the stones. I don't doubt it for a minute.

Eric wrote the jeweler a check for the full amount and slipped the ring on my finger right there in the store. It fit perfectly, and I could hardly take my eyes off my left hand. It was so sudden, so like a dream, even though I had loved Eric for quite a while. I had never been so sure of his feelings for me, but the ring was proof of them. The last reservation which had held my love in check was removed, and my love for him expanded and grew in those moments beyond all hesitation or thought of caution. From the moment he slipped the ring on my finger, I gave myself up to loving him completely.

On the way back home, Eric stopped to show me the lookout. He had mentioned it once or twice, but I had never been there. The sun had set by the time we reached it, but the clouds had broken, and the moon and stars were bright in a clear sky. It was so cold that the crisp snow squeaked beneath our boots, and our breath streamed in white clouds behind us as we ran up the steps to the platform. The moon shimmered on the still open water of the bay below, and the trees stood out black against the snow in the faint white light.

It was wonderful to be alone with Eric amidst that breathtaking beauty. Transformed by my deep love and joy, the freezing air was exhilarating, the frightful darkness mysterious, romantic, and sublime. Those moments seemed beyond improvement, a fleeting glimpse of another world, a reality subtly set apart from all that I had seen or known or even dreamed of. We kissed again in the moonlight, a deep, lingering kiss that stirred us both to the very core. Then we walked slowly back to the car, Eric's arm around my shoulders, mine encircling his waist. When we reached the car, he pulled me to him and kissed me again. I knew how much I had longed for his touch, how much this physical closeness fulfilled and expanded my love. I was caught up in emotions and sensations altogether new to me. It was all I could do to let him go so that we could drive home.

On the way back, I couldn't resist pulling off my gloves to admire my new ring. I turned my left hand in the dim light of the instrument panel, and the diamond flashed and sparkled. Eric laughed and reached over for my hand.

"Does it make you happy?" he asked.

"Oh, Eric, much more than that! I've never felt like this before," I told him, and it was true.

When we pulled into my driveway, I could see that Eric meant to simply drop me off, and on any other day I wouldn't have expected or hoped for anything more. But that night I didn't want him to leave me. I was tired of being alone, and Eric was everything I wanted.

"Won't you come in with me?" I asked eagerly. "We could have some hot chocolate or maybe some French toast. Oh, come in with me, Eric. Don't go."

After the slightest hesitation, he said, "I'd love to. Sure—I'll come in."

We ate supper together at the kitchen table. The hot food tasted especially good after our cold night walk and, for me, there seemed to be a special glow about everything. I was too much in love. Nothing was ordinary to me. Nothing seemed like familiar reality. I thought the world would never be the same again, that I would live forever in a place made bright and special and sacred by the miraculous alchemy of our love.

Later, we sat together near the fire, listening to our favorite records. We sat on the floor, Eric leaning against a chair and I resting against him. He put his arm around me and I nestled there, warm, safe, and happy. It felt so good to relax beside him, to cushion my head on his broad chest and watch the flames sleepily. It was not a time for words or thoughts. I was filled completely with a delicious feeling of love and peace, such as I had never before experienced.

It was already quite late when Eric at last stirred beside me and said gently that he must go. My unreasoning heart panicked at the prospect. We stood up together, but I threw my arms around him and kissed him warmly. His response was strong and passionate. I knew he didn't want to leave me any more than I wanted him to go.

"Stay with me," I whispered against his cheek.

He pushed back away from me to watch my face. Our eyes met and there was scarcely any need for words, though we both found them.

"My love," he murmured. "But, no. If I stay—"

"I know," I said quickly. "Yes—it will be all right."

I will never regret a moment of that night, though in the months and years that followed, on many occasions I was torn with self-doubt and self-blame. On that night, though I had no idea what price I was to pay, it seems to me I would have given the world, my life, anything, for our love, had the bargain been put to me. And, to this day, I can't say that I was wrong. Our love was so special, so precious. I can't measure its value in terms of other earthly things with any accuracy. Though in the eyes of the world I might be judged a fool, and there are those who would even say we did a wicked thing, when I look deep in my heart there is always something there that tells me these things aren't so.

Eric spent the night with me, upstairs in my bedroom. Though totally inexperienced, I longed to give him all my love and to accept his in return. My love for Eric was deep, all-encompassing. Eric was gentle and passionate, and I felt that night the full excitement, beauty, and power of our love. It was as if a whole new wonderful world was opened to me that night, a world of closeness, selflessness, complete sharing with another person, until what was his and what was mine made no difference and could not be distinguished. It was somehow different from anything I had imagined—and even better.

When I awoke the next morning, Eric was gone. I was bitterly disappointed at first, but he had left a short note for me which was full of love and expressed much of the same wonder and gratitude in my own heart. I smiled as

I read it over a third and fourth time, then, with a great effort, tucked it away in a drawer and prepared to face the new day.

There was nothing I could have done to prepare myself for that dreadful day, but as it was, it hit me so cruelly. I was in another world of joy, love, and peace, never less ready for disaster to strike—but that's what happened.

Denise came to my door around mid-morning, her cheeks flushed, her eyes blazing with anger and brimming with tears.

"You can't marry my Eric!" she screamed without preamble. "You just can't! He's mine, and he always will be!"

"No!" I gasped breathlessly. "No, that can't be. We love each other. I—I have his ring!"

She stared at my left hand, terror creeping into her voice. "That doesn't matter. It doesn't mean anything. No, it can't! Because—because I have his baby! Yes, I'm pregnant, and Eric is the father of my child!"

"That can't be true!" I told her shrilly, but terrible fears and doubts were taking over in my mind.

"Don't tell me it can't be true! I know better than you about this! How dare you? Eric has been mine for years. We would be married by now if you hadn't come along, laying a trap for my poor Eric, who never wandered before or loved any other girl. But he'll marry me now! I have his baby, and that will make all the difference to him. You wait and see!"

With that, she turned and fled back down the drive. I stared after her uneasily, not yet reduced to tears, because I still believed this story would be proven false. Yet I was deeply shaken and disturbed. I didn't know who to turn to or what to do. I wanted Eric to deny this, yet I hesitated to confront him with Denise's charges.

I didn't have to worry about this for very long because Eric came over about half an hour later, before

I had made up my mind what to do. I could tell by the look on his face that he knew what had happened, and I fell into his arms, exclaiming, "I'm so glad you came back to me!"

He held me comfortingly for a moment, then I stepped back from him and said carefully, "Come in and sit down, Eric. We need to talk."

We sat together on the sofa and I told him quickly what Denise had said to me. My voice shook with pain and I would not meet his eyes until I had finished speaking. I wanted him to see trust there, but I knew if he read what I felt it would be doubt and fear.

"Tell me it isn't so, Eric. That's all I need—just to hear you say it isn't true," I said weakly. The stricken look on Eric's face frightened me, and every second of silence disheartened me more.

At last Eric began, carefully. "I don't love Denise. That much of her story I can deny to you absolutely. After knowing you, Lily, I know that I never loved her. But, for a long while, I tried to make myself believe that I did. Try to understand. We grew up together. Mother always wanted me to marry Denise, to unite our family with the Robinsons. She's a pretty girl, and charming in her own way. Until now, now that I know what love really is, I had no strong objection. Our marriage was what both Denise and Mother wanted, and I thought it would probably work out for the best. But then I fell in love with you, Lily, and it changed everything. I know now that I don't want to marry her, because I don't love her—and I never will."

"But what about the baby, Eric?" I asked quietly. "Is that part true?"

"I—I don't know, Lily," he admitted.

"What do you mean you don't know?" I blazed at him. "Do you mean to tell me it's possible? That's all I want to know!"

"Don't, Lily, don't be this way," he pleaded, but I

was too hurt to respond to his pain. If only I had been cooler, more understanding. If only I had listened to him. But I was hurt and disillusioned and angry. I couldn't accept him as he was, as a man with human weaknesses, capable of making mistakes, yet still worthy and deserving of my love.

"Tell me if it's possible!" I demanded savagely.

"Yes, it's possible," he murmured miserably. "But I don't know that it's true. I don't think she does either. She hasn't been to a doctor. Can't you see? It's just a desperate trick to hold me!"

"Can't you see that's not the point? When did it happen? Last month? Last week? I thought you loved *me*, Eric! And all the time you were with her!"

"No, no—only once, I swear it! I did love you, even then. Oh, I can't explain! It was more than a month ago. You remember when I sold your first picture and you invited the family over, and Mother was so horrible about the money? Can't you see how ashamed and sorry I am, Lily? I made a terrible mistake! They worked on me, both Mother and Denise, in the days following that dreadful incident. I was half embarrassed to come and see you after that, and Denise took every advantage. She was afraid of losing me, Lily. She wanted this to happen! Oh, I know it's no excuse. God, I know that! But, please, Lily, don't desert me. I love you!"

"Get out!" I screamed. "For God's sake, Eric, just go! Go to her! She needs her baby's father! Go!"

"No. Please—" he whispered, but I turned my back to him and waited for him to leave. I no longer wanted him to see my bitter tears, to know my every emotion. I trembled as I heard him walk across the room and out the front door, closing it sharply behind him. Only then did I get up and run after him. I stopped, sobbing wildly against the hard door panel, then ran blindly through the house and out the back door. I kept running through the snow to the woods, dressed only in a light shirt and slacks, my feet bare. I was insane with grief. When I tripped over a root, I fell flat in the snow, and I just lay there, sobbing and clawing the snow with my fingernails.

At last I noticed that Freddy had come with me. His big furry head was pushing against my face, and I sat up slowly, fighting for control. I felt dreadfully cold, though my feet were on fire with pain, and it was desperately hard to make my way back to the house.

At last I reached the kitchen table, and I sank into one of the chairs, shivering uncontrollably. I didn't bother to get a towel and dry off. I just sat there at the table, sobbing weakly and trembling all over. Gradually I began to calm down a little, but I was soaked to the skin and thoroughly chilled. It must have been two or three hours later before I pulled myself together enough to go upstairs for a hot shower and some dry clothes.

That was the most terrible day of my life. Since then, there have been other shocks, to be sure; some even more serious than that one. But never again was I so vulnerable, so totally unprepared.

Between that day and Christmas break, when I came home to visit you, I saw Karen Norfolk only once, and none of the others at all. I gave her the picture I had framed for them, and I enclosed my engagement ring in the greeting card, without any note of explanation. Karen and I didn't discuss what had happened at all. We merely exchanged remarks about the weather and awkward best wishes. As for the present I had intended to give to the Robinsons, I put it away in a closet and sold it later in the year.

How I longed to pour all this dreadful story out to you, Kim. Many times I picked up the phone, your number in my head, but I always thought, "No, this is final exam time. Don't bother her," or, "She has papers to write. Leave her out of this." But I know now, and you must know too, that these were never the real reasons I didn't tell you. I so wanted to be self-sufficient and capable of running my own life in a reasonable manner. I was ashamed of my failure, and I didn't want to talk with anyone about it.

When we met at Christmastime, you'll remember how everything conspired to help me keep my secrets. You were down with the flu that year, and the only time I saw you, you were with your mother. We talked on the phone two or three times, and I could have told you then, but I was staying with my aunt and I didn't want her to overhear. Besides, I still really didn't want to talk about it. I know it was foolish and wrong of me, but I couldn't help thinking of how cautious and restrained you are, not impulsive and emotional like I am, and that you never would have done the things I did. I knew you would be understanding, but I still thought you would think I had been wrong—I suppose because I thought so myself.

In the months that followed, I worked very little on my photography. I kept up the arrangement with the magazine Eric had established for me by sending them two or three pictures a month, but these were photographs that Eric and I had taken during the fall or even earlier ones. I did practically nothing in the way of new work.

At first this was simply because I was depressed about Eric and too dispirited to do anything of value. However, there soon were yet other reasons. By mid-February I was reasonably certain that I was pregnant. This, of course, worried me, and I felt ill much of the time. I was constantly debating whether I should tell Eric. I wanted to tell him, wanted to admit to him that I still loved him as much as ever and needed him even more. Yet I was too foolishly proud to admit that I needed him, and I didn't want to trap him as Denise was trying to do. And then, too, I had never known for certain whether Denise really was pregnant or not. If she was, then I had no greater claim to Eric than she had. So day after day I said nothing, but sat alone in my house with the television on or records playing, thinking about my problem.

Finally, some time early in March, I received an invitation to Eric and Denise's wedding, which was to take place near the end of the month. I responded with a short note expressing my best wishes and my intention not to attend the ceremony. Knowing that Eric had decided to take this final step freed me, at least, from the incessant circular arguments and debates I had been carrying on with myself. I tried to stop thinking about him entirely. I began to think about my baby, and to realize what a great responsibility my child would be.

I began going to see a doctor in Dipper Point, not because I was having any real trouble but because I was trying to turn over a new leaf, to be a more sensible, careful, responsible person. One time in April I very nearly ran into Denise as I was coming out of his office. It turned out that Denise had been telling the truth about her pregnancy. I was glad that she hadn't seen me, and I asked the doctor the next time I saw him if it would be possible to schedule our appointments on different days. He agreed very kindly, but I could see the pity in his eyes and it upset me. Of course, the time would come when they would all know my secret. How foolish I was to think it mattered if I met Denise at the doctor's office.

When the weather began to clear towards the end of April, I started working once again. With the baby coming, I couldn't afford to let my agreement with the magazine lapse, and I had very little to send them in the way of early spring subjects. It was good to spend a few hours of the day walking in the fields and woods. The work took my mind off my other problems, and I even began to enjoy fairly long darkroom sessions. These filled the lonely evening hours, and made me feel satisfied that I was accomplishing something.

The only difficulty was that I tired much more quickly than I was accustomed to doing, and I never liked to stop in the middle of a project I had planned to complete. I didn't think I was driving myself unreasonably hard, though. I took the day off to rest if I woke up feeling below par, and I never worked late into the night as I had been used to doing. Still, when I went for my checkup in May, the doctor expressed concern because I had lost a bit of weight, and told me I must rest more. This agitated me greatly, though I raised no complaints to him about it. I had begun using work as an escape, and having to cut back the hours I spent with my photography disturbed me more than I liked to admit.

By the end of May, I was sure that my condition couldn't possibly have escaped the notice of my neighbors. My pregnancy was constantly in my thoughts, and I suppose this made me likely to assume that the others knew about it. The only reason I could see for the slightest doubt of it was that I had seen none of them socially at all. I had only waved to Karen once from a distance in town, and once I had spoken to Mrs. Norfolk in passing on the street. I was very isolated and alone.

I was surprised when Karen dropped by to see me one day early in June. I asked her to come in and talk to me. Even though I was a little embarrassed, I craved human companionship. I could tell that she had some specific piece of news, and I didn't have to wait long to find out what it was.

Denise had lost her baby. The little girl had been born prematurely and had died.

"I'm so sorry," I told her, sincerely. "Eric must be terribly upset."

"Of course he's disappointed. But Denise is really taking it hard."

To this, I said nothing. Jealousy had hardened my

heart against Denise. It was all I could do not to feel glad about her misfortune. I looked away, trying to conceal my feelings. When at last I looked up at Karen, I realized she was staring at me strangely.

"Lily," she said at last, "no one knew that you were pregnant too. How did you ever keep it from us all these months?"

"I've been keeping pretty much to myself. And it hasn't showed very long," I told her with a sigh.

"How difficult this must have been for you," she remarked with genuine concern. "You must let us help you now. There's no reason to be shy about it. Eric should be told."

"I suppose he'll find out eventually," I admitted irritably. "Besides, he is the father."

"Yes," she said slowly, the detested pity coming into her eyes. "And no one dreamed—"

"No one cared," I concluded acidly. "Please keep it to yourself for a while, will you? I'll try not to be a bother to anyone, though of course I'll need help after a bit."

"I'll be glad to help you. Don't you want Eric to know, though?"

"I don't know. I haven't decided," I told her quickly, in a bitter voice. "Please go, Karen. Please go. I don't mean to be rude. It's just. . .this surprises me, and I'm tired. Please go."

"I know," she whispered understandingly, touching my hand as she stood to leave. "But, remember, if you need anything, be sure to call on me."

I nodded silently, and she went home.

By that time in June, I had already received two or three lovely long letters from you, Kim, after school let out in May. I want you to know how much those meant to me. All during that difficult summer, I would fill countless hours reading your letters over and over, and writing answers to them. The answers were painful to write, because I hated keeping so much from you, yet I couldn't bring myself to explain what had happened. I think by then the chief barrier to this was the enormity of all the things I had concealed and the length of time I had been silent. I wanted to tell you but I didn't know how to explain, and every passing day seemed only to complicate matters more. When you finally asked if I would mind if you came up my way for a day or two, it just about killed me to put you off and make excuses, but I couldn't face it. You were so sweet and accepting about that too. I will always remember how you continued to write, how you were always my friend, even when I gave you so many reasons to question my friendship.

So the long summer wore past. The heat was terrible and there were days when I could do practically nothing until after the sun went down. I was so dreadfully alone and I felt tired and listless most of the time. Time seemed to flow over me, and I remained passive and indifferent. I cared very little about anything. My favorite phrases were "It doesn't matter" and "It makes no difference." These would pop into my head a hundred times a day, whether I kicked Freddy's water dish and had to dry up the floor or I caught myself brooding about Eric's marriage to Denise. It was my only defense, but it was a poor one, a defense springing from depression and pain.

Sometimes, when I would think about my baby, I would be almost happy. With each passing day he became more real to me, and I always knew that I loved and wanted him very much in spite of everything. I began to be impatient for my baby to be born. I would count the weeks and days on the calendar again and again. I read books on child care and bought furniture and mobiles for the nursery.

I tried to think of nothing else. As long as my mind was on my baby I could stop myself from thinking about Eric. Once in a while, though, I would fall into a bitter, sad dream about our ruined love. After learning that Denise's child had died, I would sometimes fantasize that Eric would come back to me. I even caught myself waiting for him to come to talk to me, expecting him to come, longing for it. One time this led to a stormy fit of tears and frightful rage. I felt very ill afterward, and I was terrified that I, like Denise, would lose my child. I promised myself that I would never let that happen again, and I was able to keep that promise.

As the middle of September approached, I called Karen on the phone, and we talked about plans for the time when my baby would be born. My doctor had recommended a hospital in Harbor Center to me, and when I suggested taking a room in the city for a few days, he had agreed wholeheartedly. Karen offered to come with me and even to pay part of the expenses, but I was reluctant to accept her money. I couldn't have been more grateful for her time. She also arranged for Paul to look after Freddy until I came home again. I was a little surprised that Paul would help us, but he remained a reliable friend to both Karen and myself, even though he openly sympathized with his cousin, Denise.

Karen and I stayed two nights in a room near the hospital. On the third day Timmy was born. He was a beautiful baby. But, then, I suppose mothers always feel that. I'll never forget holding him that first time, how tiny and fragile he seemed, and how proud I was, how radiant with love. The minute I saw him and touched him, I knew that something new and wonderful had come into my life, something that would more than make up for anything I had lost. Never again did I experience the terrible listlessness and depression that had eaten away at my very soul, my very will to live. From the moment I first saw Timmy and fully appreciated the reality of my child, my life had a new purpose and meaning. I no longer felt the destructive indifference which had plagued me since I lost Eric. Everything mattered to me again, mattered because of my precious child.

When I was strong enough to take over my new responsibilities as a mother, Karen came back to Harbor Center and drove me home. She was so helpful, such a good friend to me. She offered to stay with me for a few days or even weeks, but I only wanted to be alone with my baby. I didn't want anyone else to feed him or change him. Looking back, I can see how intensely possessive I was.

Timmy was always a very healthy little boy. He had a marvelous appetite and he hardly ever cried. He grew very rapidly, and the doctor was totally satisfied with his progress at every checkup. I did everything for Timmy myself. I never left him with a sitter for any reason. My whole life centered on him, and as he thrived and developed, I was contented and proud.

Finally, one day in early November, Eric came to see his son. I had known that this would happen some time, but it was still difficult for me to handle. When I saw Eric standing at my door, the months between my last horribly emotional meeting with him and that moment were as nothing. I had thought that, in all those months, I had made myself forget how much I loved him, how much I wanted him. But when I stood there beside him, taking his coat, asking him to sit down, expressing awkward sympathy because Denise's baby hadn't lived, all the old emotions came flooding back. I had to turn from him quickly to hide the trembling of my lips and to blink back the hot tears.

I knew that I had to act cold and uncaring. It cost me a great effort to do so, and at that, I wasn't sure I played the part convincingly. I refused to meet Eric's eyes and I never allowed myself to be close enough to him so he could touch me. He admired Timmy in his crib, but I didn't offer to lift my baby out for him to hold. I couldn't bear the thought of seeing my son in Eric's arms. I knew it would seem too painfully right, too painfully impossible.

At last, it was time for Eric to leave. I stood beside him at the door, trying to smile coolly, without the slightest trace of feeling. I thought I had made it through that meeting fairly well. I was just beginning to relax. Then suddenly Eric reached over to tilt my face gently so my eyes would meet his. I shook my head angrily, stepping away, but it was too late.

"Isn't there anything left at all, Lily?" he asked painfully. "Of all that beautiful love—is there nothing left at all?"

"You fool!" I lashed out. "How dare you? What if there was something left? What if there was? What could it be to us now but. . .but. . ."

Unable to finish my sentence, I burst into angry desperate tears. He pulled me to him, and though I struggled against his arms, he held me close, and I sobbed out my terrible grief and love for him, all against my own will and judgment.

"Don't cry, Lily. Don't cry any more," he soothed. Then, in a strange, quiet, purposeful tone that stilled my tears and made me look up at him, he continued, "I don't know how long it will take, or how hard I'll have to fight for it, but one day I'll get a divorce. Then we can be together, as we should be."

Eric had planted a terrible hope in my mind. Terrible because I could no longer be satisfied with my life as it was. Timmy was still a constant source of joy for me, but the sense of completeness and contentment had left me. I would catch myself in daydreams, hearing Eric's voice repeating, "I'll get the divorce." Sometimes I would lose myself in imagining what our life together would be like.

A few weeks later, Mrs. Norfolk dropped over to see

me. At first I was excited and pleased that she had come. She admired Timmy and was pleasant to me in a cool, reserved fashion. As we sat together over coffee, I began to feel uneasy. Mrs. Norfolk had become intense and nervous, and I wondered what was coming.

"Lily," she began at last, "I know how difficult it must be for you to support the burden of a young child all alone. It will be even harder when you try to resume your photography and care for Timmy at the same time. I can't quite imagine how you will manage it."

Was this an offer of assistance? I couldn't be sure, and I didn't know how to answer her.

"I suppose it will be difficult," I admitted, noncommittally.

"I've given some thought to some ways I could help you."

"How kind of you! But it really isn't necessary. We'll manage on our own, Timmy and I," I told her unconvincingly.

"That's very brave and sweet, Lily. But be honest with me. You need money, don't you?" she persisted.

"Well, I. . ." I hesitated a long moment. "I don't have much to spare, it's true. I inherited quite a bit of money from my grandfather, but I used almost all of it to buy this place. I have to make a living with my camera. The inheritance won't support us for long."

"Just as I thought!" she remarked, more to herself than to me. "Then this is my proposal."

I stiffened at the tone of her voice, wishing I had not been so open about my financial affairs. I knew by her expression and her manner that her offer would have strings attached, and I wished I could stop her from making it.

"This is what I would be willing to do for you," she said, not meeting my eyes. "I will buy back this house from you, paying half again your purchase price. And I'll send you a thousand dollars a month for one year, or even longer, if you aren't making a good living with your photography by that time. With that money, you should be able to find another suitable place, away from here, and get your life started again. You'll never be happy here, so close to Eric and Denise. I'm offering you a chance to put this behind you, to begin again. As for Timmy, why you would have no worries there. With Denise's money, the child could have anything in the world he needed or wanted, the best of everything. Eric wants his son. I think it will save their marriage. This is the best thing for everyone concerned."

I couldn't believe what I was hearing. Eric's mother wanted to buy my son for Eric. She must have heard some mention of his plans for divorce, and she hoped that by offering me this money, she could save the marriage. I was deeply hurt and angry. I didn't consider accepting her offer for a second, but I was so shocked that I couldn't speak.

At last I said, "No. No. That isn't possible. This place and Timmy—they are all in the world that matters to me. They aren't for sale at any price. I won't consider it."

As my anger rose, Mrs. Norfolk responded hotly, "We shall see! When your money's gone and you can't feed little Timmy, let alone yourself, then we'll see if you consider it! I want what's best for Eric. I want him to have his son and to get his mind off a little slut like you and give his love to his wife. Everything could be so right for him then. He would have all the money I always wanted him to have, a wonderful wife who loves him dearly, and the child she might have given him had it not been for all the pain and upset *you* caused her! You *owe* them the child, but I'm willing to pay for him."

"I'll never accept it! Timmy's not for sale at any price!" I wanted to strike her, to force her from my house, but I trembled, with barely controlled fury.

Mrs. Norfolk watched me carefully. I knew she was considering what course to take with me. When she spoke again, her tone was more gentle. "I should have known that a mother's love is stronger than common sense or practicality. I know how much you love your son. All things considered, the offer still stands, with the one change that Timmy should belong to you always. As his grandmother, I wanted him near me. I wanted to see him grow up with every possible advantage. But I know that's asking too much of you. I will pay you just as I said, if you will take your baby and move away from here, and leave Eric in peace."

I knew, then, that I was confronting a love as deep and unreasoning as my own feeling for my son. Mrs. Norfolk believed she was saving and protecting her son from me. Part of my anger died, but I held out firmly against her.

"If I believed it would be better for Eric if I left, you wouldn't have to pay me to do it! I don't want your money. I don't want to be bribed. Just leave me alone! I have to think," I told her curtly.

She had every reason to be satisfied with that meeting. She had confused and upset me. My thoughts were in a turmoil when she left, and I had no idea which way to turn. Was it possible that she was right, that I was being selfish and foolish, standing in the way of the happiness of Eric and of my son? What if I should fail to make an adequate living? What if I should cause my son years of hardship, when by a simple "yes" he could have so much? My maternal feelings fought down that line of thought. I knew my love for my son would never permit me to turn him over to Denise, no matter what material advantages she offered.

But what about Eric? Was his feeling for me now born out of pity and a sense of responsibility? Would he have been happy married to Denise if he had never known me? Would he be happy with her now if I told him I no longer loved him and removed myself from his life? How I longed to talk to him, to find the answers to these questions, and so many others. I realized that his plans for divorce were not materializing, but I had no way of knowing what he was thinking. I wanted desperately to do the right thing, and I was pathetically unsure of myself. In the end, I made no decision at all. I simply waited in silence.

As the Christmas holidays approached, a new set of difficulties took over for a time in my mind. No one at home knew anything about Timmy, and with everything so unsettled, I was not anxious that anyone should know. I had very nearly decided to call you, Kim, and explain everything. I knew that I could count on you to help me keep my secret from the others. But, at the last moment, just a few hours before I intended to call you, Karen Norfolk dropped by. She was so sympathetic and friendly, and before I knew it, I had explained my entire predicament to her. She agreed to come with me and stay with Timmy in a rented room while I made my holiday visits. So I never told you or anyone else about Timmy that Christmas.

The big house seemed doubly lonely after Christmas was past. It had been so wonderful to get out and talk with people, to eat dinner with my friends. You know I've always liked people and enjoyed socializing. I missed that particularly sharply after my friendship with Eric and his family was shaken. Even though Karen had stood by me in my time of need, and I had reason to believe that Eric still cared about me, this did little to help me cope with everyday loneliness. None of the Norfolks came to see me often, as a simple, friendly gesture. It was always for a specific, defined purpose.

For my part, I no longer visited them at all. When I went to town, which was rarely enough, I met no friends there. Some of the clerks in the little shops knew me by name, but I had made no close friends. Some of the women who had been happy to exchange trivial conversation with me before my pregnancy would pretend not to see me now that I had my baby with me. I told myself I didn't care, but deep inside I felt empty and sad. I knew I couldn't go on like that for the rest of my life.

I think it was this feeling of isolation, more than anything else, which sometimes led me to reconsider Mrs. Norfolk's offer. I wondered if I would be happier somewhere else, if I would make new friends in a new place. Yet something always held me back. I loved my house, for all its massive emptiness. I wanted to fill it with people again, to make it live. I felt there could be no place more beautiful than this land I had come to know so well, and I really didn't want to leave it. And finally, deep inside, there was a still more fundamental feeling which held me there. At that time, I put no words to it, but I know now it was because Eric was my baby's father and my true love. I never wanted to run away from him. As time passed, my wavering indecision settled into a firm conviction that I must stay.

By the end of January I was restless and impatient. I wanted to know what Eric was doing, what his mother was thinking of my long silence. I wanted them both to know that I had made up my mind. I wondered if Eric knew about his mother's offer. I suspected he did not, and that it would have angered him; that my refusal of it would strengthen his determination to regain his freedom.

Although I was still playing what seemed to be an endless waiting game, my feelings were entirely different than when I had waited for Eric to choose between Denise and myself the winter before. Then I had been too depressed to realize how much was at stake for me, and to respond to the challenge. Now I felt the terrible excitement of the gamble. Mrs. Norfolk had offered me a chance of security, if not happiness. I was prepared to turn that down, to hold out for the prize I really wanted.

I knew I was risking a great deal, but I was stimulated even exhilarated by this knowledge. I was no longer afraid. I realized that it was Eric's love I wanted, and that I was willing to fight for it. It was the only thing I really stood to lose that could hurt me. If I left, I would surely lose it. If I stayed, there was some chance I might not. The loss would be more painful if I stayed, if I really tried to win back Eric's love and failed, but that was the chance I was willing to take.

I called Karen one afternoon and asked her to drop over to talk. I wanted to tell her what I was thinking, to test my decision by her reaction to it. I was still very anxious not to do anything which might hurt either Eric or my son, but I felt a new confidence and purpose and clear-sightedness. I know that part of this change was brought about by my visit home. It had restored my belief in myself to be with people who loved and accepted me.

When Karen came over, she was more than willing to talk. I didn't even have to ask any leading questions.

"I suppose you'd like to know what Eric and Mother are up to," she said before we were even seated in the living room. "Well, Eric has his mind on a divorce, but of course Denise is determined to contest it. Mother does everything she can to discourage it, and she's climbing the walls waiting for you to decide to clear out, though I think by now she expects you aren't going to. Is she right?"

"I've decided to stay, yes," I told her easily, with no hint of the long days of indecision in my voice. "I like it here. I'm confident that I'll be able to keep up my photography well enough to pay the bills. And. . ." I hesitated briefly, meeting Karen's eyes before concluding, "I love your brother, Karen. I want to give us a chance."

She fairly beamed at me. "Wonderful! Shall I tell Eric, or are you waiting for him to make up his mind too?''

I thought for a few seconds, then said, ''Tell him, when you next see him alone. It may be what he needs to know before he can decide.''

''Yes, it'll help him, I know. Poor Eric. Between Mother and Denise—he sometimes hardly knows his own mind. But he does know it, deep down. I'll give him that much credit.''

''Do you think he'll really try to get the divorce, Karen? I know you can't be sure—but what do you think? I know Eric well. He's cautious and considerate. He loves and respects your mother and values her good opinion. In view of all of that, even if he loves me, will it matter? Or does he believe he's doing the right thing now? He's caught in the middle, I know that. I'm asking your advice. Will it be only pain for him if I stay and offer him my love? Will he only be torn, but forced in the end to say no? I don't want to hurt him, Karen. I really don't. Tell me what you think.''

For a long moment she was utterly silent, thoughtfully staring at her hands. When she looked up to meet my eyes, her expression was full of doubt and concern. ''I don't know what to tell you,'' she said at last. ''I can't promise you anything. I know Eric loves you, but there are many obstacles between you. My impulse is to encourage you to stay. You and Eric are right for each other, and I know this is the only chance that it might work out between you. But, of course, I can't be sure.''

''No, we can't be sure,'' I repeated slowly. ''But I've made up my mind to stay! You've helped me tremendously. You've given me just enough hope. I'm not looking for a guarantee.''

''I only hope I haven't encouraged you too much. But I've been honest with you, and that's the best I can do. I expect Eric will come to you when I tell him this. I'll see him tonight.''

I walked to the door with Karen, grateful for her concern, and excited by the thought that things were coming to a head. Before the evening was over, my name would be on Eric's lips. Already I was anticipating the time when he would be with me again, if only for a few moments. I knew that, when he came again, I would waste no time on reserve and pride. He needed my love, and the long months of suppressing it were about to come to an end for me—whatever the result might be.

It was three days after my talk with Karen before Eric came to me. The first evening I had waited anxiously, imagining the conversation that would take place between us, the phrases we would use, the looks we would exchange, where we would stand or sit. It was a great drama in my mind and it always ended happily with a long embrace. The following day, my sense of anticipation was nearly as keen, though my daydreams were far less vivid and specific. By the time Eric finally appeared, I had ceased planning his arrival.

He found me practically up to my elbows in a meat loaf big enough to last Freddy and me for a week. It was impossible to clean the sticky meat and tomato sauce from my fingers quickly, and as I tried agitatedly to do so, I called for Eric to come in. He came into the kitchen, where I was trying to make myself presentable, and quickly spun me around to face him. Our eyes met and I caught his excitement, flinging my soapy arms around his neck. We laughed and kissed each other, and he held me for a moment before releasing me to turn off the water faucet and dry my hands. My fingers still smelled faintly of chopped onion, but it didn't matter. Our love was more than a sweet-scented, flowery dream. The pretty speeches I had planned were all forgotten and unnecessary. It was enough that we were together.

"It's. . .it's so good to see you," I said at last. I felt the stiffness and inadequacy of the words, but Eric smiled and there was understanding in his eyes. "Come on, let's sit down. Let's talk. I'm so glad you're here!''

We sat together in the living room. Eric asked me about my work, and I told him which pictures had been published and showed him a few of the better ones I had taken that spring. My fingers trembled as I held out the prints for him to look at, and I was forced to laugh at my own nervousness, unable to conceal it. Finally, after an awkward silence, I found the courage to ask him the question which had been constantly on my mind.

"And how are things with you, Eric?. . .And Denise?"

He stood up abruptly and paced over to the window, his back to me. "It was all over between us before the wedding ceremony took place. You know that! It was a terrible mistake for me to marry her, knowing I didn't love her, but I felt responsible for the child. And, yes, Mother influenced me. I've always valued her opinion, and to her it was obvious that my marriage to Denise was the only decent and right thing to be done. No one knew about Timmy, then. I should have come to you, given you a fair chance, but I didn't think! I was weak. I was a fool. I thought that, if I came to you, I would never be able to go to Denise. I thought of you as a temptation, when all the while I should have realized— And now I've filed for the divorce, but Denise has her claws in me and she's hanging on for dear life! I pity her, but I know I can't ruin my life and yours out of pity. I can't give Denise what she wants—not really. She's hanging on to something that was never hers at all. It's taken me a long time, Lily, to realize what I've done to you—to us. Can you ever forgive me for taking so long?"

"I could forgive you for anything!" I told him, crossing to his side. He looked into my eyes, but I glanced away before continuing. "But what will happen now? Will it be very long before the divorce is granted? Your lawyer—has he given you any idea? What will happen now?''

''I really can't tell you. I don't like to be pessimistic, but I'm afraid this could take a long time. I've moved back in with Mother and Karen for the time being, and Denise is living in her parents' house. They're hardly ever at home, but Kent and Paul are staying there. That helps her a lot. In fairness to Denise, this has been very hard on her. She's been terribly upset by it all.''

''I can imagine,'' I said icily, then changed the subject. ''Well—why don't you take a peek at Timmy before you head home? I suppose you're expected for dinner.''

After Eric had looked in on his son, it was time for him to leave. Although I wanted him to stay, I knew it would be a relief to me when he had gone. He seemed to understand how I was feeling. I didn't want to touch him or be close to him, and Eric sensed this. Just before he left, he apologized briefly for his mother's offer of money, but I said nothing about it. There was a strained silence between us as he stood at the door. I took a step away from him and thanked him for coming. He told me awkwardly that he would let me know how the divorce progressed. I refused to meet his eyes, but assured him with a trembling smile that I would be waiting to hear about it.

This meeting with Eric marked the beginning of a long, fairly uneventful year for me. Because of Timmy, Eric came over to see me quite often, at least once a week. I was very pleased by this, as I wanted my son to grow up knowing and being loved by both his parents, but it was also difficult for me. I loved Eric very deeply, but under the circumstances, I would not permit myself to speak of this or show it. At first he would tell me of the various snags his divorce suit was encountering, but this was inevitably a distressing topic of conversation, and as time went on, he no longer mentioned it frequently. There were times when I hardly knew what to say to him, and I felt acutely uncomfortable in his presence.

I think it was only because we were such good friends that it was possible for Eric and me to make it through this extremely trying period. We knew each other well and we helped each other over the rough spots with jokes and remembrances of the time we had spent together before we had ever been lovers. I suppose you may well wonder at my caution and my strict morality. You know, even for me, it's kind of hard to explain. As far as what other people thought of us, I'm quite sure Mrs. Norfolk and Denise believed we were carrying on a scandalous, intimate affair, so my restraint was useless in that regard. I think I felt as I did because I never again wanted to be hurt as I had been before. I couldn't face so complete an involvement with Eric again until I was sure that it would be a lasting one. Eric was very understanding about this and very patient.

During the spring months, Eric began helping me with my photography occasionally, as he had done before. We took Timmy and Freddy with us whenever possible, but sometimes this could not be managed. Then Karen would come over to my house to stay with them for a few hours. This was a great help to me, and I was grateful to her.

I had decided to concentrate on photographing the wild mute swans that lived in the bay area. Many of the graceful white giants were unafraid of people, particularly those members of the flock that lived in a large, communal group in a river near Harbor Center. The boldest of the swans would take bits of bread from my fingers, and I needed no special long-focus lens to capture their beauty on film.

After several days of observation, however, I realized that even more striking and spectacular pictures might be taken on the inland lakes with my telephoto lens. The flock on the river included no mated pairs of swans or newly hatched cygnets. Swan families were to be found only in the more isolated spots, away from the main flock. Eric and I located and photographed several such families before the summer was over, sometimes near their nests, amid stumps and reeds, sometimes swimming in formation on the open water, the elegant parents bracketing the downy, gentle young ones.

On one lake that we visited, there were two nesting pairs. The male swans, fierce and protective of their own families, would spar with each other like great warships, their wings billowed over their backs in an attitude of aggression, their necks magnificently arched in defiant S-curves. Some of the pictures we took of these symbolic battles came out extremely well.

My favorite picture of the swans was taken very early one morning, with the sun coming up a fiery rose. Eric and I heard the faintly haunting, whirring sound of swans in flight as we sat on the shore of a quiet cove with our camera. We had been watching a pair of swans and their two young gliding across the burning surface of the lake, a breath-takingly beautiful sight. The new arrivals came to rest in the cove, but at a respectful distance from the family we were watching. The two swans which had just flown in appeared to be a mated pair, but they had no young. The wings of both these swans billowed up into an aggressive posture as they approached the family, and the adult pair we had been watching responded by raising their wings above their backs in magnificent flowers of plummage. The tiny cygnets peeped fearfully as their father advanced toward the approaching pair. As we watched, the two males drew very close together and confronted each other with loudly beating wings. Their mates eyed one another fiercely, also, hissing and puffing up their plumage to maximum size.

Eric and I watched, fascinated, and quietly snapped pictures and checked our meter readings. Then, as suddenly as this assault had begun, the two swans parted, and the pairs drifted back together. The pair with the cygnets glided swiftly away from us, but the intruding couple stopped in front of us, their wings still high and full, their necks arched in perfectly matched S-curves. For a brief moment, the two came together, head to head, as if in a kiss, their necks outlining a perfect heart, each swan forming one half of the shape. This striking configuration was mirrored before the swans on the brilliant water, the reflection slightly troubled by the fast-dying turbulence of the recent confrontation, but unbroken by any windblown wave. The intense color of the sunrise, the perfection of the swans' pose, the emotion of the moment, all combined in a brief glimpse of unbelievable beauty.

I loved this picture above all the others Eric and I had taken. Eric was with me when it was processed too, and I know he felt the same intense joy in it that I did. When I sent it in to the magazine, I put both of our names on it, though Eric insisted this was unnecessary. It was our picture—not mine. Increasingly, I had begun to feel that Eric deserved credit for his work, and that was the photograph that pushed this feeling into a conscious thought.

I would have been astounded had the magazine rejected that picture, so it was not really a surprise when I received my monthly envelope in the mail from them. I opened it casually, at first merely glancing at the contents, but I quickly realized this was more than the usual check and short, polite note of acceptance. The letter was considerably longer than usual, the check several times the amount I had expected. I was so excited I could hardly read the letter, but when I calmed down enough to comprehend it, I was even more overcome. Our picture had been placed in nomination for a significant national honor, and Eric and I would both receive a great deal of recognition in photographic circles because of this.

It was not long before this turn of events was drawn to the attention of Denise and Mrs. Norfolk. I had not thought how it would seem to them when my name appeared with Eric's on a photograph credit. I had been delighted and thrilled by our mutual success, but the neighbors regarded it in a different light. The two women came storming over to my house, eyes blazing, cheeks flushed. Their anger no longer intimidated me. I very nearly didn't care about it at all by that time.

"You, you—hussy!" Mrs. Norfolk fumed. "Bewitching my Eric and flaunting your wickedness shamelessly!"

"How dare you link your name with his in public?" Denise added, a sob in her voice. "It's bad enough the way you carry on here, and I know it! But now everyone knows!"

The faint wail in the last words aroused no pity in me. I smiled a faint, cold smile. "We took the picture together. It is a professional relationship acknowledged in the magazine—nothing more."

"Damn you to be so calm!" Denise screamed at me. "He's my husband—*my husband*, do you hear me?"

"For how much longer?" I asked her cruelly.

Mrs. Norfolk raised her hand to slap me, but I stepped back quickly. "Leave me alone," I said sharply. "What Eric and I do is our business and I don't have to stand here listening to you."

"All right! All right!" Mrs. Norfolk snapped. "I've tried to help you in the past, offered you every possible assistance, but no more! You'll see what I can do!"

I shut the door in their faces. My pulse was racing but I was angry, not frightened. Mrs. Norfolk's threat hit my ears with an empty, flat sound, for she had never helped me and I didn't see how she would hurt me. I tried to calm myself as I climbed the stairs to Timmy's room. He had been awakened by the loud voices, and I needed to soothe and reassure him. I found strength and peace as I rocked my litle boy in my arms, murmuring sweet lies to him. "Everything's all right, everything's fine," I crooned until I almost believed it myself.

Eric and I were drawn closer by that incident. I found out later that his mother had treated him in almost the same way she had treated me. When I told him about it, I merely said that Denise and his mother had been upset by the appearance of our names together in the magazine, but he had understood how much I left out in saying this and had been touched by my omissions. We continued to work together and to submit our work jointly. We didn't seriously discuss any other alternative.

When it had been several months since Eric had mentioned his divorce to me, I began to be impatient for it to be settled. I hated to bring it up, but at last I couldn't stop myself any longer. I had to ask him about it. I was instantly sorry I had spoken. Eric looked very grim and there was little encouragement in what he told me. I tried to cheer him up about it, to act as if it didn't matter, but I knew he could see through it, and we both felt miserable trying not to show our feelings. I vowed to myself never to open up that topic again.

As far as our career was concerned, it was a very important year. Eric and I enjoyed a great deal of success. Not only did our pictures sell, but we also won our share of awards and honors. Our names were becoming fairly well known. Other magazines took an interest in our work, and the magazine which had first published my earliest pictures was anxious to express its appreciation as well. I was excited and inspired by it all. I loved my work, and the recognition was sweet.

Personally, it was a desperately frustrating year. In spite of the time we spent together, both Eric and I were conscious of the barriers between us, the painful void in our lives. We watched our son grow, but we could not live together as husband and wife. We loved each other, but I firmly refused to show or acknowledge it, and Eric respected my wishes. Sometimes at night, in spite of all the reasons I made to be happy, I would shed silent tears of loneliness and longing, but I never let either Timmy or Eric see them.

Although the tension between Mrs. Norfolk and myself had never been more extreme, there was still one strong link between us. Timmy was her grandson, and eventually this fact began to carry some weight with her. I had no way of knowing exactly what it was that changed her attitude. It might have been Karen's subtle persuasion, Eric's calm persistence, or some other factor I could not even guess. But, for whatever reason, when I next saw her again late in the summer, she made every effort to be civil, if not friendly. She seemed very anxious to establish a new relationship of peaceful co-existence with me, and I was relieved by this, and more than willing to forget the threats and insults of the past.

More and more, Timmy and I began to be accepted into the Norfolk family, while the closeness Mrs. Norfolk and Denise had shared diminished. Mrs. Norfolk invited us to dinner on Timmy's birthday in September, and it recalled memories of our past friendship to all of us. I was encouraged enough to invite the three Norfolks to lunches and suppers after that, and they almost always accepted. It was good to have people in my house again. The old sense of family I had valued when I first became friends with the Norfolks had returned, and this made me very happy. I couldn't help thinking that this change might even mean that Eric's divorce was at last going through, but I was waiting for Eric to tell me about it himself.

That year, when I came home for the holidays, Timmy stayed with the Norfolks. The five of us celebrated Christmas early so we could share Timmy's delight in the decorated tree, the festive packages, and the turkey dinner his grandmother prepared. The week of separation seemed long to me, but I was satisfied and at peace with my relationship with Eric's family. I knew that they all loved my son.

It was impossible for me to forget the bitter anger that had existed between Mrs. Norfolk and myself, and this was equally true for her, but we both made every effort to accept and understand. Eric and I talked at length about Mrs. Norfolk's relationship with Denise and her reaction to the situation we had found ourselves in following Timmy's birth. Eric helped me to see how difficult it had been for his mother to remain impartial. Denise had been almost like her own daughter from the time she was a little girl. I saw how Eric's mother had dreamed of that marriage for years, and how her loyalty was naturally to Denise. I could understand and sympathize with her disappointment when those precious plans fell through. I held nothing against her, but I couldn't help feeling a pressure to compete with Denise, to prove myself as desirable a match for Eric as the millionaire's daughter was in Mrs. Norfolk's eyes. This is still a strain between Eric's mother and me, but I hope it will be overcome in time.

At any rate, Mrs. Norfolk has resigned herself to the failure of that marriage. The match she has foremost in her mind these days is one between Karen and Kent. As you most likely have had an opportunity to observe already, the chances of success for this scheme are very slim. Karen is openly hostile to the idea, and Kent seems obligingly indifferent.

The deep rift between Denise and Eric has caused hard feelings between both Kent and Denise and the Norfolks. Kent and Denise are very close. They stand by each other consistently. Yet the ties of friendship between the two families are decades old. Mrs. Norfolk, particularly, wishes for a healing between all of us. I know that.

If there's any possibility for this to happen, it lies in Paul. Paul has remained more objective than the rest of us, perhaps because he is less personally involved. He has made every effort to blame no one and to help all of us. When I was ready to hate Denise or Mrs. Norfolk, when they turned with rage against Eric and me, Paul always tried to be a good friend to everyone. I didn't realize till much later, when Karen told me about it, that it was Paul who had gone out of his way to encourage Mrs. Norfolk to accept Eric's divorce, and that he had also tried to persuade his cousin not to fight it. At the same time, he had been interceding with Karen and Eric in Denise's behalf, seeking their understanding and compassion for the cousin he loved as a sister. There were times when this diplomatic effort irritated Kent and Eric particularly, but, in the end, I know we will all be grateful to him for trying to keep us from destroying the bonds of friendship that have grown over the years.

Dear Kim! I can't even imagine what you must be feeling as you approach the end of this incredible account. I can only hope that what I've said will make our present situation clear to you, as it could not have been clear before. How wonderful it feels to confide all this to you! In spite of the current dangers, as I write these last pages, I feel sure and free. It's such a weight off my mind to share everything with you, to feel that this is no longer a deep and bitter secret but a problem to be faced and resolved.

I have yet to comment briefly on the threats and dangers you undoubtedly will have sensed by the time Eric and I return. I firmly believe that there will be no real danger to you. Otherwise, I would be a most false friend to lure you here in my absence. I can't believe that Denise would act against you. Please don't feel that I have betrayed you or used you. In fact, my need is desperate. I know you'll understand this and accept what I've done as only what I had to do.

Within the past year, the divorce was at last finalized. I didn't know about this at the time, but immediately following the termination of the marriage, Denise went completely to pieces. She was devastated by her loss and would speak to no one. A few days later she attempted suicide. Paul found her locked in their garage with the car running and saved her.

Later, when Eric and I began making definite plans for our marriage, her destructive anger began to be turned against others. She plotted to kidnap Timmy from his playpen while Eric and I were taking pictures one morning. I can hardly bring myself to remember the nightmare terror of that incident. Paul brought Timmy back to us unharmed and pleaded for our understanding of his cousin, but I was frightened as I have never been any other time in my life. Then there were anonymous notes—petulant and disturbing at first, but becoming vindictive and threatening.

Eric and I had decided to wait to get married in the hope that, given time, Denise would be able to accept it more calmly. We had no wish to hurt her more than was necessary. Eric was afraid any action on our part might drive her to some desperate move. Paul and Kent repeatedly implored our patience. We all felt that, with time, she would become more stable. She was seeing a psychiatrist. Eventually the notes stopped and Paul admitted that she seemed to be better. Eric said that we had waited long enough, and we once again set a date for our wedding. It was to have been in April.

When Denise learned of our plans, she once again became frantic. She confronted Eric and me at my house, screaming incoherently that she would kill me, or kill my baby, or take back her own child from us. Sometimes she believed that I had stolen her baby. At other times she remembered that Timmy was my son and despised him. It was a dreadful, traumatic scene. Eric and I were helpless to reach her. At last, Kent came over, wondering where his sister was, and persuaded her to go home with him.

It was a terrible time for Eric and me. We talked about moving away, but neither of us wanted to do that. We canceled our plans once again, but a skull and crossbones appeared on the hood of my car, and flowers were uprooted from our garden and strewn about the lawn, sometimes forming words—threats and obscenities.

The strain was unbearable to all of us. Mrs. Norfolk broke into a tirade of blame and anger against us one afternoon, which hurt me deeply. I was tired of waiting, tired of the pressure. I finally pleaded with Eric to take me away and marry me without an elaborate ceremony. We set a secret date and told each other that Denise would cope better when our marriage was an indisputable fact.

In the months between our canceled April wedding date and the new, privately determined date in July, Denise truly seems to have improved. We've all begun to hope that she has at last come to terms with the situation calmly and realistically. Paul and Kent are encouraged by her ability to cope at home. She has even begun to associate with Mrs. Norfolk and Karen once again. Understandably enough, she still has difficulty retaining her composure in the presence of Eric or myself, but Paul assures us that she seems very much herself under other conditions. Eric is totally encouraged, and not only hopes but believes that she will accept our marriage. I hope to heaven I'm wrong—but if I were not apprehensive that this step we are taking will precipitate some drastic reaction, I wouldn't be writing this letter to you now, Kim. I just don't know what will happen, and in the event that Denise reacts badly, I want to be able to tell you everything quickly.

We planned our wedding trip around your visit, Kim. I wanted someone staying in my house while we were gone. I hoped that, since she didn't know you, Denise's attention might be diverted from us by your arrival. When we leave Timmy with Mrs. Norfolk, we will give her specific instructions to entrust Timmy to you in the event of trouble, since you would be able to remove him from danger quickly, perhaps even without Denise's knowledge.

I feel so much easier about leaving Timmy, knowing that you will be here to help. Unfortunately, Eric doesn't agree with me wholeheartedly in this. He has been reluctant to involve you, especially since you are unaware of the situation. Yet he steadfastly opposes any suggestion I make that we enlighten you beforehand. He wants to leave Timmy in his mother's care. I don't entirely trust his mother to be as cautious as she should be, as she no longer believes Denise capable of any dangerous or threatening action. For that reason, too, I need you to be here. I couldn't bear to leave Timmy here otherwise.

Well, it won't be long now. A very few more days, and you will be here, and Eric and I will be married! Of course, by the time you read this, a great deal more may have happened. Let me thank you in advance for all you will have done for me by that time. In fact, unless things show signs of going wrong, I probably will be telling you this story rather than giving it to you to read. I have written this out in case the situation demands that you know everything quickly. I can envision some difficulty in finding enough time to tell you all this under such circumstances. At least now you know what you're dealing with, and you will be in a better position to protect yourself and to help my son. Forgive me for allowing you to step into a situation like this so totally unprepared and unwarned. Necessity has forced me to presume, perhaps unpardonably, upon your friendship and your love, which I have always relied on and treasured, and held equally in my own heart for you.

Lily

It was very late by the time I finished reading Lily's letter—nearly two o'clock. My eyes stung with fatigue, but I turned back through the pages, rereading an occasional passage. So many things had fallen into place. I could understand Mrs. Norfolk's attitude toward me, now. She had felt, as Eric did, that she could handle the situation alone. She had resented my presence because it represented Lily's apprehension and lack of trust. It was a relief to understand the reason behind her coolness toward me. I felt that this also explained the arguments I had overheard between Lily and Eric.

Until that evening, it would have been difficult for me to accept Lily's statements about Denise. I remembered the picnic at the lake I had shared with the Robinsons, and how friendly Denise had seemed. I realized that I should have suspected that friendliness. I should have seen that Denise and Kent were trying to get close to me for a reason. Though they had never cared for Lily, I had accepted them naïvely at face value.

Now I understood Denise's flirtation with Eric, her tears, Lily's fear when Denise had been alone with Timmy. Even Denise's elegant clothes fit into the pattern now that I understood it. She had dressed that way deliberately, to remind Mrs. Norfolk and Eric of her millions. I thought apprehensively of the pranks which had been performed since my arrival. I could not doubt that Denise was behind them. Lily, too, had realized the danger. That was why she had given me the letter tonight.

I remembered the story Denise had told me of Paul's tragedies. There had not been one allusion to any of that in Lily's account. I wondered how much, if any, of that story had been true. If it was all a fabrication, I could see how cleverly it had worked. That story had acted as a wedge between Paul and me, a barrier which had kept me from learning the truth and minimized my effectiveness as Lily's protector. The Norfolk's had deliberately withheld information from me because they had not wanted outside help or interference. Paul had wanted to talk to me. I remembered his phone call now. But, because of Denise's warning, I had made it difficult for him.

Kent! The thought was like a searing pain. All the easy confidences I had shared with him, the trust I had felt in him—how sorely misplaced it had been! He had been Denise's co-conspirator. I had played right into their hands, telling Kent everything I knew. No wonder Paul suspected me! He knew that Kent and I had formed an alliance. How should he know that I had merely fallen blindly in love? I felt sick at the thought. I understood Kent's reserve now. He didn't really care for me—he had only wanted to use me. Tears came to my eyes, but I blinked them back, thinking furiously.

Lily, Lily. What horrors you've been through, and never a word to me. Dear God, Lily, couldn't I have helped you in some way better than this? How could you shut me out so? Why?

I knew why. I had been so caught up in my own life, my own world, that I had hardly given Lily any thought during these past years. My friend had needed me and I hadn't been there at all. I turned out the light and lay quietly in the black misery of my own private hell, suffering with her old pain and my own helplessness to have alleviated it.

Suddenly my thoughts sharpened from this emotional turmoil. I sat up quickly, my heart beating faster. The dead girl in Harbor Center. Someone had mistaken her for Lily. Denise! Denise had killed her! Hadn't Kent called me that night and asked if I had seen her? Had that been the night? I thought it was. The thought horrified me. The shadowy fears and threats took on the complexion of a terrible, real violence. I wondered what the future held and how we could best be on guard against it.

Because I was very tired, I tried to rest, but I was far too tense for sleep. I stared watchfully at the empty darkness of my room, then forced myself to close my eyes. But I couldn't shut off my thoughts. They ran over and over Lily's story and the new interpretations it gave to my own experiences since my arrival. I awaited the sunrise with impatient apprehension, but when the earliest light played behind the curtains, I was at last asleep.

Chapter Ten

I awoke with a start when someone tapped lightly on my door. I knew it must still be fairly early in the morning and that I had not slept long, for it took me several seconds to shake the dull heaviness and rouse myself to answer. The door began to open before I had managed an invitation, but as Lily closed it behind her, I sat up slowly, smiled, and mumbled with faint irony, "Come in."

"Sorry to wake you," she whispered, "but I wanted a chance to talk." She was dressed for the day and fully alert, but she looked tired, as if she hadn't slept well.

"No problem," I asserted, crossing to the window to let in the light and fresh air. It was going to be another warm day, even hotter than the day before. The air was heavy with a hazy dampness, and the weak early morning breeze was already too warm to dry the faint moisture from my face. "Another hot one," I commented, turning back to Lily.

"Yes," she acknowledged with a slight frown of displeasure, settling herself uncomfortably in the yellow chair. "It's murder in this bandage."

I picked up Lily's journal nervously and ran my fingernail down the spiral binding. "Interesting reading, this," I began cautiously.

"I'm very glad I wrote that, now," she told me with assurance. "There was so much you needed to know. It seemed the best way.

"Yes, unless. . ." I let my voice trail away.

"Unless I had told you sooner," she supplied correctly.

I laughed, shaking my head at her. "Of course, that was my thought. But it doesn't matter now. I only wish I could've helped you. There must have been so many times it would've helped just to have someone to talk to about things. I wanted to be the one you relied on for that. But, I know—I was too far away, too involved in other things. I'm sorry, Lily, I'm really sorry." My voice broke, and I stopped, looking away.

"Don't," she said almost sharply. "I don't have to listen to that. It wasn't your fault, and I won't have you stealing my own guilt from me. Do you hear?" Her eyes met mine steadily, admonishing, demanding forgiveness.

"All right," I said, smiling shakily.

"Well, that's all right, then," she sighed with relief.

"What are your plans now, Lily? I mean, it's pretty obvious that things can't go on as they are. Look at you and Freddy, your bandages, crutches, and cast—and due to no accident. It seems to me that Denise has got to be stopped. She's dangerous, not only to you, but to all of us. Who knows what she'll do next? She should be hospitalized before she does anything more. Though it's already too late for someone, a stranger we don't even know! Why was nothing done before?"

Lily looked at me helplessly. "You're right, of course. That's what should be done. How clearly a person can see things, if they just step back a little. . . But surely Eric and I have no authority, and Kent does everything he can to believe Denise is all right. He and Paul have fought many times over that. But he loves his sister. Kent would sacrifice anything to protect her."

"It can't be allowed to go on," I insisted firmly.

"Eric and I are going over to talk with Mrs. Norfolk

and Karen about what can be done this afternoon. He agrees with me that the time has come when we have to act to protect ourselves. I hope that Paul will come over to stay with you and Timmy. I'm terribly apprehensive about what may happen today. You can almost feel disaster in the air," she shuddered, smiling nervously.

"Don't be melodramatic," I admonished her with an uneasy laugh.

"You don't fool me, Kim. I know you feel it too."

"Well, at least your plans are under way. But are you sure we shouldn't call the police? I don't see what we can do to stop her, without help."

"That's what we have to decide this afternoon. I know Mrs. Norfolk will be against it. Incidentally, I told Eric about giving you this information. He wasn't too thrilled, but at least he knows. I think it forced him to take the situation seriously, in a way. We can't just try to ignore it any more. I only hope we aren't too late."

"Why would it be too late? With so many people aware of Denise's trouble, I should think we could protect you," I reassured her.

"Yes," she agreed reluctantly, as she stood up to go.

"I'll be dressed in a minute and get breakfast for you," I offered, as she made her way to the door.

"Wonderful. I'll get Timmy ready. Maybe we can go for a drive this morning. Anything but waiting in this house doing nothing."

"What about your journal? Do you want it back?" I asked, following her to the door.

She hesitated in the open doorway, turning back to look at me. I held the book out to her, but she seemed not to see it. "Keep it," she said finally. "I wrote it for you. For whatever it's worth, I want you to have it."

I was surprised and puzzled. My eyes questioned her as I folded the slim notebook to my chest, schoolgirl fashion, but her smile told me nothing.

"Get dressed," she said. "I'm starving."

I slapped her shoulder playfully with the notebook as she turned to go, and pushed the door shut behind her.

Minutes later, I ran down the stairs, already feeling the oppressive heat of the day by the time I reached the foot in my denim cut-offs, sleeveless cotton blouse, and sandals. The four of us ate a quick breakfast of cold cereal and fresh fruit. Eric requested iced coffee, and Lily and I followed his lead. It was too hot to think of eating or drinking anything warm. I noticed that Lily's appetite had deserted her in those few minutes I had spent getting dressed and putting the food on the table. She picked at the icy melon and sipped her coffee delicately. She fussed over Timmy incessantly, encouraging him to eat his cereal, helping him to bites of melon, extolling the virtues of a glass of milk in the terms children understand. I became uneasy, watching this flurry of motherly love, and my eyes met Eric's across the table. He said nothing throughout the meal, but his eyes in that moment chilled me. They were cold, suspicious, harshly assessing. It was a relief when the meal was over and we could get away from the house.

We took my car because I wanted to put some gas in it. Eric sat in the back seat with Freddy and Timmy. He was less than enthusiastic about the whole venture and would offer no suggestions about where we might go. Lily was too keyed up to care where we went, and, as I was behind the wheel, our route was left soley to me.

I turned right onto the road and we went past the lake toward Dipper Point. The water was still and pale, mirroring the burnt-out blue and white of the hot sky. The light was peculiarly intense and glaring in spite of the thin overcast of haze.

I felt like apologizing for my car's lack of air conditioning, but before I roused myself to break the silence in the car, I noticed Kent walking along the road, headed home. He carried a small sack of groceries in one arm, so I knew he had just come from the store. I wondered idly why he hadn't taken the boat, especially on such a hot day. He waved to us as we slowed down and passed him, and I waved back, but Lily and Eric did not. It was an uncomfortable moment for me. In spite of what I had just learned from Lily about Kent, I had felt a little involuntary surge of pleasure at the sight of him. My color rose in confusion, and I muttered, "I'm sorry," under my breath to Lily. She glanced at me sympathetically but said nothing.

There was a heavy quiet over the surrounding countryside. Even the little brown field sparrows one would expect to see flitting in the grasses or chirping on the fenceposts were invisible and still. When we passed a farmhouse, I noticed a clothesline hung with limp towels. There was no breeze to dry them, not even enough to stir the grasses by the roadside or to set the leaves rustling in the trees. Two little children sat motionlessly on the porch steps. They watched the car as we went by, but no one waved. Everything was as silent and static as a painting or a photograph. Only our car disturbed the illusion of timelessness which hung over the scene with the diffused, relentless blaze of the white, sunless sky.

"When this breaks, there'll be a storm," I predicted. My words hung about us like a prophecy of doom.

"It's hardly ever like this up here," Lily reminded me. "Much less frequently than at home. And we never have tornadoes."

"Most likely it'll spend itself over the Lake," Eric remarked.

These casual observations served to lighten the tension between us. I flicked on the car radio before the silence could press in on us again. Lily punched through the buttons idly, then twisted back through the channels with the tuning knob. The choked-off snatches of country and western songs, interspersed with sudden loud bursts of amplified guitars and phrases from commercials and weather reports grated unpleasantly on my ears, but I made no complaint.

It was Eric who protested from the back seat. "For heaven's sake, Lily, settle on something, can't you?" She instantly stopped fiddling with the knob and punched one of the buttons decisively, then settled back with a sigh while we listened to a toothpaste advertisement which I had lately found to be intensely annoying. I reached over and turned the volume down.

At last we reached the residential section of Dipper Point. I saw a few children on the porches, but there were no spirited games of tag or jump-rope. Even the dogs were quiet, sleeping in the shade. I drove past the depot restaurant where Kent and I had eaten lunch, and stopped the car for a moment to look down at the harbor.

"It must be beautiful in winter too," I remarked. "I'd love to see those pictures you told me about, Lily. They sounded fantastic."

"Yes, I'll show you," she told me abruptly, and I realized that I had startled her by this allusion to her journal, though I hadn't intended it.

I could pick out the *Betsy Ann* even from our high vantage point. Before I could stop myself, I was pointing at the boat and chattering uneasily, "There's the *Betsy Ann*. Kent took me out in her one time. He says he'd like to fix her up and run a tour service."

Lily gave me a long, thoughtful look. "He told you that?"

"Why, yes. We talked about new upholstery and varnishing." Something in her face made me stop.

"That's Paul's dream really, not his," she said flatly.

"Paul's? But Paul never said anything," I protested.

I started the car again and drove through the little town towards the filling station. When we passed the grocery store, I thought uneasily of Mr. Blair's remarks

227

of the day before, but I said nothing to Lily and Eric about them. I parked outside the Indian crafts store and hurried in to pick up another totem pole for Lily like the one that had been smashed. She was surprised and delighted by the little gift, as I had hoped she would be.

"But how did you know so quickly what you wanted? Eric and I just said you'd be in there till noon!" she laughed.

"Well, I'd picked one out before, actually, but—it was broken. So I just found another like it."

"Well, I love it. Thank you." She beamed at me. Then she turned to show the little figure to Timmy, and I started up the car, feeling satisfied and happy. I could tell the little gift had pleased Lily, and this delighted me. It was reminiscent of days long past, when we could make each other smile by pulling an extra candy bar out of a sack lunch or putting together a few rhymed lines which we shared with each other alone. The smallest things could sometimes be the truest tokens of friendship. I rejoiced at the knowledge that this still could be so for us.

Finally, I pulled up beside the gas pumps, turned off the engine, and stepped out of the car to unlock the gas cap, which had been a little gift from my father during the first critical fuel shortage. I wondered idly as the attendant filled the tank whether there would be more talk of rationing next winter, and for how many years the world's petroleum supplies would last.

I snapped out of this abstracted speculation when I noticed the second attendant wiping the windshield of another car. I knew I had seen him somewhere before, but for a moment I couldn't remember. Then I realized that he was Dick Blair, and remembered Lily pointing him out to me as he and his wife had passed us in the red Volkswagen. Yes—and he was the grocer's son. I wondered uneasily if he would recognize me and pass remarks to me that Lily or Eric might overhear. I stepped as far away from the open car window as it was reasonable to do. As I had anticipated, when Dick was writing up his customer's bill, he made it a point to step out of his way to speak to me.

"Kim Harris, isn't it?" he asked with assurance. "Heard any more from the police? I would hate to see you get yourself in trouble around here. Small town— rumors spread quick."

"No, Mr. Blair, they haven't been in touch with me a second time. I'm sure there will be no trouble. But thanks for your concern." I gave him a piercing look and a hard smile. The other attendant was asking for my credit card, and I signed the bill and left without speaking to Dick again.

"I didn't realize you and Dick were already acquainted," Lily said when I got back in the car.

"We weren't. The only time I've seen him was when our cars passed on the road."

"But he seemed to know you. What was he saying?" she persisted.

"Nothing really. Just small talk. He probably knew who I was because you're with me. It's a small town. News travels fast," I echoed Dick's reminder. Then I abruptly changed the subject. "Shall we drive to Harbor Center, or is that too far for now?" I asked.

"Oh, let's go," Lily said quickly. "It'd be fun."

Eric leaned his head back on the seat and shut his eyes. I decided not to press for his encouragement.

The road to Harbor Center took us along the shore of the bay, a route I particularly enjoyed. Seagulls spiraled and dipped above the muted blue-gray of the water, and the far shoreline was softly blurred by the hazy light. A few small boats dotted the unusually calm and smooth expanse of the lake. A sailboat stood, virtually motionless, near the middle of the bay, its colorful red and blue sail subdued by the intervening distance and the heavy, moist air over the water. Eric and Lily pointed out boats to Timmy, and they made a game of counting them as we headed toward Harbor Center.

By the time we reached the stretch of highway which had been built up with a representative of practically every major national fast-food chain within the past several years, it was time to stop for lunch. I pulled into the parking lot of the restaurant that had been the favorite of our high school crowd back home, and after debating our orders for a few minutes, went in to buy hamburgers, french fries, and shakes. There was quite a line, but it moved rapidly, and the people seemed happy and excited. Most of them were on vacation. The atmosphere was one of rush and fun. I enjoyed the laughter in the crowd and the smiling hustle of the young people who served the customers.

When I went back to the car with the food, even Eric seemed a little more relaxed. We enjoyed our lunch in the car, and everyone had a good time, as if our problems had been left behind and temporarily did not exist. Timmy bubbled enthusiastically, for eating out was an adventure to him.

We could see the bay clearly from the place where our car was parked, though the highway passed between the shore and the parking lot. There was a long breakwater built out into the lake, and Lily told me that during the Fourth of July celebrations, fireworks were set off there.

"We watched the fireworks over there under those trees this year," she told me, pointing. "Eric came over here and bought us some soft drinks. So Timmy remembers this place—don't you, Timmy?"

Timmy clearly did remember, and I smiled happily. My choice had been perfect.

As soon as we finished eating, Eric commented that we should be heading back, and took the sacks of cups and wrappers to a trash barrel. Timmy kept his shake.

I wanted to see if I could find the lookout on the way

back, but I was afraid of taking too much time, so I asked Eric if it would be out of our way. He assured me that it wasn't, and promised to help direct me past it, though we had no time to stop. I enjoyed following a different route. I wanted to fix clearly in my mind the roads between the lookout and Lily's house, especially. The place fascinated me, and I wanted to be sure to know how to find my way.

As soon as we arrived back at the house, Lily and I took Timmy upstairs for his nap. The morning had been exciting for him, and he was a little tired, so he settled down to sleep quickly and peacefully. By two-thirty, Lily and Eric were ready to head over to the Norfolks' to talk with Eric's mother. Paul came walking up the drive just as they were leaving, and I heard Lily thank him for coming over before they got in my car and pulled out.

I opened the door for Paul, smiling hesitantly and murmuring, "It's good of you to come." The resentment I had felt because of Paul's attitude toward me was gone, and I hoped that we could talk and straighten things out.

"Lily suggested that I come over. I think she's probably right," he began doubtfully as we walked into the living room to sit down."

"How's Denise today?" I asked him.

"On the edge, I would say. Just hanging on. Kent doesn't see it. He empathizes so completely with her that he can't see it when her perfectly normal feelings of rejection and hurt grow into something more excessive and dangerous. But I'm afraid for her. Lily has never allowed herself to understand how terrible Denise's grief and anger really are. Lily doesn't sympathize with her. You have to understand—Denise's life has been torn apart by this. She suffers, Kim. I don't condone what she's done to Lily and Eric—threats and malicious tricks—but I do understand them. Denise is suffering more than anyone else. No one seems to care or understand that, except Kent, of course. She has no one else."

"I can see how dreadful all this must have been for her," I admitted sympathetically. "There's been so much pain for everyone—yet no one meant to hurt anyone else deliberately. No one was really at fault. It just happened, that's all—nobody was really to blame."

"Yes, you're right. But when someone is hurting, as Denise is, they look for someone to pay back for their pain. Denise wants revenge sometimes. Don't kid yourself. She hates Lily and Timmy—sometimes even Eric. Lately she's even begun to hate you, because you're an obstacle to her revenge. There are times when she would even turn against me. But then, you have to admit that Lily is the same way a bit. She blames Denise. She never tried to understand her and she never will. If she stopped to see how Denise has been hurt, to really feel the pain she's caused my cousin, it would spoil the little dream world she's built around Eric. She needs to believe that it was Denise's fault if Eric hurt her. But, of course, it wasn't. She isn't to blame for loving him, any more than Lily is."

"If Denise really loved him, she'd let him go. She wouldn't put him through this," I asserted with conviction.

Paul considered that for a moment, studying me thoughtfully. At last he said, "That might be true for you, Kim. But there are many kinds of love. Denise's love is never selfless. She isn't one to sacrifice. She would love to please Eric, to charm him, to make him happy. That's what love means to her—the gratification of being able to give pleasure. Lots of men would love to be in Eric's place. They'd cherish her, admire her, and find happiness together. With Eric it was never that simple. And Kent can never forgive him for turning his back on Denise's love as if it were something of no value, when to Kent, his sister is the most precious thing in all the world.''

"I think I offended Kent very deeply last night," I told Paul reflectively. I wanted to talk with him about Kent. "Lily, as you know, doesn't trust Denise at all, and I'm afraid we both acted very suspicious of her. During the party, Denise took Timmy upstairs to bed, and Lily wasn't aware of it until some time later. When she realized what had happened she was frightened, and I bolted up the stairs to check it out. Kent saw that, and he was angry because we didn't trust Denise alone with Timmy."

"I saw what happened. Lily was obviously frightened, and you reacted to that. Kent had no reason to blame you. Besides, Lily's fears are at least partly justifiable."

"But, all the same, he was upset about it. I'm really sorry to have hurt his feelings, no matter how unavoidable it was."

"I don't think he holds that against you. Really, I don't. You've been good for Kent, Kim. I think, for the first time in a long while, you've given him something to care about besides Denise. Because of you, he can put things in a clearer perspective, at least a little bit. Take this morning. Although he won't listen to anyone else's apprehensions about Denise, he admitted to me that he was worried about what she might do. I think in a way you've opened his eyes. So don't worry that he's holding that against you. I don't think he does."

"That means a lot to me, Paul. Thanks for telling me," I said. Our eyes met directly, and I felt that we had become good friends in these few minutes. Then a little flush of unexpected color rose in Paul's face, and he looked away, embarrassed. I was momentarily puzzled, but I pretended not to notice.

There was one other topic I desperately wanted to clear up with Paul but I hardly knew how to introduce it. This was Denise's story about Paul's life. I wanted to know what the truth was and to explain to him why I hadn't asked for his help during Lily's absence, but had always turned to Kent. Yet, without knowing how much of Denise's story was true, it was awkward to bring it up.

"Paul, there's one other thing I need to talk with you about. I don't know quite how to begin, but there are some things I need to know and some things I should tell you." I hesitated for a moment, and Paul encouraged me to go on.

"When I first arrived here, Kent and Denise went out of their way to be friendly, and they invited me to go to the lake with them for a picnic. While I was with them, Denise made a special point of talking to me about you. She told me quite a story about your past, and ended up by warning me to keep quiet about Lily's troubles where you were concerned. If you don't mind, I'd like to know how much of what she told me was true. If it is true, I hate to bring it up. It's just that I need to know."

Paul looked surprised and angry as he urged me to continue. I told him what Denise had told me about his father's death, his mother's suicide, his marriage to Sara, and the automobile accident. Denise had asked me not to upset him by mentioning Lily's absence, and I had avoided him because of this protective request. I could tell by his face as I spoke that most of the story was incredible to him, and I knew that my suspicion that Denise had invented it was correct. When I had finished, he shook his head grimly.

"That explains so much," he began. "I wondered if it was my imagination—why you should avoid me. Now I see. And that incident with the fire in our back yard, the incident with the boat—they were contrived to make Denise's story credible to you. But I didn't understand. I played right into the part.

"Most of the story isn't true. My parents both died when I was very young. I have no memory of them.

There was a girl I cared for when I was in school, but it didn't work out, that's all. We never got married. She fell in love with someone else. I was a little depressed about that, but nothing unusual. Denise made up the whole drama to suit her own purposes. And, obviously, Kent played along with her."

"At first it all seemed to fit so well that I didn't question it," I told him. "But later, the more I saw you, I began to wonder. Yet how could I ask? I was afraid to—until today, when I was virtually sure."

"Yes, I see how it was," he assured me, and there was an eagerness in his tone, an excitement of discovery.

He was about to say something more, but we heard someone running toward the house. I flew to the window to see Karen hurtling herself towards the door. I ran to open it for her, and she burst in, breathless from running, tongue-tied with fear.

"Hurry. Hurry!" she gasped. "They're coming. Take Timmy away."

"What's happened?" I asked, but Paul stopped me.

"Get Timmy, quick! We'll take Eric's car. I've got the keys."

I ran upstairs and tried not to frighten Timmy by my urgency and haste as I woke him from a sound sleep. Karen had remained in the living room, staring out the window with fascinated terror. She still stood so as I headed toward the door, but before I reached it, Paul was coming in.

"It's no use. It won't start. Cut wires," he snapped quickly, his eyes flashing. "We'll take the short cut to the lake and take the boat."

There was no time to hesitate, no time to ask questions or even to think. Karen was too panicky to speak calmly. She could only repeatedly tell us to hurry. Paul and I ran out the back door and across the yard to the woods. I scarcely noticed Timmy's weight in my arms. I had never run so swiftly in my life. We splashed across the stream, taking no time for the stones, and raced on toward the lake. As we reached the shore, my heart was pounding, and I could scarcely breathe. The color drained from Paul's face as he stood ahead of me, noticing that the boats were gone.

We stood for a moment in stunned disbelief, fighting to catch our breath and collect our thoughts. I remembered meeting Kent on the road that morning, and realized with a sickening jolt that he had probably left one of the boats moored across the lake at the store. But there was no time to waste. Paul took Timmy from my arms, for I had suddenly begun to feel the effects of such strenuous exertion. He ran back the way we had come, and I concentrated on trying to keep up with him.

When we reached the stream crossing, Paul turned on to the other path that headed away from the house. This path was far more overgrown from lack of use. The bushes scratched against my bare legs, and branches caught at my clothes and hair and whipped against my face as I ran. At last we came out of the dense thicket into the rolling hills of an open field. I could scarcely go on. Paul was yards ahead of me, but he too was tiring badly. The wild raspberry vines tangled profusely about my feet, tearing my skin as I tried to run, causing me to stumble. It was so hot, and the air was so heavy, that I could hardly breahe.

When we heard the sound of cracking branches behind us in the dense underbrush, Paul turned to me, and I could see he was nearly as exhausted as I was.

"Hide with Timmy—there, in the boulders." He pointed. "I'll try to lead them on."

I took Lily's child and found the strength to carry him the few yards to the mass of rocks Paul had indicated. We dropped down out of sight, and I prayed that Timmy would be silent, though tears of fatigue and fear spilled over onto my own cheeks.

It was but a matter of moments before I watched

Denise and Kent run past. They were gaining on Paul quickly. Our run to the lake had cost us dearly. Paul held his arms out awkwardly, as if he carried the child, and stumbled on ahead of them. He had not run very far beyond the rocks where Timmy and I hid when a last treacherous vine snared his ankle before he could reach the clear grass. I choked back a cry of sympathy and terror and watched with horror as Kent and Denise closed in on him.

I could hear very clearly what was said, for there was a deadly stillness all about us. There was no sound of wind or bird calls, only the heavy pounding of my own heart, and the painful struggle of my labored breathing.

"Where are they?" Denise demanded shrilly. Her voice was thin and high from running, but clear and steady.

"Where you'll never find them," Paul bluffed, pulling himself to his feet. "You might as well give up, Denise—whatever it is you think you're doing."

He had scarcely steadied himself on his feet before Denise flew on him, striking him blindly on the chest and arms with her fists. "You must tell me! You must!" she wailed. Paul staggered back a step or two before he caught hold of her wrists and checked her fury.

"Stop it!" he commanded her. "Get control of yourself, Denise. What are you thinking of, to act like this? Why should you care where Kim and Timmy are? They don't concern you, Denise. Let them alone."

"No. No. They're talking. I know they're talking! Mrs. Norfolk and Eric and Lily. They don't trust me. They hate me. They want me put away. I know it. I know it. Let go of me! Let go of me!" She pulled violently away from Paul, and the two men watched her with horrified fascination. "I have to have the child. So they can't do that to me. I won't let them do it. If I have the child, then I can bargain, I can deal. I can make them promise. Eric will promise to help me if I have his son. That's why. I must find Timmy. I must find my baby. My baby.''

She turned about, looking wildly in all directions, and I could have cried for her. She was so beautiful, even in this strange, tormented frenzy. Her dark hair flowed about her shoulders, standing out sharply against the bright white of her loose terry-cloth beach dress, which billowed as she turned, then settled against the slim, graceful lines of her body. She stopped, looking at the rocks where we hid. For a moment I thought she saw me, but then she looked away.

"Kent," Paul said desperately, "Kent, can't you take her home? What are you doing, to let her do this? This won't help anything. You've got to know that."

"Everything'll be all right," Kent said calmly to Denise. He crossed slowly to his sister's side. "No one understands." He gave Paul a hard look that I could not interpret.

Suddenly Timmy was crying in my arms. I pressed his face to my chest, but the wailing reached Denise's ears and she began to walk toward the rocks.

"Hush! Hush!" I said quickly, but it was too late. I settled Timmy down behind the boulder and climbed out to confront Denise. Paul moved to stop her, but Kent blurted out, "Be careful, Paul," and Denise pulled away. Her hand slipped into the pocket of her dress, and she drew out a gun.

"God, no!" Kent said, and I realized that this was what he had been afraid of. He had known about the gun and had hoped he could prevent her from using it. "Denny—sweet Denny, don't do this! Please, honey. Give it to me, Denny." He held out his hand for the gun but she held it away from him.

"Don't, Kent. It will make her give Timmy to me. I want my baby."

"He's not your baby, Denise. He doesn't belong to you. You've got to listen to Kent," I said.

"That's right!" Denise said harshly. "He's not mine! I want to kill him! He spoiled everything! Or maybe it was you! Yes, you! I'll kill you! Just as I killed Lily. Yes, I killed Lily!"

"Shut up, Denise! Stop it! You didn't kill anyone. It was a sailing accident!" Kent broke in desperately.

I felt a moment of panic before I realized they were talking about the girl in Harbor Center. I was stunned by the realization that Kent's theory of the sailing accident was but a flimsy cover-up for Denise. I knew then that Denise had really tried to kill her. Then I saw that she was pointing the gun directly at me.

"Oh, no, Denny! She isn't worth it! Nothing's worth it! You'll ruin your whole life!" Kent cried fearfully. His eyes met mine, and I saw his fear for me there, and I understood, despite the words he used.

"Shut up, Kent! I have to!" Denise wailed, and tightened her grip on the gun threateningly. Kent threw himself between us and the gun went off. Paul snatched it from Denise's hand, but he was too late. I heard Denise sobbing as I fell to my knees besides Kent and cradled his head in my lap, running my hands over his still cheeks.

"Oh, no, oh, no," I moaned, seeing the blood seeping into his shirt around the bullet wound. "Please, no."

"Kim, Kim, how badly is he hurt? Calm down! How badly is he hurt?" Paul asked. He held Denise as she sobbed helplessly against his shoulder. I wished that he would come to help me.

I was shaking all over, but with trembling fingers I tried to find a pulse in Kent's throat or temples, or to feel the faintest breathing. "I don't know. I don't know, Paul. I think he's dead." I was suddenly, unreasonably terrified of the still face in my lap. I longed to get up and run away, to fall in the grass and cry out my fear and pain. But I sat very still, holding

Kent gently, my tears falling soundlessly on the motionless face.

Denise sat on a boulder, wailing uncontrollably, and Paul knelt beside me to examine his cousin. At last he touched my shoulder gently and whispered, "It must've hit his heart. He's gone."

"He saved my life," I told Paul numbly. "He loved me, Paul. He died for me. It was my fault. I should have known better what to say to her. I said the wrong things. And now he's dead—and it's my fault!"

"Hush! It's not true. It wasn't your fault. Denise had the gun, not you. You loved Kent, and he was lucky for that. You mustn't blame yourself," Paul soothed me.

Even in my grief and confusion I could see the strain in his eyes, the fear that he would be unable to reach me. I checked the torrent of agonized self-blame I felt, and tried to hold back my tears. "It's all right," I managed at last. "I'll be all right."

"Can you stay here with Timmy and Kent, Kim? I know it's asking a lot. Will you be all right?"

I nodded silently, settling Kent's head against a thick tuft of grass, and going to Lily's son. Paul gave me a concerned look before turning back toward Lily's house with Denise, and I tried to respond with a brave smile, but failed in the attempt.

When Paul and Denise were out of sight, I sat down on the rock where Denise had been sitting, holding Timmy in my arms, his face against my shoulder, so he couldn't see Kent's body. I stared at Kent's face, rocking slowly back and forth with the child. I felt hollow and weak inside. There were no tears even in this emptiness. I sat quietly and waited in the bright, hot day, unconscious of the passage of time.

I was startled when Dr. Jacobs knelt down beside Kent. I hadn't heard a sound of his approach, but, snapping to awareness, I saw that Eric, Paul, and Karen had come with him. Paul asked in a subdued voice if I was all right. I nodded silently. We waited for Dr. Jacobs to complete his examination, but I felt no real tension or curiosity. I had held Kent's dead face in my hands. I knew. When he straightened and turned to us, shaking his head regretfully, Karen moaned softly, but I felt nothing.

I wanted to get back to the house, take a cool shower, and go to sleep. I had never been so tired in my life. My ankles were covered with crusty, dried blood, and some of the scratches were still open and stinging. I stood up, on slightly wobbly legs, and carried Timmy over to where Karen was standing.

"Let's go back," I said to her dully, then, turning to look at Eric and Paul, "you'll bring Kent, now?"

They nodded silently and I turned to go. I didn't want to stay to watch them struggle with the awkward weight of his body as they put it on the stretcher. Karen walked beside me. I could see the tears glistening in her eyes.

When we reached Lily's back yard, Karen persuaded me to continue on to the Norfolk residence. Lily was staying there with Mrs. Norfolk, and Denise was sleeping in one of the bedrooms upstairs. Dr. Jacobs had given her a sedative. Karen offered to take Timmy from me, as she had done before as we walked home, but I refused. My arms ached with fatigue, but I insisted on carrying the child.

Mrs. Norfolk opened the door for us, and I realized for the first time how dreadful I must look. She drew in her breath sharply and exclaimed, "Kim, dear!" putting her arm about my shoulder and leading me into the living room.

Lily sat tensely on the edge of her chair, one hand rested on her crutches. She glanced at my face, but her eyes quickly riveted on her son. I crossed to her chair, barely able to feel my legs beneath me, and settled the little boy in her outstretched arms.

"Here's your baby, Lily," I murmured thickly.

"Here's your baby."

Lily smiled as she folded the little boy to her, talking to him and laughing with relief. "Thank you, Kim." I turned and walked out to the front porch, but I didn't stop to answer. I saw alone on the front porch swing and watched as the three men brought Kent's body up the drive, up the steps, and into the house. A few minutes later I followed them inside.

Dr. Jacobs and Eric were standing at the foot of the steps. Paul came out of the Norfolks' guest room and pulled the door shut behind him. He looked very tired as he walked past us and up the stairs. Dr. Jacobs sighed heavily, watching him, then turned to me.

"Let me give you a sedative," he said kindly, reaching into his bag. I shook my head in refusal, but he pressed two pills into my hand. "Take these. You'll feel better." Then he followed Paul upstairs to see Denise.

Eric had gone on into the living room, where Lily and Timmy were looking through some magazines. I could hear Mrs. Norfolk and Karen in the kitchen. I stood alone in the foyer, staring at the guest-room door, then crossed to it quickly and slipped inside.

It was very dim in the room, for the shades were pulled. I stood with my back pressed against the door, thinking feverishly, "I loved you, Kent. I loved you." I thought of the night we had walked to the lake together and how gently he had held me. I remembered how gloriously alive I had felt in those moments, and I knew that even for Kent it had been something more than an illusion. Somehow I longed for an impossible communication, a confirmation of my own feelings, but, though I stared intensely across the room, there could be no answer for me there. I tore my eyes from the sheeted mass on the bed and lurched from the room as hurriedly as I had entered.

Karen met me in the hallway and put a glass of cold lemonade in my hand, leading me into the living room. She urged me to sit down and I did as she told me. I was thirsty and I drank the icy liquid quickly, despite the queasiness I knew would surely follow.

I watched Lily and Eric and Timmy laughing together across the room, and it was as if they were in another distant world. When Karen went back to the kitchen, I set down the glass and hurried from the house, slipping out quietly when Lily and Eric didn't notice.

Lily's house was unlocked, as Paul and I had left in such a hurry, and I knew it made no difference any more. Freddy greeted me with tail wagging, and I patted his head as I passed him on my way to the stairs. I realized I was still clutching the pills Dr. Jacobs had given me, and I dropped them in the hall wastebasket.

I showered quickly and changed my clothes. I was going to lie down and try to sleep, but I felt restless. I snatched up my purse and ran down to my car. Eric had brought it back to Lily's drive, perhaps when he had brought Dr. Jacobs to the house. I couldn't remember seeing the doctor's car. I slipped behind the wheel and pulled out of the drive. I scarcely knew where I was going. I simply drove.

At some subconscious level, my mind directed the car to Lily's lookout. As I pulled into the lot, I felt relief that no other cars were there, satisfaction with this destination, which I had never consciously determined. I left the car and climbed slowly up the steps to the platform. I reached the railing and leaned against it heavily, staring almost unseeingly at the long drop to the water below. Thunderheads were forming over the bay, but where I stood it was still hot and windless.

As I stared down at the harsh gray water, the nebulous agony of my stricken heart found words in my mind. "My life is nothing," I thought. "So small, and empty, and broken. All the years, the years. And what am I? What have I got to show for it? So alone. I never loved any man as I loved Kent. I loved Kent. And now there is no one, no one at all. I look at Lily and only feel more alone. She doesn't see. She has her life and I have nothing. The world has nothing for me."

The wind was rising about me. I dimly felt it on my face, in my hair, and heard it vaguely in the trees. The gray water below no longer looked harsh and dead, but violent, savage, punishing. The waves pounded on the rocks and lashed the air as they broke. I leaned out into the wind, fascinated by the rabid water.

Horatio's lines in *Hamlet* rushed into my head.

What if it tempt you toward the flood, my lord,
Or to the dreadful summit of the cliff
That beetles o'er his base into the sea, . . .
The very place puts toys of desperation
Without more motive, into every brain
That looks so many fathoms to the sea
And hears it roar beneath.

Then Hamlet's "I do not set my life at a pin's fee," and

How weary, stale, flat, and unprofitable
Seem to me all the uses of this world!"

Suddenly I was no longer alone. I could hear the professor's voice reading the lines, and feel the power of his emotion and the author's in mine.

And I remembered other things. I remembered Matthew Arnold writing out "the sick fatigue, the languid doubt," and felt again a kinship as the lines came to me.

Who never deeply felt, nor clearly willed,
Whose insight never has borne fruit in deeds,
Whose vague resolves never have been fulfilled, . . .
Who hesitate and falter life away. . ."

Was I not such a one? Yes, all my life, yes. Until I fell in love with Kent, and then, for once in my life, I was sure of my feelings and expressed them freely. It was so beautiful, and Kent made that beauty possible for me. What can my life be, now that he is gone?

> "A thing of beauty is a joy forever:
> Its loveliness increases; it will never
> Pass into nothingness."

Keats's simple words struck me powerfully, piercing the dull numbness of my frozen grief and stirring some deeper inner core of hope.

The storm was very nearly upon me. I watched the frothing water and the thrashing branches in the early dusk. Thunder sounded over the bay, and sharp lances of lightning hurtled from the clouds to the surface of the water. "It will never pass into nothingness," I said aloud, against the tearing wind. Hope and doubt rose in me, an unbearable longing that at last broke forth from me in healing tears.

The warm summer rain poured down heavily on my shoulders as I wept into my folded arms, leaning against the railing. I loved the rain and the wind. I lifted my face and let the fresh, drenching torrent of the storm mingle with and wash away my tears.

"Shantih shantih shantih," my whirling brain supplied. The peace which passeth understanding. A cry of desperate hope. But, no, it was no part of me. Could such peace be found in the waste land of my life? I was tired. I didn't know.

I turned back toward the steps and my car just as Paul reached the platform.

"Kim!" he cried out with relief. "Kim, I was so worried for you. No one knew where you went, and then the storm—"

"I'm all right," I told him quietly. "I needed to be alone."

"I know," he whispered gently. We were standing close to each other, near the railing, for Paul had crossed quickly to my side. He hesitated, meeting my eyes, and I felt that he was trying to sense whether his presence might comfort me or if I viewed it as an intrusion.

"I'm glad you're here now, though," I admitted truthfully.

He put his arm around my shoulders and we walked back to the parking lot. He had come in Dick Blair's Volkswagen, but I noticed gratefully that no one else was in the car. Paul opened the passenger door for me, but I hesitated, murmuring, "I don't want to leave my car here."

"All right. But let's get in for a minute. We can talk better."

I slipped in and leaned my head back against the headrest gratefully, closing my eyes. The rain pounded on the windshield glass, but it was the kind of steady sound that we could talk under easily. When Paul opened the other door and took the driver's seat, I glanced over at him and noticed how the water ran in streams from his hair, trickled down his face, and dripped from his saturated clothing.

I laughed quietly. "We're soaked to the skin, both of us. I was crazy to come out here in this weather."

"Oh, I've always enjoyed a good summer rain. Perhaps not so thoroughly as this," he smiled.

"How do you happen to have Dick's car?" I asked.

"It's the only one that was left in working order. Denise had Dick 'fix' all the rest, even Kent's. You were out in yours, so they couldn't tamper with it. It seems Dick has helped Denise pull off quite a few of her little tricks. But not killing that girl. He swears he knew nothing of that, and I believe him."

246

"Do the police know Denise did it?"

"Yes. There was no way to protect her any longer. Of course there'll be a trial. I expect she will be hospitalized though. If only I could have made Kent see his way clear to do that earlier. It's such a waste."

"I'm sure you did all you could," I told him gently.

He forced a smile and cleared his throat, then changed the subject. "And what are your plans now, Kim?"

"I'll be going home as soon as possible," I told him. There's nothing for me here, I thought to myself. I felt a strong need to be with my parents, to sort things out again.

Paul glanced away and began to speak, as if he felt he were saying things we both might regret, but which had to be said. As he went on, his eyes met mine, asking for understanding. "There's one thing I really wanted to talk with you about. It hardly seems the time, but maybe I've already waited too long. I want you to know. You'd have seen it, known it, sooner, if it hadn't been for Denise stepping between us, Kent pressing for your confidence. Kent wasn't the only one who cared about you, Kim. You've come to mean a lot to me too. Don't say anything. I know you don't love me now. But won't you think about staying here a while? To give us a chance?"

I watched his kind, anxious eyes, and I knew I should have seen this coming. I looked away from him, hating to hurt him, as I knew in my heart I must do. I hesitated, faltered. It was too soon. I still loved Kent. I couldn't think of any other, yet; possibly not for a long time.

"I don't know," I said at last. "But, Paul, thank you for telling me." We tried to smile at each other.

"Let's go back," I said, to break the awkward silence. Even the rain had stopped.

I got in my own car and drove back, the Volkswagen

ahead of me. Paul turned in to the Norfolks' drive, as Denise was still staying there. I went on alone to Lily's house.

There was still a faint light in the western sky, for the clouds had cleared as the sun set. Lily and Eric and Timmy had come out to sit on the front porch in the fresh, cool air after the storm. Lily rested her head on Eric's shoulder, and Timmy leaned against his father's knee, his face lifted to smile up at his parents. A sad little smile flickered across my face as I thought what a picture that would make for Lily's collection. It was enough that I had seen it. But I knew that in the morning I would be going home.

THE BLUE KEY
Kathalyn Krause

PRICE: $2.25   T51536
CATEGORY: Mystery

The sacred jade altar was missing from Simon Turner's collection of art. His niece, Mae, was pitted against unknown enemies who believed she knew where the altar had been taken. The ruthless killers had already struck once, and Mae knew she had to find the jade before they found her!

MERCHANT
OF MENACE
John Stevenson

PRICE: $1.75   T51507
CATEGORY: Adventure

"The Merchant of Menace," according to rumor, had developed a way to set off earthquakes at will. On the trail of the mysterious "Merchant," magazine writer Rod West stumbled on an incredible plot of mammoth proportions. If the "Merchant" were not stopped in time, his diabolical device could destroy millions of lives, and fragment the entire surface of the globe!

THE HAMMERWORD TECHNIQUE
By Marv Sprouse

PRICE: $2.25 T51496
CATEGORY: Adventure (original)

Helmut Daiger possessed one of the finest minds in postwar Germany. But this almost Nazi-like modern German uses a subliminal brainwashing technique to plant the seeds of an evil plan in the minds of opposing military leaders across Europe and Asia. Following the murder of a U.S. psychologist and the outbreak of hostilities in the Middle East, CIA agent Crimson Mitchess discovers Daiger's trail and sets out in pursuit of the mysterious scientist. But she has only a few days to find him before the world will be brought to the brink of all-out war!